Th Wor

A Liturgical Mystery

by Mark Schweizer

SJMPBOOKS

Liturgical Mysteries
by Mark Schweizer

Why do people keep dying in the little town of St. Germaine, North Carolina? It's hard to say. Maybe there's something in the water. Whatever the reason, it certainly has *nothing* to do with St. Barnabas Episcopal Church!

Murder in the choirloft. A choir-director detective. They're not what you expect...they're even funnier!

The Alto Wore Tweed
The Baritone Wore Chiffon
The Tenor Wore Tapshoes
The Soprano Wore Falsettos
The Bass Wore Scales
The Mezzo Wore Mink
The Diva Wore Diamonds
The Organist Wore Pumps
The Countertenor Wore Garlic
The Christmas Cantata
The Treble Wore Trouble
The Cantor Wore Crinolines
The Maestro Wore Mohair
The Lyric Wore Lycra

**ALL the books now available at
your favorite mystery bookseller or sjmpbooks.com.**

"It's like Mitford meets Jurassic Park, only without the wisteria and the dinosaurs..."

Advance Praise for *The Treble Wore Trouble*

"When the end comes, you'll wish you'd bought this book to burn for heat."
Beth Brand, author

"Guaranteed to be funnier than your church's mission statement."
Bruce Schoonmaker, college music professor

Much like Thor's mighty chariot-pulling goats Tanngrisni and Tanngnjóstr, Dr. Schweizer has clip-clopped across the bridge to Asgard and nibbled the shrubbery of heaven.
Beth and Bill Batson, avid readers

"I love this book and it loves me. Yes, I know this love is wrong. So very, very wrong ..."
Linda Tinkler, life model

"Schweizer has, with great self-discipline, turned himself into the thinking man's Easter Bunny."
Richard Shephard, Chamberlain, York Minster

"If I actually had free will, this book would have changed my life!"
Mark Ardrey-Graves, Metaphysical Determinism Society

"If you only buy one book this year, then get something else. Like maybe something by Beth Moore or Max Lucado.
Martha Hatteberg, Bible Study aficionado and incidental character

"This is not all bad, except as literature."
Helen Byrd, school teacher

"What a gem ... so good my mind grew wings and walked away!"
Sir Ron Cooke, Book Reviewer, Mrs. Miggins Coffee Club

I lost twenty pounds and started dating a lingerie model! This book didn't help, I just wanted everyone to know."
Dr. Cleamon Downs, retired church music professor

"I'm reading this book on *Kindle*, so I won't ever see this review anyway."
Susan Clarke, choir member

The Treble Wore Trouble
A Liturgical Mystery
Copyright ©2012 by Mark Schweizer

Illustrations by Jim Hunt
www.jimhuntillustration.com

All rights reserved. No part of this publication may be reproduced, stored in a retrieval system or transmitted in any form or by any means electronic, mechanical, photocopying, recording or otherwise, without the prior written permission of the publisher.

Published by
SJMP BOOKS
www.sjmpbooks.com
P.O. Box 249
Tryon, NC 28782

ISBN 978-0-9844846-6-9

June, 2012

Acknowledgements
Nancy Cooper, Betsy Goree, Beverly Easterling, Kristen Linduff, Beth McCoy, Patricia Nakamura, Donis Schweizer, Liz Schweizer, Richard Shephard, and Holly D. Wallace

Sing Me to Heaven
Music by Daniel Gawthrop, Poem by Jane Griner
used by permission

Prelude

Three thousand miles away, Marsha suddenly woke to the sound of beetles scurrying and the smell of sewage and couldn't help thinking that, if she had only gone to choir practice instead of that Beth Moore Bible Study, none of this would be happening: the First Methodist youth group wouldn't have been eaten by cannibals, and she wouldn't be left with only seven toes or be locked in a Peruvian jail with a large, unhygienic woman named Adelgonda who liked having her feet rubbed.

* * *

"The difference between a good writer and a bad writer is merely the distance of a few participles."

"You don't say," said Meg, glancing up from the book she was reading.

"I'm absolutely convinced," I said.

Meg was curled up on the overstuffed leather sofa in front of the fireplace, her legs tucked under her. It was where she might be found on any given evening after the dishes had been washed, the dog fed and she'd finished watching her daily DVR recording of *Worldwide Exchange*. The program came on at four in the morning and featured in-depth coverage of business and investment issues, something that Meg, as a financial advisor, was keenly interested in. I, on the other hand, was not. I enjoyed watching a football game, or the NCAA basketball tournament, or even one of those home renovation shows, but sitting through an hour of financial information every day was tantamount to torture.

When I asked why she didn't get up at four to watch the program live, Meg rolled her eyes. "Oh, puh-lease," she'd groaned. "There's nothing happening at four in the morning that's going to affect anything that I do. I just like to keep up." So, unless I had other pressing business, as soon as Meg settled in with her book, I sat down at my typewriter and tried to tickle the muse.

"Hayden Konig," Meg said, peering over the pages and doing her best impression of a schoolmarm, "do you even know what a participle is?"

"No," I said, "but I could look it up."

"I think you should."

Sitting at the typewriter, I immediately decided that I couldn't be bothered. I put my fingers onto the keys and felt a gentle warmth emanating up through my hands. Imagination? Perhaps. But, as far as I was concerned, writing was more than inflated pronouns, furtive oxymorons, and grumpy infinitives. Writing was magic, and, although the magicians were many, my favorite had an historical link to this particular machine.

Raymond Chandler.

Raymond Chandler was my literary hero. A giant in the 1940s, he, along with Dashiell Hammett, embodied the hard-boiled fiction writer. Chandler was good. No, he was the best, and Philip Marlowe was his character — a wisecracking, hard drinking, tough private eye with a contemplative, more philosophical side. A man who loves women and enjoys poetry, but wouldn't think twice about jamming a roscoe in some sap's button and squirtin' metal.

"Would you like a glass of wine?" asked Meg. "I'm getting one for myself." She'd unfolded herself from the sofa and set her book down on the coffee table.

"No wine, thanks, but will you bring me a beer?" I asked.

"I certainly will. Any preference?"

"Nope. Surprise me."

Meg and I have been married for three and a half years. Before that, we'd been an exclusive item since she moved into town nine years ago. She is a few years younger than I, and, according to almost everyone in our little burg of St. Germaine, North Carolina, I "married up." They would get no argument from me.

Mrs. Megan Konig, née Farthing, had been married once before, and so was one union ahead of me. I hadn't planned on marrying at all — not being one of those unmarried men who was "resigned" to bachelorhood, but one of those who enjoyed it. I'd had the freedom to do what I wanted. I lived in a log cabin on a couple hundred acres. I was rich, thanks to an invention I'd come up with that had nothing to do with my actual job — a job, by the way, that I loved. Life was good.

But life was even better now. Now I had all those things and a beautiful wife besides. I watched as she walked to the kitchen. Baxter, our tricolored Mountain Dog, dutifully got up from his rug in front of the fire and followed her, hoping, I supposed, that maybe Meg had forgotten that she'd just fed him and would therefore offer him another piece of leftover duck with blueberry glaze. It was a forlorn hope, but one that Baxter never failed to exhibit. If Meg headed to the kitchen, the big dog was on her heels, tail wagging in optimistic expectation. I heard the rattling of bottles as Meg rooted around in the fridge, the sound of the door closing, the clink of a wine glass, and a few moments later, Meg was coming back into the living room with a glass of red wine in one hand and a bottle of BottleTree Blonde in the other. Baxter followed at a respectable distance, his tail now low, flagging his disappointment. He made his way back to his rug, sniffed it once or twice to make sure no other dog had sneaked into the house and usurped it while he was otherwise occupied, then stretched out and settled back into his torpor. It was the blazing fireplace that sent him snoring. It did the same thing to me. Keeping a fire going in early March was a given here in the mountains of North Carolina. Although we'd had the occasional warmish day in February foreshadowing an early spring, this year, like most, there was still snow on the ground.

Meg set my beer on the desk beside the typewriter and went back to her comfortable perch on the sofa. She was the prettiest woman in three counties. Shoulder-length black hair framed a face with high cheekbones, a beautiful smile, and dancing blue-gray eyes. As for her figure, well, with the possible exception of Cynthia Johnsson, the mayor of St. Germaine and an expert belly dancer, Meg would be far and away the favorite in any "over-forty" beauty competition in the state. Cynthia might win the talent competition, with her belly dancing and all, but Meg would garner extra points during the personal interview. Whenever Pete Moss (Cynthia's significant other) and I argued the point, Cynthia and Meg insisted that we're both sexist pigs. Still, a pig knows what a pig knows.

"Thank you very much," I said, taking a sip of the amber brew.

"You're very welcome. Did you look up 'participle' yet?"

"No. I'm much too busy. What are you reading?"

She held up the book so I could see the cover, a cover I knew well. "It's your copy of *The Big Sleep*."

"My Raymond Chandler, first edition, hardback copy signed by the author with mint condition book jacket?" I asked nervously.

"No," said Meg with a laugh. "Your cheap, non-signed, 1978 Books-A-Million facsimile copy."

"Whew," I said, letting out my breath in relief. "That was close. How do you like it?"

"I like it," said Meg. "I've seen the movie, of course. The book is better." She tapped a finger on her chin, pondering for a moment. "You know, I can see where you come by some of your phraseology in your own so-called writing."

I fairly blushed with pride. "Yes, Raymond and I are as alike, yet unalike, as two dissimilar peas in a pod."

"Exactly what I'm talking about," said Meg.

In addition to owning several volumes of signed first editions by Raymond Chandler, I was also typing on the very typewriter that he used to write the book that Meg was reading for the first time. I had bought this 1939 Underwood No. 5 through an on-line auction. After a thorough refurbishment, it worked like new. If hard-pressed to conjure the spirit of Mr. Chandler, I could also don his own grey fedora, circa 1952. These literary procurements, as cool as they were, were the purchases of a law enforcement professional with too much disposable income. Meg's words, not mine. Since she'd taken charge of our investment portfolio, our assets had steadily grown, despite the down market. She never complained when I had these flights of belletristic fancy and spent a few thousand dollars here or there.

"Listen to this," said Meg, brushing a strand of hair away from her face. "Here's an example. *A case of false teeth hung on the mustard-colored wall like a fuse box in a screen porch.*"

"Nice," I said, with a smile.

"Nice?" said Meg. "What does that sentence even mean? Who would hang a case of false teeth on the wall? And since when do false teeth come by the case? Wouldn't someone get a 'set' of teeth? Even in 1939?"

"It's all about context," I insisted.

"Okay, I see your point," Meg agreed, "but a *case* of false teeth? It sounds like something that came right out of your liturgical mysteries."

"Don't worry," I mumbled, "it will."

Baxter let out a gentle woof in his sleep and his hind legs twitched as if he were dreaming about chasing one of the deer that frequented the pastures in which he was fond of running. Meg reached a leg over to where he was lying and scratched his belly with her foot. He immediately rolled onto his back and gave a happy groan but never opened his eyes.

I might be worried about Meg's criticism if writing were my career. Luckily, it isn't. As I mentioned before, I'm a law enforcement professional. Police chief of St. Germaine, North Carolina, a small town in the northwestern part of the state, nestled deep in the Appalachian Mountains. The SGPD consists of three officers: myself; Lieutenant Nancy Parsky, a fine officer who could probably run everything by herself if worse came to worst; and Dave Vance, who did most of the paperwork and answered the phone. We're not that busy most of the time.

But I have an avocation as well. No, not writing. Music.

I'm the organist and choirmaster at St. Barnabas Episcopal Church. This is the best use of my undergraduate and first Master's degrees in music. My second graduate degree accounts for my job as police chief. None of these degrees count at all toward my propensity for writing bad fiction. That came naturally.

"How's your story coming?" Meg asked. "I haven't heard any typing for a while."

"I'm almost ready," I said, looking at the paper peeking around the roller of the typewriter, waiting for the lone sentence to cajole me into continuing. It was a good start, and yet ...

"I have to mull these things," I said. "Mull and cogitate. Then some rumination. This is my process." I took a sip of my beer. "BottleTree Blonde," I said. "A lovely choice. Delightfully light, crisp and effervescent with just enough weight for some complexity. Yeasty, yet not too heavy."

"Now you sound like Bud," Meg said, laughing. "Get back to work. The choir is waiting for the next story. You heard Marjorie at choir rehearsal. If there's no story next week, there's likely to be a mutiny."

I had been fashioning musical detective stories for the choir at St. Barnabas for the better part of five years. Beginning with *The Alto Wore Tweed*, I'd worked my way through the choir — the Baritone, Tenor, Bass, Soprano, and Mezzo — then rounded it out with the Diva, the Organist, and the Countertenor.

"You're right," I said, and pulled the paper from behind the platen of the old typewriter. I replaced it with a fresh sheet. "Time to get moving. Maybe I need some inspiration."

"Did you look at those Chandler quotes I left on your desk?"

"Yeah," I said, leering at her with my most potent ogle, "but I was thinking about *other* inspiration."

"Forget it, Bub. I'm reading."

I picked up the quotes that had appeared in *Harper's* magazine a few months back. These were unused in his stories, but had been found in his notebooks. Apparently Raymond Chandler collected similes the way I collected rebuffs. I typed one onto the page in front of me.

```
A face like a collapsed lung
```

I smiled and tried a few more.

```
A nose like a straphanger's elbow
His face was long enough to wrap twice around his neck
A mouth like wilted lettuce
```

I knew what I had to do.

```
            The Treble Wore Trouble
                  Chapter One
```

Magic.

Chapter One

"God is a comedian, playing to an audience too afraid to laugh."

"Who said that?" asked Nancy.

"I said it," replied Pete. "You just heard me."

Pete and Nancy were sitting across from me at the Bear and Brew. He lifted the pitcher of amber brew from the middle of the table and refilled his own glass, then Nancy's. Pete's pint glass had "Old Speckled Hen" printed on it, Nancy's had a Guinness logo, and mine advertised Newcastle Ale, all of which had nothing to do with what we were drinking. The pitcher contained Corona, the cheapest stuff in the place. It was Pete's contention that when you ate a really good pizza, you should always drink cheap beer. Not bad beer. Just cheap.

Pete Moss wasn't cheap by nature. As the ex-mayor of St. Germaine and the owner of the Slab Café, he had made some wise investments over the years. He looked like an aging hippie, complete with graying ponytail, one small earring, Hawaiian shirt (winter or summer), faded jeans and sandals — either with or without socks, depending upon the snow on the ground. He might look like a love-child from the '70s, but he was a Reagan capitalist from the minute he had to pay his own Social Security taxes. Pete was always on the prowl for the next Big Idea.

Cynthia Johnsson, Pete's longtime love interest, was up at the counter giving someone heck over our botched order of garlic knots which we should have been enjoying while waiting on our extra large Black Bear Special pizza. Cynthia was a waitress by trade and therefore had no patience for shoddy waiting. That Cynthia was also the current mayor of St. Germaine didn't mean she could give up her day job. After a vigorous and, some might say, "hilarious" campaign and subsequent election, Cynthia discovered that the position of mayor paid very little, certainly not enough to live on, and so continued her full-time occupation as a professional server — one of several ladies who did so. All of them worked in almost every eatery on the square, depending on their schedules and who happened to be busy. The Bear and Brew, the Ginger Cat, and the Slab Café all shared the town's female wait staff. In addition, Cynthia performed as a belly dancer, available for parties, class reunions, Shriners' conventions, and bar mitzvahs. She also gave belly dancing classes at the library when summer was approaching and the women of St. Germaine remembered that they might have to don a bathing suit at some point and thought that some hip and belly wiggling might have a positive effect.

Meg, the other member of our party of five, had excused herself to make a phone call to her mother and was just outside the brew pub. I could see her through the front window, holding her phone to her ear. It was cold out. Her breath was visible and escaped in puffs when she spoke. When she was listening, her head bobbed slightly and she smiled. Her free hand held the lapels of her overcoat tight against the stiff breeze. She hadn't taken the time to button it when her phone rang and she decided to take the call outside. I watched the snow come up in little eddies as the wind travelled down the sidewalk and whipped around her legs. Meg's black fur cap was indistinguishable from her hair, especially in the dim light of the nearest streetlight, several yards away. It gave her the appearance of a 1940s movie star or maybe an exotic Russian spy. After a few moments, she finished her call, dropped her phone into the pocket of the overcoat and pushed open the front door of the restaurant to come in out of the cold.

"I think it was Voltaire," I said to Nancy, picking back up the conversation.

"Nah," said Pete. "I thought it was Voltaire, too, but it turned out to be H.L. Mencken. It's on my Quote-of-the-Day calendar."

"That was my second guess," I said.

"It's freezing outside," said Meg. She took off her coat and dropped it over the back of one of the empty chairs at the table. Her hat followed. She ran her fingers through her hair and shook her head as if trying to rid herself of the cold. "Brrr," she said, sitting down beside me and scooting me over on the bench. "Hey! I'm starving. Didn't we order some garlic knots?"

"Cynthia's getting them," Pete said, then pointed at me and himself in turn. "Hayden and I are busy quoting Voltaire and H.L. Mencken. We're intellectuals, you see."

"The secret to being a bore is to tell everything," Meg quipped.

"There's no need to get personal," said Pete. "I didn't tell everything." He took a sip of his beer and smacked his lips in appreciation.

Meg laughed. "I was quoting Voltaire," she said.

"Oh," said Pete. "That's okay, then."

The original Bear and Brew, located just off the square in St. Germaine, had started its life as the Kellogg's Feed store in the 1920s. But "original" this building was not. Almost three years ago, the fiery finger of God had smote the old Bear and Brew and burned it to the ground for her owners daring to petition the city to sell beer on Sunday. There had been protests and picketing and the issue had finally been decided by the voters in favor of Sabbath sales, but not before lightning and the ensuing fire had consumed the modern day Gomorrah.

The antique feed store itself had provided the ambiance for the restaurant long before "country store chic" had become de rigueur: wide plank floors stained with neatsfoot oil, fertilizer, and saddle soap; old wooden counters nicked and carved by countless penknives; pickle barrels with checkerboards affixed; metal signs advertising everything from tractor parts to windmills to chicken feed. There had been a jukebox in the corner, the kind that still played 45s, good solid tables, and wooden chairs left over from the Great War. When the Bear and Brew opened, the local beer aficionados discovered a place that made their dreams come true. There were twenty-two micro brews and six national brands on tap, an even better selection in bottles, and pizza that became famous across the state in a matter of months.

The new Bear and Brew had been constructed on the footprint of the old structure and included as much character of the original as modern building codes would allow. The design still embraced the Appalachian barley barn motif, but also now included an up-to-date kitchen, clean bathrooms that worked, and a definite drop in the rodent population. Old, original signs had been replaced with reproductions — new tables built out of reclaimed lumber and sawdust was sprinkled on the floor at regular intervals. One thing that hadn't changed was the pizza. It was still delicious. The Black Bear Special, for example, was made with the restaurant's homemade bear sausage — ground bear meat mixed with secret spices and a bit of pork — topped with black truffles, mushrooms, a double helping of mozzarella cheese, and Black Krim heirloom tomatoes, grown locally. All things considered, as far as the customers were concerned, the fire hadn't been such a bad thing.

Cynthia returned to the table with steam coming out of her ears. "Amber Jo didn't turn the order in," she said in disgust. "She thought we wanted it brought to the table with our pizza. Now, why on earth would we want garlic knots at the same time as our pizza? I told her to forget it."

Nancy snorted, having even less patience with inefficiency than Cynthia did. She smoothed the front of her shirt and straightened her badge. Nancy, unlike me, dressed for duty in her police uniform. I favored khakis and a flannel shirt.

Nancy's winter uniform was much the same as her summer outfit: official dark brown pants with a tan stripe, and a long-sleeved, tan uniform shirt with dark brown lapels and pocket flaps. The evidence of her office, her shield and her gun, were displayed prominently, the SGPD badge on her breast pocket, a Glock 19 9mm in a black auto-locking holster on her belt. She favored a black leather trooper's jacket in the winter, or, if the snow was really coming down, her law enforcement issue parka, but wouldn't wear a hat unless it was bitterly cold, preferring to simply tie her brown hair back in a ponytail. When the temperature outside reached ten degrees or so, Nancy would eschew pride for practicality and reach for the muskrat trapper-style hat that she'd bought in Canada some years ago. Her opinion was, however, that this hat bestowed upon her the "Fargo" look, and, although this was a movie that she found hilarious, it was not a look that she was eager to cultivate.

As second in command at the St. Germaine Police Department, Nancy was all business when duty called, and being one of the two police folk who answered calls in the township (the other being myself), "duty" usually called her first. I lived a good ten miles from town, and Nancy didn't mind the responsibility. Dave would handle the occasional emergency if Nancy and I were both unavailable, but that was a rare event.

St. Germaine was a town that didn't have many emergencies, if you didn't count the murders. According to Dave and Nancy, murders weren't really emergencies, the damage having already been done. Still, a dead body demanded a police presence, and we had to go and sort things out, collect crime data, look for clues, that sort of thing. We had a good closure rate on murder cases. We should. We had enough practice. When Pete had been mayor, he'd come up with a good town slogan: "St. Germaine, come for the murders, stay for the shopping!"

A town of fifteen hundred souls, St. Germaine was larger than it appeared at first blush. The downtown square — the part of town that gave St. Germaine its structure — was built around Sterling Park. The street that ringed the park and passed in front of all the downtown shops, City Hall, Noylene's Beautifery, the Slab Café, the Ginger Cat, Eden Books, St. Barnabas Episcopal Church, and a few other buildings was Sterling Park Court, but everyone called it the "The Square." If someone wanted to send a letter to St. Barnabas Church, the address would read: St. Barnabas Episcopal Church, The Square, St. Germaine, North Carolina. This flew in the face of the U.S. Postal Service, which generally demanded actual street addresses, but the Postmistress of St. Germaine, a fine southern lady named Mary Miller, didn't seem to mind, and all the mail was delivered in a timely fashion.

Outside the square, the town meanders into the surrounding mountains, tree-lined streets snaking their way into the hills and hollows. There is a Piggly Wiggly grocery store, many churches, a drug store, small businesses, Christmas tree farms, a library, nearby summer camps, a couple of cemeteries, a fur farm, and many, many residential avenues — all things that create a community.

"Ah, here we are!" exclaimed Pete, seeing Amber Jo hoist a large aluminum platter from the counter and look our way. "Dinner is almost served."

A few moments later we were divvying up the pie and digging into a sumptuous repast.

"My," said Cynthia, "this is everything that *Our State* magazine said it was."

"That review last month?" asked Nancy. "You haven't eaten here since then? This Black Bear pizza is the best thing since their last thing, whatever that was."

"The Polar Bear Special," said Meg. "Alfredo sauce, fresh spinach, sun-dried tomato, artichoke hearts, feta, provolone and mozzarella."

"You have the menu memorized?" I asked.

"You bet," Meg said, happily.

"You've been busy," Cynthia said.

"It's the truffles that makes this great," declared Pete. "That and the bear sausage. But mainly the truffles."

"These are mostly mushrooms," said Meg, holding one of the black, shapeless blobs aloft on her fork. "There may be a smattering of shaved truffles, but I'm almost sure that what we're tasting is just some truffle oil. Real truffles would be cost prohibitive."

"It's true," I said. "Truffles are very expensive."

"Which is why I've called you all here," said Pete. "And why we ordered the Black Bear Special."

"Why?" said Cynthia.

"You see," began Pete, "as you may or may not know, last week a Mr. Willard Shady from Troutdale, Virginia, was digging a grave for his cat, Frisky, under a large oak tree, and dug up a white truffle weighing just over two pounds."

Nancy swallowed the last bite of her pizza, and chased it down with a gulp of beer. "Is that a big one?" she asked, taking another slice and putting it onto her plate. "Two pounds seems sort of big. Bigger than a turnip, anyway."

"About the same size as Frisky's head, I'm told," said Pete. "Anyway, Mr. Shady sold his truffle in New York City for one hundred eighty thousand dollars."

"Are you kidding?" said Meg.

"Nope," said Pete. "The size is the key. Truffles go for six to seven thousand dollars a pound normally, but if you find a big one, the sky's the limit. Here's the thing ..." Pete looked around the table, smiling. "Troutdale is fifty-three miles due north of St. Germaine, well within the acceptable geographical norm. Therefore, according to Hiram Kennedy, our extension agent, there is no reason why truffles shouldn't be growing here in St. Germaine or the surrounding areas."

"So what causes truffles to grow where they do?" asked Nancy.

"No idea," said Pete. "Spores or something. That's not the point. The point is, how do we find them?"

"Pig?" I said.

"Exactly," said Pete. "We're going to need a truffle-pig. Then we're heading up into the mountains. I asked the game warden. He doesn't care about roots. Any truffles we find are ours to keep."

The Appalachian Mountains are the oldest chain of mountains in North America and run from Newfoundland down to Georgia. In our area — here in northwestern North Carolina — we are blessed with majestic mountains, deep forests, rocky crags, breathtaking waterfalls, and sparkling lakes. Little towns are nestled all along the range, but most of the land is still undeveloped, much of it being part of the National Park system. If Pete could take a pig into the parks, and if there were truffles to be found, he might just get lucky.

"These days, some people use dogs," I said. "The dogs don't eat the truffles they find."

"Too slow," said Pete, dismissing the idea. "A pig is faster and has a better nose. She can smell truffles three feet under the ground. Don't worry. I can keep her from eating the merchandise."

"Why a her?" asked Cynthia. "Can't you use a boy pig?"

"Nope," said Pete. "Has to be a sow. I've done the research. A girl pig is attracted to the smell, because a truffle smells like a boar's sex hormones."

"Eeew," said Meg. She stopped eating and stared at her half-eaten piece of pizza with a look of dismay.

I took it from her hand. "Are you telling us all this for a reason?" I asked, before finishing the remains in a single bite.

"I want to know if you guys want to invest," said Pete.

"You're buying a pig?" asked Cynthia, surprised. I suspected that this was the first she was hearing of it.

"*We're* buying a pig, honey," said Pete.

"Don't you 'honey' me!" said Cynthia. "I don't want a pig."

"Too late," said Pete. "She's on the way."

"On the way from where?" asked Nancy.

"From France, of course," said Pete. "Gascony."

"How much does this imported pig cost?" demanded Cynthia.

"She's highly trained," explained Pete. "She has one of the highest truffle ratings in France."

"Truffle rating?" said Meg with a giggle.

Cynthia narrowed her eyes. "How much?" she repeated.

"Umm ..." said Pete. "Did I mention her pedigree? She is a full-blooded Mangalitsa, a breed originally from Hungary, but now ..."

"Pete ..." warned Cynthia.

"With the shipping, six thousand."

"Dollars!?" screeched Cynthia.

"She'll pay for herself in no time," said Pete. "Really." He picked up the last slice of pizza and took a big bite.

"I'm in," I said.

Meg stared at me.

"What?" I said to her, splaying my hands. "I've always wanted to invest in a truffle-pig. It's been a lifelong dream of mine."

"Mine, too," said Nancy. "Count me in. If we don't find any truffles, at least we can have bacon."

Chapter 2

St. Barnabas Episcopal Church is a place where miracles occur, if not with regularity, at least every few decades or so. The church had been founded in either 1842 or 1846, depending on which faction you believed — the Winslow Coterie or the Entriken Cabal. Actual records don't exist any longer for reasons that will soon be made clear.

Two of the matriarchs of St. Barnabas are Wynette Winslow and Mattie Lou Entriken, both now in their seventies, and, although they have been fast friends since childhood, they have differing narratives as to the founding of St. B.. They are both lifelong members of the parish, as were their parents, grandparents, and great-grandparents before them. In matters of church history, their collective memories are relied on almost exclusively, and in almost all cases their chronicles tended to jibe remarkably well. Except when it concerns this one thing.

Wynette Winslow and her coterie have held that the church was founded by Father Alastair Crawly in 1842. She has made this assertion because she had in her possession a letter that had been passed down through her family, a letter written to her great-grandmother by the very same Alastair Crawly who, in 1862, had been captured by the Union forces in Virginia and sent to Alton Prison in Illinois. In this prison letter, explains Wynette, Alastair Crawly declares his longing to return to his beloved town and "take up the reins of that great work so eagerly begun those two decades past."

For Wynette, the math is simple. 1862 minus two decades puts the founding date at 1842. This, and the avowed attestation by her sainted forebears, is enough for Wynette.

There are three problems, according to the pundits, with Wynette's dating of the founding using the aforementioned correspondence. The first is that Alastair's "great work" written about in the letter didn't actually mention St. Barnabas Church. Therefore, the reference might be to his fledgling ministry, with the actual founding of the church to have occurred later. Secondly, "two decades," although specific in one sense (the meaning to be taken as exactly twenty years), is vague in another. "Two decades" could be easily be construed to mean "about twenty years, give or take a few on either side."

The final problem is that there is no letter. No letter she can produce anyway. Wynette lost it or misplaced it, but she is adamant about the contents.

Mattie Lou Entriken (as well as the rest of the Entriken Cabal) dismisses Wynette's great-grandmother as a floozy who was always trying to cause trouble. She can say this with certainty because Father Crawly was Mattie Lou's grandmother's uncle and Mattie Lou's Grandma Gertie had said that Wynette's distant relative, known to the Entriken clan as "Betty the Blue Ridge Bombshell," had no business writing letters to a married man whether he was in prison or not.

Mattie Lou's proof consists of a printed bulletin from 1896 that advertised, in the "announcement" section, a need for firewood, a plea for prayers concerning Arthur Ackerman's cow, and an announcement about the upcoming celebration of the Golden Jubilee. Mattie Lou's math is as exact as Wynette's, setting the founding date for the congregation as "St. Barnabas Day, 1846." Unfortunately, her proof has the same drawback as Wynette's. That is, it can no longer be found.

"It's here somewhere," said Mattie Lou. "When I'm dead, y'all can go through all this stuff and find it if you want."

Adding to the problem was the fact that Wynette's mother and the Winslow Coterie were in charge of planning the centennial celebration, and so the church commemorated the event in May, 1942. The sesquicentennial followed in 1992. This cemented the 1842 date.

All bickering aside, clearly the community of St. Barnabas formed just about the time that St. Germaine itself became a township. The old wooden church survived the Civil War, when many of the town's buildings did not, by serving as headquarters for Colonel George Washington Kirk. Kirk had been charged with holding the mountain passes of Deep Gap and Watauga Gap for General George Stoneman as he marched through North Carolina in March of 1865. Although Kirk's men were Union sympathizers from the area, both they and Stoneman's soldiers had little regard for the locals and engaged in stealing, general destruction of property, killing animals, burning buildings, and destroying all courthouse records. The church building was spared for another thirty-four years.

In January, 1899, the first of our legendary miracles occurred when the church caught fire. The miracle wasn't that the church didn't burn to the ground. It did. The miracle wasn't that no one was hurt, although no one was. The miracle (verified by a photograph!) was that when the congregation showed up on the lawn on that frigid Sunday morning after the Saturday night fire, their despair changed to wonder as they gathered around the altar of St. Barnabas — a six hundred pound oaken altar with a marble top that should have been destroyed in the flames, but was instead sitting outside in the snow, across the street in the park, the communion elements all in their place. The episode was credited to the work of angels.

It was this altar that became the centerpiece of the new church building this time made of stone and mortar instead of pine clapboard, and based on the familiar American design.

The church was in the shape of a cross. The main part of the church, or the nave, was filled with pews on either side of a center aisle. The transepts formed the arms of the cross and contained pews as well, these facing inward. The altar was in the front. Over the years it had moved from where it stood against the front wall in the days when the priests celebrated with their backs to the congregation, to a few yards beyond the chancel steps, as the church rethought its liturgy and the priests offered the Great Thanksgiving facing their flocks. The choir loft was in the back balcony, accessible by steps found in the narthex, known by other denominations (and motels) as "the foyer." Two hidden doors in the front paneling offered access to the sacristy — the room where the clergy put on their vestments and where communion was prepared. The pews could accommodate about two hundred fifty worshippers.

It was a lovely church.

It burned to the ground on Thanksgiving weekend four years ago.

The fire began during a Thanksgiving Pageant and again, a miracle occurred. Two miracles, actually. The first was thanks to the St. Germaine Volunteer Fire Department. This time it truly *was* a miracle that no one was hurt, since the church was packed with people. Against all odds, the volunteers made sure everyone was out of the building and contained the fire to the church building itself, even though there were many other structures in the immediate vicinity. Most of the congregation — in fact, the entire town — watched in horror and deep sadness as the building was consumed and fell inward in a conflagration of flames, sparks and smoke.

Rising out of this chaotic scene was the second miracle of the night, the one that the town still talks about and the one that made all the papers. On the morning after the fire it was discovered that while everyone was occupied with the bedlam that was the town square, the altar of St. Barnabas — the same holy table that had been part of the church since the beginning — had once again been moved from the burning building into the park across the street. When the congregation gathered the next morning, intent on having a service of thanksgiving, they found the altar amongst the fallen leaves, the communion bread and the wine right where they were expected to be.

The rebuilding of St. Barnabas took a little over a year and a half. The new building was a copy of the old, even down to the stone that had been ordered from the same quarry as the turn-of-the-century structure. The grounds were expanded to include a meditation garden in the back and, although some differences had been made in the office area, by and large, members of the church in 1950 would have recognized the St. Barnabas they knew without any trouble.

During the past twenty-two years that I've lived in St. Germaine, St. Barnabas Church has enjoyed the ministries of more than a few clergy and lay persons, including thirteen priests, full-time, part-time, and interim. I, myself, have not enjoyed them all. As in any working environment, I've had great friendships with several of them, a good working relationship with a few, an uneasy truce with two or three more, and a tooth-grinding tolerance of the rest. Over the years, though, I've learned to keep my head down and stay out of their way.

I've been the part-time organist and choir director since I moved to town. I found myself in St. Germaine thanks to my college friend and roommate, Pete Moss, who at the time was the mayor. The town was looking for a police chief, and my master's degree in criminal justice and administration was just the ticket. I also have a master's in musical composition from UNC Chapel Hill, and that, paired with certain organ performance skills, landed me the position at St. Barnabas almost immediately. I marry the two professions by keeping a J.S. Bach organ score in my office at the police station and a Glock 9 mm in the organ bench. I find it handy in keeping the tenors in tune.

As the organist and choir director, I'm invited to all the staff meetings. As the police chief, I've been in the habit of politely declining. When Gaylen Weatherall was the rector, I did manage to get to three meetings a month. When she left us to become the Bishop of the Diocese of Northern California, I scaled back my involvement in worship planning, leaving it to those full-time staff members and the Worship Committee. I still picked the hymns and chose the music for the service, but, as far as the other aspects of the service were concerned, well, I left that to the other parties.

When Gaylen had prevailed upon Meg to take the position of the Senior Warden, Meg had done so willingly and executed the office with aplomb and capability. She'd been reelected a couple of times, but when the Rt. Rev. Weatherall took her leave, Meg retired from the position and from the vestry. When Meg retired, so did my regular attendance at worship meetings.

Now, two interim priests and a year and a half later, the church had called a new priest to be the rector of St. Barnabas. I hadn't had anything to do with the process, and neither had Meg. We'd spoken to the candidate, of course, and I had a meeting with her when she came in to interview, but, really, I knew nothing about her other than what her curriculum vitae indicated.

Dr. Rosemary Pepperpot-Cohosh

Born:	1964
Married:	Herbert (Herb) Cohosh (23 years)
Children:	None
Hometown:	Fonda, Iowa
Education:	*Bachelor of Arts,* Iowa Wesleyan College
	Masters of Divinity, Wartburg Theological Seminary
	Doctor of Ministry, Pacific International University

Ordained:	1998, Evangelical Lutheran Church in America (ELCA)
	2004, Received into the Episcopal Church, Diocese of Iowa
Employment:	Walmart Associate
	Assistant Pastor, Augustana Lutheran Church
	Self-employed clothing design consultant
	Supply priest (Episcopal)
Turn ons:	Long walks on the beach, puppies, sunsets, rainbows, sharing feelings, unicorns

    Okay, I made that last one up, but I suspected that I wasn't far off base. We'd been exposed to the ministry of the Reverend Pepperpot-Cohosh, known to her parishioners as Mother P, since last November, and she was steadily, with the help of her husband, (also a bona fide Lutheran pastor), molding St. Barnabas into the vision that they had for the church universal.

    How did a Lutheran pastor become an Episcopal priest? Pretty easily, as it turns out. The Evangelical Lutheran Church of America came into full communion with the Episcopal Church several years ago, meaning that each churches recognizes the clergy of the other and allows them to function in each other's parishes. Mother P officially transferred from the clergy roster of the Evangelical Lutheran Church to that of the Episcopal Church with the blessing of both bishops, after serving as a supply priest in the Diocese of Iowa for a couple of years. That she'd never had a full-time charge in the Lutheran church didn't seem to bother anyone. When she saw the opening advertised at St. Barnabas, she applied, and four months later was offered the job.

    It is well known throughout the Episcopal church that each parish operates as a little fiefdom, with the parish priest as the overlord. The vestry has the final say and can overrule the priest's wishes, but usually this doesn't happen unless things get really out of hand. Mother P had come to St. Barnabas just before

Advent, and, to her credit, had left us alone to continue as we had through Christmas, content to celebrate the Eucharist each Sunday, offer prayers, visit the sick and bereaved, and get to know the lay of the land. Now, though, as Ash Wednesday loomed less than a week away, it was clear that Mother P was ready to begin exercising her despotic prerogatives.

Chapter 3

The Treble Wore Trouble

It was a dark and stormy night, dark like the oil slowly oozing out from under the 1954 Chevrolet Bel Air sedan parked in front of Tad Grassfin's mobile home where he'd moved the old jalopy in hopes of selling it (four hundred dollars "as is"), and stormy like the courtship of Norwood Wenzell and Lucy Hickenlooper who used to make out in the back seat of that same Chevy until Norwood went off to Korea and Lucy married Tad in a fit of pique, and now, fifty years later, Tad needed the four hundred to pay for his glaucoma medicine; but this is not Tad's story, nor even the story of Norwood and Lucy (who died together in a motel room in 1965, but don't go jumping to conclusions, they were just friends), it just starts out dark and stormy like that.

Three thousand miles away, Marsha suddenly woke to the sound of beetles scurrying and the smell of sewage, and couldn't help thinking that if she had only gone to choir practice instead of that Beth Moore Bible Study, none of this would be happening, the First Methodist youth group wouldn't have been eaten by cannibals, and she wouldn't be left with only seven toes, or be locked in a Peruvian jail with a large, unhygienic woman named Adelgonda who liked having her feet rubbed; but this isn't Marsha's story either, although hers is pretty interesting, but rather short (hint: it ends badly for Marsha in another twelve minutes or so).

* * *

"In just two sentences, you have almost single-handedly destroyed the English language as we know it," said Meg, reading the typewritten page I'd handed her. She was sitting at the kitchen table nursing her first cup of coffee and had been thumbing through yesterday's copy of the *St. Germaine Tattler*.

"Thanks," I said. "It took some work. I like to think that Raymond Chandler would be proud."

"He would not be proud."

Meg held up the piece of paper distastefully in two fingers and I took it from her.

"I am not dissuaded," I said, reading back over my prose. "This is only the beginning. I have many more locutions at my disposal."

"I'm sure you do," said Meg, "but put some pants on, will you?"

"Hey! I'm wearing my hat at least."

"Raymond Chandler's hat. Don't you have to go to work today?"

"It's Saturday," I said. "I've got time to finish this chapter, run, shower, and make it to the office in time for donuts."

"What time would that be?"

I shrugged. "Ten? Ten-thirty?"

"You're running?"

"Yep. Gotta get back into it. The snow's almost melted and we should see temperatures in the high 40s today."

Meg tapped the newspaper in front of her, "Did you know that Mildred Kibbler found a rabid possum in her garbage can? It got away when she tried to shoot it. That's right next door to Mom."

"Two questions spring to mind," I said. "Number one: what made her think it was rabid?"

"According to the article, there was a lot of foaming and snapping."

"I'm sure there was," I said. "But what about the possum?"

"Oh, ha, ha," said Meg, sarcastically.

"Second question: how can you miss hitting a possum in a garbage can?"

"Don't know. It's not funny, though. What if that possum *does* have rabies and it gets into *Mom's* garbage can?"

"Have no fear. She's a far better shot than Mildred Kibbler."

There was no doubt that Meg's mother, Ruby Farthing, *was* a better shot. I'd taken her target shooting several times up on the ridge above the cabin. Ruby was a natural markswoman with a ·410 gauge shotgun, preferring the old-timey "point and shoot" method, cradling the stock under her arm rather than bringing it up to her shoulder. A .410 was very small, a kid's gun really, but it was fine for Ruby who didn't like the kick of a bigger gun, but wanted something handy in the house. I could throw a potato into the air and Ruby would blow it apart from twenty yards ten times out of ten. I was sure she could hit a possum in a garbage can.

Ruby Farthing is now in her seventies and still a beautiful woman. Like Meg, she's tall and willowy. She has the same smile, the same blue-gray eyes, and the same incorrigible sense of mischief. Unlike Meg, her once-black hair has turned to a shimmering silver gray. Also, unlike Meg, she can shoot. That she is a savant with a ·410 shotgun irks her daughter no end.

"I'll check it out when I get to town," I said. I waved my story at her. "Right now, I have to strike while the ineffable inflatus is fragrant upon me."

Meg looked up from the newspaper. "The what?"

"The ineffable inflatus," I said smugly. "To quote Elizabeth Barrett Browning. See? This is why I'm a writer and you are but a financier."

Meg smirked at me. "Take Baxter when you go running," she said.

***

I lit a stogy, looked out the window into the dark storminess and smiled as I remembered another Marsha, long ago — a Marsha who, as I recalled fondly, also had a Chevy, glaucoma, four hundred dollars, and a girlfriend named Adelgonda — which, I thought as I puffed on my cheroot, tied up the similitude nicely. My high school English teacher would be proud.

I'm a detective, a Liturgy Detective, duly appointed by the Bishop, baptized into eleven denominations, and pre-absolved by His Holiness himself. Things were slow, and my bank account was into negative numbers. I needed some work, a case, and if the bishop wasn't going to throw some moil my way, well, it was every gumshoe for himself.

Suddenly the door opened and there she was, all dressed in black, the very image of St. Grizelda of Guacamole, her long yellow-orange hair flowing over her shoulders like Velveeta cheese sauce cascading onto a bed of nachos, making my stomach sing "La Cucaracha" while my gall bladder used my kidneys for castanets.

"Marilyn," I hollered, "hold my calls."

"No one is out there," said the woman, giving a nod toward the empty desk outside my door. "The note on the desk says she's gone for the day."

She glided across the wooden floor like a skater: one skating on ice, not wood, even though she wasn't wearing skates, not even roller skates, which would make more sense indoors because ice skates would carve these pine boards like a carrot peeler and I'd want to refinish them the same way I wanted to treat this dame, strip her veneer, run my hands over her smooth, naked planks, and fondle her the way Norm Abram fondles a piece of wormy chestnut on "This Old House."

"My name is Carrie," she crooned. "Carrie Oakey." Her hips moved to a melody of their own, a siren's song that beckoned a palooka's thoughts into dark, smoky bars where saxophones honked out a living like brass-plated geese begging for nickels: "C'mere, big boy," they beckoned on the upswing, then, on the backswing, made a dozen promises I knew they could keep.

She squiggled into a chair, crossed her legs, and hiked her black dress up over one knee, then hiked it a little more and showed me more thigh than my "Victorious Secret" Bible-lingerie catalog.

"Hiya, Toots," I said, picking up the cigar that had fallen from my mouth. "What can I do for you?"

"I hear that you're a Liturgy Detective. And I need help."

* * *

I left the story hanging in the typewriter and headed to the bedroom for my running gear. Baxter was already outside chasing whatever wildlife he could scare up, and even with two hundred acres to roam he was in no danger of getting lost. His current interest was an otter that had appeared in the river just after Christmas.

Our house began life as a log cabin in 1842, the same year that St. Barnabas Church was founded, if Wynette's account was accurate. The log portion of the house was a twenty-by-twenty two-story cabin purportedly built by Daniel Boone's granddaughter and her husband in Old Landing, Kentucky. The logs had been numbered, taken down, trucked to North Carolina, and reassembled on the property. Along with the cabin came some pretty impressive documentation which, if it can be believed, placed Daniel Boone in this very cabin at least twice in his life while traversing the Bluegrass State. The census report from 1880, which I'd also found, showed that there had been eight people living in the cabin including two servants.

Now the cabin serves as the den with the rest of the house built around it. The stone fireplace in the den has an elk head hanging above the mantle — a trophy from a hunting trip out to Wyoming once upon a time. The elk had been joined a few years back by a stuffed buffalo that stood in the corner, a Christmas present from Meg that she'd gotten from a Western-themed restaurant going out of business. This was now the extent of the animal decor. All other bearskins, raccoon tails, beaver pelts, cow skulls, and miscellaneous shells, feathers, fur, and teeth had been relegated either to Nancy's house or the storage shed. Once Nancy mentioned to Meg that she would rather enjoy having a bearskin rug in front of her fireplace, I watched as the trophies of my bachelorhood disappeared one by one.

Not that I minded too much.

Meg had a good eye for decor and knew what I liked. The house had never looked better. After we had gotten hitched, she'd overseen some redecorating and renovations that included a new, updated, fancy kitchen, a master suite, a heated garage, as well as polishing up the old cabin. I'd never needed a garage for my old pickup truck, but Meg's Lexus was a different story. Her car needed heated floors, ambient overhead mood lighting, chamois polishing cloths made from the skins of unborn goats from the Carpathian Mountains, and some kind of wax squeezed out of baby sea turtles. My 1962 Chevy truck, on the other hand, was happy just not to be left in the middle of the river — something I'd done once or twice.

I finished tying my running shoes and went out the bedroom door that opened onto the back deck. A long whistle produced

Baxter, tearing across the field, his ears flapping and his tail straight out behind him. He'd been down at the river, but my whistle brought him running. I didn't wait for him. I ran down the steps and took off jogging up the drive, knowing that he'd catch up with me in a couple of moments.

My morning run, three days a week, took me on a two-mile loop. I used to do a five-mile loop, but I couldn't really tell any difference in how I felt after doing just two miles as opposed to five. The plain fact was that I felt just horrible after either one. This had to do, I suspected, with the aging process. My goal in continuing to run is to stay in the same size clothes for a few more years, the fact that I'd switched to expando-pants a few years back notwithstanding. Expando-pants, I believe, are possibly the most significant fashion breakthrough since the whalebone corset. Side gussets hidden in the waistband allowed a three-inch differential and made Thanksgiving dinners a pleasure once again. After Pete Moss discovered this extensible apparel and filled me in, we never looked back, although both Cynthia and Meg were ready to disparage them as "maternity pants for men."

Baxter lost no time in closing the gap. I was puffing uphill and he passed me like I was standing still, before crashing into the mountain laurel and disappearing. I didn't see him again for the better part of the run, but then, as I turned for home, he lurched out of the undergrowth in front of me, licking his chops, and wagging his back end furiously. I knew that look. Baxter wasn't adept at catching live varmints, but he was perfectly willing to follow his nose and devour almost any small animal that had expired or was otherwise defenseless. By the fur still clinging to his muzzle, I suspected rabbit, or maybe a nest of baby rabbits, and decided not to tell Meg.

Baxter is one of two animals that shares our home. Invited animals, anyway. Living out in the hinterlands, we were bound to have our share of mice, snakes, bats, the occasional raccoon, and whatever other critters gravitated toward the warmth of the house during the winter months. Our other invited guest isn't entirely domestic but is happy to share our space. He is a barn owl. Archimedes.

I trotted across the field and headed toward the house. I'd put up a small barn in the last couple of years to house some tools. Meg kept her gardening equipment in there; I had a small tractor and an ATV — a four-seater Kawasaki Mule that I used to drive around the property and survey my realm. The little barn was also Archimedes' secondary hangout. I glanced up into the eaves as I ran by. He wasn't there. I hadn't seen him for a couple of days, but that wasn't unusual, especially when the snow began to melt. With no leaves on the trees, chipmunks and mice were easy pickings.

Archimedes spent most of the winter in the house, perched on the head of the stuffed buffalo. If you didn't know better and happened into the room while he was resting, you might assume that he was part of the decor. A moment later, though, you'd be startled as he launched himself soundlessly into the air and glided though the house into the kitchen, where he'd land on the sill and trigger the electric eye that opened the window allowing him access to the great outdoors. He returned the same way. Over the years Archimedes had granted us stroking privileges but we knew that, despite his appreciation of the supplemental mice we offered him as a treat, he was a wild creature. He came and went as he pleased, and that pleased us.

I huffed up to the front door, stopped and bent over, my hands on my knees, trying unsuccessfully to catch my breath. Baxter had his nose on the doorjamb, just waiting for a gap that he could exploit and shove his bulk through, heading into the house. Not looking up, I turned the knob and felt, rather than saw, Baxter bolt into the front hallway. Several minutes later my wind returned and I stood up, took my shoes off outside (something that never happened pre-Meg), and carried them back to the bedroom. I opened the back door, tossed the muddy shoes in a heap on the deck, peeled off my clothes and went into the bathroom to shower.

Chapter 4

I climbed into my truck and pointed it toward town. It was a ten mile drive that usually took about twenty minutes. The only thing in the truck that could be considered new was the stereo system. I turned it on and the sound of one of Handel's coronation anthems, *The King Shall Rejoice*, filled the cab. The choir had given me this and a few other CDs as a Christmas gift, and I was working my way through them. The piece for choir and orchestra that I was listening to was written for the crowning of George II. It was my second favorite of Handel's coronation anthems, but the one with the best final movement. The double fugue — two melodies simultaneously played against each other right from the start — ended in a three minute Alleluia section that was to be played while the king was being crowned. Very impressive.

My truck rattled its way down the mountain roads and, as the final Alleluias sounded, I pulled into my parking place beside the police station. A Saturday in St. Germaine, in early March, was generally what we in the law-enforcement profession called "dull." There were no tourists to speak of. The skiers, if there were any left, had headed up to Sugar Mountain, or maybe Beech, but with the temperature climbing I thought the number of folks choosing to brave the slopes might be slimming.

I parked the truck and went into the police station. It was on the square, next to the Town Hall and just across one of the side streets from the Slab Café. Dave was sitting behind the counter, busy typing on the old Dell computer, either filling out the monthly reports we needed to file with the state to keep some of our funding intact or updating his Facebook page. It was hard to tell with Dave. Still, he always got the reports finished on time, and neither Nancy nor I had any desire to tackle them. So however Dave managed his time was fine with us.

"Donuts?" I asked, as I came in.

He looked up. "In your office, boss," he said. "I stopped by the Piggly Wiggly about an hour ago. Amelia threw in a few extras 'cause they were made yesterday."

"I hope you ate those old ones," I said. "I've been waiting all morning for a fresh bear claw."

"Already finished those old ones off. There's nothing better than a free, day-old donut." Dave smacked his lips and hit a button on his computer keyboard. The printer lit up and started putting out paper.

"The monthlies," Dave said. "Our hard copies. I've already filed the electronic ones. And you'll be happy to know that I did buy some bear claws."

The SGPD reports needed to be filed by the 21st of each month for the month previous. Not a problem. Dave had them done with hours to spare.

"Thanks," I said. "And thanks for doing the reports. Anything of a constabulary nature afoot?"

"Not a thing," said Dave. "No calls and no messages."

Dave was dressed, as usual, in his pressed khaki trousers and a light blue button-down oxford shirt, covered with an argyle sweater vest. His tan jacket was hanging on the freestanding coatrack beside the front door. Dave didn't carry a gun, but had a badge somewhere in his desk that he might be able to find, if pressed.

"Anything on a rabid possum at Mildred Kibbler's house?"

"I read about that," said Dave. "But she hasn't called. If she sees it again, I suspect we'll get a 911."

"I told Meg I'd check."

"Oh, yeah," said Dave. "That's next door to Ruby, isn't it?"

I nodded and went into my office. There on the desk was the box of donuts. I opened it.

"Dave," I called. "Here on my desk seems to be a large, supposedly full, box of donuts. A dozen in fact, if the label is to be believed. Plus the extras that Amelia tossed in."

"Yeah?"

"Yet, when I open this box, there is but half a bear claw left."

"Well, yeah," said Dave. "But it's a fresh one. You're lucky I saw your truck coming around the square. Otherwise ..."

"I don't know how you keep your schoolgirl figure," I said, my disgust apparent. "I run fifteen miles a day and have to wear expando-pants. You sit behind a desk, eat donuts by the hundreds, and never gain an ounce."

"It's a gift," said Dave. "Like my unassuming good looks."

I stuffed what was left of the pastry into my mouth. Almonds, apples, and frosting in a deep-fried fritter that was still warm. Delicious, but none too filling.

"I'm going to the Slab," I announced. "Gotta get some breakfast."

"I'll just finish up here," answered Dave. "Then I'm done for the day. Okay with you?"

"Okay," I said. "Have a good weekend. You heading over to see Collette?"

Dave smiled. "Yessir. It's about an hour drive down to Wilkesboro. I'll be back on Monday morning."

Dave and Collette Bowers had become an item again after Collette had shown up in town after a hiatus of a few years. They had been engaged before that, but Dave's age-old infatuation with Nancy, resulting in a dalliance that Collette found out about just before the wedding, ended that betrothal in a flurry of anguished carnage. When Collette found out about Dave's betrayal, she proceeded to destroy the interior of the Slab Café where she was employed as a waitress, culminating the episode by almost killing her soon-to-be ex-fiancé with a sugar shaker. After the breakup, Collette found a fundamentalist church and, following the church's founding Biblical principle of "name it, claim it," decided to "name" Dave and "claim" him as her anointed helpmate. It didn't work out that time either. After disappearing the night of the St. Barnabas fire, Collette showed up a third time, this time dressed in Vampire Gothic complete with black leather, blood jewelry, and spiderweb tattoos. Christian fundamentalist to vampire — quite a change for a shy girl from Hickory. Dave was intrigued and, although Collette didn't make the trip back to St. Germaine very often, he was happy to visit her in Wilkesboro.

And, of course, Nancy had given up on Dave.

* * *

The cowbell hanging on the door of the Slab banged against the glass door and announced my arrival. The restaurant wasn't full, but there were two busy tables and a man sitting at the counter wearing insulated bib overalls. I didn't recognize the counter guy, but the folks at the tables I knew well.

"Good morning, Chief," called Len Purvis, when he saw me. His wife, Roweena, acknowledged me and waved, but didn't extend a greeting due to her mouthful of scrambled eggs. Seated next to Len was Gwen Jackson, their neighbor and the town veterinarian. "Morning, Hayden," she said, in between sips of coffee.

The other table was occupied by Billy Hixon and two of his landscaping crew, Randy and Lester Kleinpeter. Randy and Lester were brothers who had grown up in St. Germaine. They had worked for Billy all through high school during the summer breaks and on Saturdays. When they graduated, Billy hired them full-time since it was clear that they wouldn't be attending college. Both of them were chowing down on eggs, bacon, grits, baked apples, biscuits, gravy, and whatever else Pete had in the kitchen. They were big boys with big appetites, and since the boss was paying they didn't mind having a good meal.

Billy, on the other hand, was watching his weight. This was information that his wife, Elaine, shared with me last Wednesday at choir rehearsal. Billy, never a small man, was under doctor's orders to lose thirty pounds. Elaine had indicated that, if the past few days were any indication, this was not going to be a pleasant few months. Billy was looking at a plate that had a stalk of celery on it. That was all. A stalk of celery. He wasn't eating it, just looking at it in disgust.

"This is stupid," Billy said as I walked up. "Look at this thing." He picked up the stalk and waggled it at me.

"Why don't you dip it in this gravy?" suggested Randy. He pushed the bowl of thick brown sludge across the table.

Billy growled.

Billy Hixon's Lawn Service, in addition to having a lot of small, personal accounts, also had several large annual accounts that funded the company through the winter months. He was responsible for the grounds of St. Barnabas. The rumor was that he charged the church the usual rate plus ten percent, then gave the percentage back to the church as his tithe. I didn't know for sure. Billy also took care of Mountainview Cemetery, St. Germain's oldest and most beloved garden of eternal rest; the Bellefontaine Cemetery, known locally as *Wormy Acres*, due to the founder of the enterprise being Woodrow "Wormy" DuPont; Sterling Park; and Camp Daystar, our Christian nudist camp, to name but a few. Although December, January, and February were slow, the yearly contracts kept the money coming in, and once March arrived (whether it was still winter or not) the crews were in full force. There were leaves to dispose of, lawn thatching to do, fertilizer to spread, plant nurseries to contact, equipment to sharpen and refurbish — any number of things.

"I'm sorry," I said to Billy. "That's a pretty awful-looking breakfast."

"Oh, I've already had breakfast," he said. "Elaine made it for me before I left this morning. A boiled egg and half a grapefruit."

"Coffee?" I asked.

"Prune juice."

I shuddered. Noylene came over to the table with a plate of pancakes and set them down in front of Lester.

"You share these with your brother," Noylene said. "I ain't bringing you no more."

"Mmmph," grunted Lester, his mouth full. Randy reached across the table, skewered two of the pancakes with his fork, and dragged them to his own plate. Lester grabbed the syrup and smothered the remaining flapjacks in maple sweetness, then passed the bottle across to Randy, who was slathering butter in between the golden disks.

"Those boys can eat," observed Noylene.

Billy sighed, dipped his celery in the gravy, and took a bite. It didn't crunch.

The cowbell on the front door clanged again and I looked up to see Brother Hog waddle in with little Rahab in his arms.

Rahab Archibald Fabergé-Dupont was two years old. To be more precise, two years and three months. According to my sources, i.e. Meg, the age of any baby over three months old, but under two years, is designated in months; Little Prissy is seventeen months old. Bobby Clyde is twenty-one months old. After the age of two, the division goes to half-years. This keeps up until age ten or so. Beyond that, a yearly milepost is sufficient until the age of forty. Then, whichever decade the person currently haunts is close enough, as in "Meg is 40ish." So Rahab was two, going on two and a half.

Rahab is the precocious (and some might say "insufferable") offspring of Noylene Fabergé-Dupont-McTavish and the Rev. Dr. Hogmanay McTavish, known to his friends as "Brother Hog." The boy is lacking the McTavish hyphenation at the end of his surname for the simple reason that Noylene and Brother Hog weren't married at the time of little Rahab's birth. They were married now, but Noylene hadn't gotten around to changing the birth certificate.

Brother Hog had always been suspect of his son's forename. Yes, it was both Biblical and Old Testament, but Rahab was a *female* prostitute in the book of Joshua. Noylene had named the child in the hospital and thought the name sounded exotic. An exotic name for an exotic baby. Rahab, you see, had been born with a tail — a caudal appendage, the obstetrician called it. Not common, but it sometimes happens, and the doctors usually take care of it right away. Noylene wasn't so sure. Maybe this was a sign from God. Maybe little Rahab should keep his tail until he reached an age where he could decide for himself whether he wanted it or not. In the end, Noylene agreed to let the doc snip the little rascal's rudder. Once the surgeon offered Noylene a two-for-one tail snip/circumcision deal, she was on board. Noylene never could resist a bargain.

Brother Hog was a born-again preacher, first and last. He had spent most of his professional life in an evangelist's tent, but had also taken a turn as the pastor of New Fellowship Baptist Church here in town. He had grown more rotund since he'd first set up his tent in Sterling Park several years ago, but one thing hadn't changed: his trademark hairstyle. It was a coiffure fancied by TV preachers, used-furniture salesmen, and the insane. To call this particular hairdo a "comb-over" would do it a gross injustice. Brother Hog's crowning glory manifested its entire expanse from the right side of his scalp. The gray hair swooped up and around his brow, circled his head once, then twice, then terminated in a cluster of sprigs glued down with half a can of hairspray. Noylene, now being married to Brother Hog and having firsthand knowledge, affirmed that, unwound and unglued, the lonely tress was about two feet long.

After resigning his ministry at New Fellowship Baptist when Rahab was born — Hog's name on the birth certificate identifying him as the father hastened his departure — he went back to seasonal evangelizing in the spring and the fall. This was more Hog's style. As a full-time tent evangelist, he'd been on the road fifty weeks a year. It was a pace he no longer wished to keep and since he was now Noylene's husband, he didn't have to.

Noylene was quite the entrepreneur. A self-made woman, she had little education but made up for it in drive, determination, and gumption that was unmatched by anyone I knew. Along with being one of the professional waitresses in town, a few years earlier she'd opened Noylene's Beautifery, An Oasis of Beauty, taking advantage of her God-given talent of granting beauty to others less fortunate than herself. Pete, then the mayor, had been skeptical about the name of the salon. He thought the tourists might not appreciate the down-home flavor. I'd had a different view.

"Look on the bright side," I'd told him. "With a name like Noylene's Beautifery, she'll either go out of business in two months, or it'll become a bizarro, cutting-edge, cult-like styling salon that people will flock to. Noylene will be charging three or four hundred dollars a haircut. Either way, it's win-win."

We were both wrong. The Beautifery settled down into a successful, small-town beauty parlor. A year later, Noylene got a small business grant from the state to perfect her Dip-N-Tan, a contraption invented by her son, D'Artagnan, where her customers could hang from a bar and be slowly lowered by a winch into a vat of tanning fluid. It didn't take long before the women of St. Germaine (and some of the men) were walking around town, summer or winter, looking as though they had just returned from Rio de Janeiro. Above the vat, Noylene had placed a sign:

I am dark, but comely, O ye daughters of Jerusalem ...
Song of Solomon 1:5

Noylene felt that it was always good to have a Bible verse to fall back on. In fact, she had several verses from the eighteenth chapter of Leviticus that, taken together, explained why it had been perfectly acceptable for her to marry her cousin, Wormy DuPont. They were divorced now, chiefly due to Wormy's incarceration for the murder of Russ Stafford during a Bible School reenactment of the Stoning of Stephen. He'd grown jealous of Russ (playing the part of St. Stephen), whom he thought to be the father of Noylene's unborn baby, and took the occasion to pummel him to death with a rock. After his conviction, Noylene sold the cemetery, filed for divorce, had the baby, married Hog, and never visited Wormy, not even once. She'd made a pretty penny on the cemetery, and rumor had it that she'd also sold some mineral rights up on Quail Ridge where some diamonds had been found. Noylene had nothing to say about that.

All things considered, the Rev. Dr. Hogmanay McTavish was happy being a kept man.

"C'mere, baby," said Noylene, holding out both hands to take Rahab from her husband. Rahab hadn't been a small baby and now wasn't a small toddler. He was a pudgy fellow who owed more of his looks to Hog than to Noylene. The little guy reached across the gap and climbed into Noylene's arms. She grunted softly as the baby changed hands.

Rahab's parents had been at odds about the youngster's immediate life goals, Noylene gravitating toward "potty-training," with Brother Hog leaning heavily in the direction of "Baby Evangelist." A Baby Evangelist, according to Hog, was a better draw even than a Scripture Chicken, Hog's last evangelical enticement. The Scripture Chicken had been trained to choose a scripture from an overlarge Bible resting on a table in the middle of the stage. Then, once the scripture had been "pecked," Brother Hog would preach his message. Hog had some favorite passages to be sure, and the bird generally picked those with the help of a little seed-corn. But, if the chicken varied from the script, Hog was good enough to massage almost any Biblical reading into fitting his *sermon du jour*. Bother Hog hadn't had a Scripture Chicken since the untimely demise of Binny Henn, his favorite, mistakenly eaten on the last night of one of his revivals. Hog had tried to train a couple of other chickens after that, but his heart just wasn't in it.

Now, though, Brother Hogmanay McTavish had new fire and it stemmed from his son. It seemed as though Little Rahab was a natural with a microphone. Hog discovered this one day when Noylene was at work. He'd given Rahab an old microphone to play with to keep the boy quiet while he was watching a rerun of an old Oral Roberts crusade. Rahab, a gifted mimic, took the microphone, held it to his mouth, and strutted around the living room of the trailer screaming into it and waving his copy of

Baby's First Old Testament. That his hollering was unintelligible made little difference to Hog. Unintelligible wasn't a problem. He knew opportunity when he saw it and immediately grasped how a toddler on a stage "preaching in unknown tongues" would be an even bigger attraction than his chicken. All Rahab needed was a glossolalian interpreter, and who better than his own father? Hog knew exactly what his own son was trying to say if only he could say it. Just then Pat Robertson, another TV preacher, came onto the screen and said, "There's someone watching who needs to get back into the ministry. This is a *Word of Knowledge*. God says that you need to get back out there and take your family with you." Well, it couldn't get much clearer than that. It was a sign, if ever there was one.

Noylene was not convinced. She didn't like the idea of her baby boy preaching to the masses. Pete and Cynthia had a bet on which parent would prevail. Cynthia's money was on Noylene. Pete said that he saw the look in Brother Hog's eye and that Noylene didn't stand a chance.

"He's a helluva preacher," said Pete, "and he makes a good argument. Who is Noylene to stand in the way of the Gospel? If God and Pat Robertson have told Hog to take that baby on the road, I doubt that Noylene's got much say."

"We'll see," Cynthia had replied.

"Good morning, Chief," said Rosa Zumaya, coming into the room from the kitchen, wiping her hands on a towel. Rosa was a plump woman and I'd never seen her without a smile on her face. If I had to guess, I would say that she was in her late forties. Her black hair was tied into a bun at the back of her head, and her face was as devoid of lines as a twenty year old.

I sat down at our table near the back of the restaurant. It was generally conceded to be the St. Germaine Police Department table, but if Pete had actual paying customers we were ousted without ceremony. The red-and-white-checked vinyl table cloths were identical on all the tables. The chairs were wooden and upholstered with red Naugahyde. The four booths along the side wall were trimmed in the same fabric. Ditto for the upholstered chrome stools at the counter. The counter top was white but had a beat-up look to it. The floor was tiled in a checkerboard black-and-white linoleum. All the tables and the spots at the counter were topped with a ketchup bottle, mustard bottle, Tabasco sauce bottle, salt and pepper shakers, sugar shaker, and an aluminum napkin holder. The menu was on a board fixed to the wall behind the counter, but you could get anything you wanted at the Slab. That is, if Manuel had the ingredients, and he usually did. Manuel Zumaya was Pete's cook, and he'd been working at the Slab Café for a couple of years. Before Manuel arrived, cuisine had been marked by respectable diner fare — burgers, sandwiches, fries, a good breakfast, lunch specials, and the like. I could even get a Reuben sandwich if I felt the need. Since Manuel had taken over the kitchen, epicurean expectations among the breakfast and lunch crowd had risen dramatically. With his wife, Rosa, they had transformed the Slab into an eatery worthy of Pete's delusions. Rosa did most of the prep work in the kitchen, made coffee, waited tables — whatever was needed — but mostly, she invented recipes. And *what* recipes!

"I'll have some pancakes," I said to Rosa, as she filled my coffee cup.

"Apple cinnamon ricotta pancakes or cherry macadamia nut pancakes?" Rosa said. "We have both today."

"Really? The first one, then."

"I think you'll love them." Rosa smiled, then disappeared through the kitchen door. A moment later Pete came out, saw me, walked over to the table, and sat down. Hog took the adjacent table. Noylene had hauled Rahab into the kitchen to say hello to Manuel.

"How you doing, Hog?" Pete said to him, giving him a nod.

"Tolerable," answered Hog. "How 'bout some coffee?"

"Hmm," said Pete, looking around for a waitress, even though he knew both of them were in the kitchen. "Yeah, sure." He got back up and found a coffee pot behind the counter on a burner, then made the rounds: Hog first, then the counter guy, then the Purvises and Gwen Jackson, then Billy's table.

He dribbled the last half cup into a Kleinpeter brother's cup. "Gotta get another pot," he said.

"Don't worry about me," said the boy. "I'm full up."

Noylene came back into the dining room with Rosa right behind her. Rahab was hanging onto Rosa's neck with one hand and pushing a banana into his mouth with the other. Pete went back to the coffee station and replaced the pot. He picked up a full pot, looked around the room, then set it back on the burner and walked back over to my table.

"Your hotcakes'll be up in a few," said Noylene. "You want whipped cream on those?"

I shook my head. "Nope," I said, then turned to Pete, who had found his chair again. "What's the word on our pig?"

"Should be here from France any time. I don't have a final delivery date yet. There's apparently a bunch of quarantine stuff she has to go through."

"You're getting a pig?" said Billy. "A fancy French pig?"

"Yep," I said. " A truffle pig."

"Truffles, eh?" said Brother Hog. "You know, Little Rahab there drinks truffle-milk." He gestured at Rahab, who was stuffing the remaining stump of the banana into his cheeks like a chipmunk. He looked as though he'd be saving most of this banana for later.

I watched as Len, Roweena, and Gwen perked up at the mention of a fancy French pig. Or maybe it was the comment that Rahab was partial to truffle-milk. Didn't matter. Like most eateries in small towns, conversation across tables was a given. Everyone's participation was invited.

"I've never heard of truffle-milk," said Roweena.

"It's my fault," said Noylene. "The boy wouldn't drink cow's milk. Oh, he'd drink goat's milk, sheep's milk, probably yak's milk if I could get it. So one day Manuel was messing around with truffle oil in the kitchen and gave a dab to Rahab on his finger. The boy went crazy. Sucked on that finger like it was the last full teat on the dog. He sobbed when Manuel finally had to pass him off and get back to cooking. Anyway, I tried a few drops in his bottle and he took to it like a rat to a raincoat. He's been drinking truffle-milk ever since."

"Makes sense," said Gwen. "Truffles have a very distinctive flavor."

"Cheaper than goat milk, I'll bet," added Len.

"You ain't just whistlin' Dixie," said Hog. "Goat milk costs more'n beer." He paused. "Or, so I've heard."

"Did y'all know that yak's milk is pink?" asked Billy. He was still contemplating the remains of his celery stick, swirling it in the gravy.

"I did not know that," said Roweena, thoughtfully. "Good information, though. I expect it'll come in handy one day." Noylene nodded her agreement.

"Hang on," said Pete, looking at Noylene. "A rat to a raincoat?"

Chapter 5

Easter was going to be late this year. When Easter fell in March, we might be fighting the snow to get to church. But when Easter was deep into April, we generally had beautiful weather to accompany it. On this Sunday morning, with Fat Tuesday, Ash Wednesday, and all forty days of Lent to look forward to, the weather didn't look too bad, and the groundhog had promised us a quick resolution to the frosty season. Although Punxsutawney Phil didn't give us a specific date, an early spring should be right around the corner.

I was ready to head for church. Meg was not. "Five minutes," she said. I knew that meant fifteen. It was no problem. We had plenty of time before I needed to warm-up the choir.

"What are you going to give up for Lent?" Meg called from the bedroom.

"I don't know yet. I still have a couple of days to decide."

"I'm giving up chocolate."

"That sounds good," I called back. "I'll give up chocolate, too."

She walked out of the bedroom, at the same time working to fasten a silver cross around her neck. "You should give up cigars."

I thought for a moment. "Nah. How about asparagus?"

"Cigars."

"You can't make the decision," I said. "That's not the way it works. It has to be a personal commitment made through hours of prayer and long contemplation. Otherwise, it doesn't mean anything. How about if I give up crossword puzzles?"

"Yes, I can tell that took a lot of contemplation," said Meg. "Here, help me with this necklace, will you? I can't get the clasp to catch."

She handed me the cross, spun around, and lifted her hair off her shoulders. It took me a moment to figure out the clasp, but she waited patiently.

"Done," I said.

"Thank you very much. Now, about those cigars ..."

* * *

Transfiguration Sunday is celebrated at St. Barnabas on the last Sunday after Epiphany. It is the same in most of the liturgical Protestant denominations in the U.S. The actual *Feast of the Transfiguration* is on August 6th, coincidentally the anniversary of the dropping of the first atomic bomb on Hiroshima, but we are happy to celebrate it in communion with the rest of our Episcopal brethren on the Sunday before Lent begins.

It's a big Sunday. A major feast day. The Gospel lessons are revelations of the identity of Jesus as the Son of God to his disciples. Jesus takes Peter, James, and John with him and goes up to a mountain. Once on the mountain, Jesus "is transfigured before them; his face shining as the sun, and his garments became white as the light." The prophets Elijah and Moses appear and Jesus talks to them. Just as Elijah and Moses begin to depart from the scene, Peter begins to ask Jesus if the disciples should make three tabernacles for him and the two prophets. But before Peter can finish, a bright cloud appears, and a voice from the cloud states: "This is my beloved Son, with whom I am well pleased; listen to him." The disciples fall to the ground in fear, but Jesus tells them not to be afraid. When they look up, Elijah and Moses have disappeared and Jesus instructs the disciples not to say anything to anyone until he has risen from the dead, which, of course, they don't.

In Christian teachings, the Transfiguration is unique among the miracles of Jesus in that the miracle happens to Jesus himself. It is a pivotal moment in the narrative, and the setting on the mountain is presented as the point where human nature meets God: the meeting place for the temporal and the eternal, with Jesus himself as the connecting point, acting as the bridge between heaven and earth. It is the origin of our expression "mountaintop experience." With such symbolism and these wonderful texts in three of the four Gospel accounts, one might find it odd that the sermon for the day was listed in the bulletin as "Cloudy With a Chance of Meatballs."

"That's a children's book from the '70s," said Georgia Wester. She sighed and slid her bulletin into the front of her choir folder. Georgia owned and ran Eden Books on the square. She was also on the altar guild.

"I'm sure that Mother P will make it all clear," Meg said. "The title is probably very clever in context."

"I'm sure it is," Marjorie said. "Hey! We should change the anthem to *On Top of Spaghetti*." Marjorie was a tenor and no fan of Mother P.

"On top of spaghetti," sang Mark Wells, and the rest of the basses joined in immediately in the time-honored campfire classic: "All covered with cheese. I lost my poor meatball, when somebody sneezed."

"Kyrie, eleison," added Bev Greene. "Meatball, eleison."

"We're doing the piece we've rehearsed," I announced. "I wrote it and we're singing it. It's the price you pay for having a genius as a choir director."

"I like the anthem fine," said Rebecca Watts from the alto section, "but this story is off to a bad start." She waved her copy of *The Treble Wore Trouble* at me. I'd printed it on the back of the Psalm.

"I know a girl named Carrie Oakey," said Varmit LeMieux, reading and talking at the same time, a talent he'd probably discovered only recently. We all knew he couldn't *sing* and read at the same time, a drawback that hampered his choir participation considerably. But he wasn't in the choir to sing. He was in the choir to keep an eye on his wife, Muffy.

"You do not know any girl named Carrie Oakey," snapped Muffy.

Muffy and Varmit had joined the choir soon after they moved to town. Actually, Muffy joined the choir. Varmit tagged along.

"I think I do," said Varmit. "Doesn't she sing in a bar we used to go to? The name sounds pretty familiar."

Muffy huffed out a great sigh of exasperation, then decided to ignore Varmit. She turned her attention to the rest of the choir. "Are all y'all planning to come to the play? We open a week from this coming Friday. Three performances — Friday, Saturday, and a Sunday matinée."

The St. Germaine Little Theater had a long and distinguished history, dating back to 1934. It began as the St. Germaine Footlight Club (named for that grand old community theater in Massachusetts) and specialized in Gilbert and Sullivan, as well as some turn-of-the-century melodramas and contemporary plays. The Footlight Club was the first theater in North Carolina to present *Our Town* in the mid 1940s and had Walter Brennan come in to headline the production. Walter's sister, directing the show, prevailed on the Oscar-winning actor to take the role of the Stage Manager. Since then the name of the company has changed, and artistic visions have come and gone. We still have a board of directors, though, and the theater puts on two productions a year.

"What's the show?" asked Marjorie.

"It might behoove us to look at this music," I said hopefully.

"Nah," Marjorie answered. "We don't need to go over this anthem again. We've got it cold." Being the only female tenor gave her a sense of propriety. That she kept a flask of something-or-other in the hymnal rack of her choir chair gave the rest of us pause. We did not ask, nor did we tell. Marjorie was in her late seventies at least.

"You don't know? We're doing *Welcome to Mitford*, adapted by Robert Inman from the books by Jan Karon." Muffy gave Marjorie a deliberately puzzled look. "It's been in the paper about a dozen times. Didn't you see my picture on the front page on Friday?"

Marjorie said, "I don't read the paper."

"You should. Anyway, I'm playing Miss Cynthia Coopersmith. That's the lead. Christopher Lloyd is playing Father Tim Kavanagh *and* he's directing the production. He's very talented."

"I'm sure you'll have tickets available for sale next week," I said.

"Oh, sure!"

Muffy LeMieux had married Varmit and moved to St. Germaine so they could help run Blueridge Furs, a fur farm that specialized in a registered, hybrid animal called a Minque®, a genetically engineered cross between a nutria and a South American pacarana. Muffy was a singularly beautiful redhead, a feature often overlooked by many women due to her mildly irritating personality. It was a feature not overlooked by many men, personality or not. She favored angora sweaters, short-sleeved in summer, long in winter, of the sort that might have been popular in Marilyn Monroe's heyday, stretch pants, high heels, and overly large "mall hair."

"Muffy?" Nancy said the first time we met her. "What an *interesting* name. Is that spelled with a 'y' or with an 'i'?"

"A 'y'," Muffy had answered. "Although I spelled it with an 'i-e' when I was in high school. You know how sometimes you can dot the 'i' with a little heart?"

Nancy nodded.

"But then I changed it back. It was too hard to remember."

Muffy was a wannabe country singer and she had been told, on numerous occasions, that she sounded almost exactly like Loretta Lynn. I almost had the twang out of her choral sound. Almost.

"Let's look at the Psalm first," I announced. "Then the anthem."

* * *

The service went off without much of a hitch. Dr. Mother Rosemary Pepperpot-Cohosh's sermon was about how the Transfiguration story sounded just about as crazy as the sky raining meatballs. In the end, she suggested that we might just as well embrace the mystery of it all and give up our "Cloud Control." I thought she missed the point, but during the sermon I decided what I'd give up for Lent. I'd give up snarkiness. No criticizing the sermon. No snide remarks about the liturgy or lack thereof. Forty days of "going along" with the church program, whatever that may be. Now *that* was a Lenten discipline. I'd tried it before and failed. This time I was determined.

"Here's my plan," I told Meg, as I drove her to her mother's after church. "I shall give up liturgical snarkiness for Lent. I shall give Rosemary my full support in as far as I am able. I shall not criticize her preaching, nor her ministry."

"No way," said Meg. "You can't do it."

"I certainly can," I said. "If you can give up chocolate, I can give up snarkiness."

"Want to bet?"

"Oh, yes, I'll bet."

"Okay," said Meg. "If I win, you have to go to a health week with me."

"What's that?"

"A week at a medical facility that specializes in fasting, cleansing, colonics, massages, aroma therapy, reflexology — that sort of thing."

"You're kidding, right?"

"I am *not* kidding," said Meg. "It would be very good for you."

"It would not be good for me. It would kill me."

"It certainly wouldn't kill you. You'd feel better after."

"What do I get if I win?" I asked.

"What do you want?"

"Hmm. If I win, you have to cook me hamburgers three times a week for seven weeks. All the way from Easter to Pentecost."

"Sure," said Meg. "Why not? The burgers would probably finish you off, but I don't really have to worry, do I? There's no way that you're going to let Mother P have carte blanche with the worship services."

"Watch me," I said with a grin.

I dropped Meg off and drove home, cleansing my ecumenical palate by listening to some recordings of different choral settings of *O Nata Lux de Lumine*, the ancient hymn for the Feast of the Transfiguration — two by Renaissance composers, Thomas Tallis and Christopher Tye, and three by contemporary composers, Morten Lauridsen, Seth Garrepy, and Guy Forbes.

O Light born of Light,
Jesus, redeemer of the world,
with loving-kindness deign to receive
suppliant praise and prayer.

Thou who once deigned to be clothed in flesh
for the sake of the lost,
grant us to be members
of thy blessed body.

When I drove up to the cabin, I was refreshed. Refreshed enough to make myself a sandwich and sit down at the typewriter, now to the music of Cole Porter. Raymond Chandler would have listened to this, I thought. I took a bite of the sandwich, then another, and reread my previous effort. It was good, I thought. Maybe not Raymond Chandler good, or even Dashiell Hammett good, but certainly Carroll John Daly good. I clicked the paper in behind the roller and continued.

* * *

"I hear that you're a Liturgy Detective," she said, "and I need help."

Her eyes were limpid pools, her nose was a limpid sausage, her ears were limpid cartilaginous extrusions. I nibbled on one in anticipation.

"Everyone needs help, Sweetheart," I purruped. "But it'll cost you."

"Two hundred a day plus expenses," she said, dropping two C-notes on the desk. "That's what your ad says."

"That's about right." I settled back in my chair, tucked the cash inside my shorts, and chomped down on my cig. I remembered that ad. Marilyn talked me into placing it in the local rag when business got so bad we were charging the roaches rent.

"Okay," I said. "What's the chisel?"

"I have a baby naming company called 'Bible Babies.' We supply new and interesting Biblical baby names for upscale, desperate parents who want something unique yet presumptuous."

My eyes went as crazy as Michelle Bachman and Rick Perry's love-child. "Go on," I said, eyeing the sausage.

"I mean, there are plenty of Joshuas, Jacobs, Jordans, Rachels, and Elizabeths. But where are the Dalmatias, or the Gomers, or Doeg the Edomites?"

"Dunno," I said, thinking about lunch.

"There are over sixty thousand Biblical names," said Carrie, "and today's busy parent needs help to navigate through that mine field. Most of the parents think that their baby's Biblical name means 'Beloved of God,' or maybe 'Gift of the Lord.' But you have to be careful. For instance, 'Courtney' literally means 'Yahweh's Mud Pie,' but what parent wants that on a decoupaged plaque? With 'Bible Babies,' they get a lifetime warranty."

"How about Nergalsharezer?" I said, my mind wandering to a prom-date I once had. "What does that mean?"

"Don't be horning in," she warned, then continued. "All of a sudden, we get a notice from the Attorney

General that all the Biblical names have been copyrighted."

"☻?" I asked in surprise.

"And now we have a cease and desist order." She reached inside her purse, pulled out a piece of paper and pushed it across the desk. I recognized the stationery. It came from the Bishop.

* * *

Nice, I thought. *Nice.*

Chapter 6

Fat Tuesday: the only holiday for the horizontally challenged. It was the day before Ash Wednesday and therefore (traditionally) a day of excess. Mardi Gras parades — the best ones — were held on Fat Tuesday. Drinking and debauching are the orders of the day as we gird our loins for forty days of fasting and prayer. Fasting and prayer have mostly fallen by the wayside, but the drinking and debauching have certainly been embraced, insofar as Mardi Gras goes.

In the church we've managed to avoid the imputation of "fatness" by announcing that we choose to celebrate "Shrove Tuesday" instead: "shrove" from the verb "shrive," meaning "to grant absolution." A pancake on Shrove Tuesday would taste as sweet and make you just as fat. We eat pancakes just before Lent begins because, as severe and high-minded Christians, we eschew sugar, fat, flour, and eggs, items whose consumption is traditionally restricted during the penitential season, and so, ingest them in abundance on the day before. Sort of like a "last meal." One last sugar high.

All this is historical trivia and has nothing whatsoever to do with what we actually do or why we do it. Serving pancakes in the parish hall at St. Barnabas on the Tuesday before Lent is done to raise money for the youth mission trip to Costa Rica. I suspect that most churches have the same or a similar agenda. I myself choose to eat pancakes all the way through Lent, but that never stopped me from eating them on Fat Tuesday ... I mean *Shrove* Tuesday ... as well.

The pancake meal began at four in the afternoon and continued until six, catering to whoever happened to walk in. The event had been advertised, and since it had been an annual tradition for a number of years, was well attended. Single folks, married folks, old and young, parents with their children, whether they were parishioners or not, all enjoyed a great pancake supper for the price of a donation. And people tended to be generous.

I chose a seat next to Bev Greene. She waved me over as soon as I cleared the line with my paper plate stacked with three pancakes. On the table was a bowl of yellow not-quite-butter and a bottle of Aunt Jemima maple syrup. Coffee was also being supplied, and the coffee was good — Community Coffee from Louisiana. We had it shipped in.

"How are you this evening?" I asked Bev, as I took my seat.

"Let me just tell you," said Bev, grimly.

"Uh-oh," I muttered.

"You know what a 'blended' service is, right?"

"Yes, I do," I said.

"Get ready then. You're about to get one."

I sighed.

Bev was our Parish Administrator. Some time ago, the church voted to hire an administrator to free up the rector for more priestly duties. No rector since then had argued the need, since it was no skin off their nose and work that they didn't have to do. The administrator was in charge of writing checks (although she didn't keep the books), scheduling, handling all personnel issues (at the behest of the rector), and all sundry chores that fell under the job description as "other duties as required."

"Mother P has decided that the season of Lent might be a good time to experiment with alternate forms of worship. You know, I'm not sure I want to do this anymore."

"It's only for six Sundays," I said. "A finite period. Six Sundays and done."

"Really? That's how you think it will go? Six Sundays and done?"

I shook my head, rethinking my proposed Lenten discipline of ecclesiastical détente. Could this be a test?

"Nope," I said. "I don't believe that's how it will go."

"We're having a meeting in the morning. A staff meeting. I wish you would come."

"Yeah, okay. What time?"

"I'm going in to see her at nine. The full staff meeting is at nine-thirty."

"I'll be there, but I'm not sure I can do anything. It's her call."

Bev smiled. "You're intimidating. You reek of snoot."

"I could shower," I suggested.

* * *

I'd avoided staff meetings, worship meetings, vestry meetings, and almost every other meeting I could think up an excuse to get out of after our last rector left to become bishop of Northern California. Since I was on the staff, I suppose I was invited to attend, with or without prior notice. Mother P — Rosemary Pepperpot-Cohosh — was surprised to see me come in. Her eyes widened for a moment, then she said, "Hayden, so glad you could make it this morning." She was sitting at the head of the table in the conference room. To her right was Kimberly Walnut, the Director of Christian Formation. Kimberly had been at St. Barnabas for a few years, and her ideas for improving the church service had barely been held in check by Bev after Gaylen departed. Kimberly owed more of her worship proclivities to the Methodist denomination she grew up in than the Episcopal denomination that had hired her. Her style was not, as we Anglicans are fond of saying, "high church." She wanted to feel things, she said, and feel them deeply.

There was no love lost between Kimberly Walnut and Bev, but Bev had been under orders from the vestry not to fire anyone in the absence of a permanent priest. Once Mother P came on board, Kimberly Walnut found an ally on whom she could rely.

On Mother P's left was Herb Cohosh, her husband and a full-fledged Lutheran pastor. Joyce Cooper had taken the job of treasurer last year but still served on the Worship Committee. She sat next to Herb. Marilyn, the church secretary, came in and sat down next to me at the other end.

"We might as well get started," said Mother P.

"Where's Bev?" asked Joyce. "I just saw her a few minutes ago."

"Bev resigned this morning," Mother P said, with just a hint of sadness. "We'll miss her leadership. *I'll* miss her leadership. But we must press on." She brightened. "I'll meet with the vestry this week and we'll look at our long-term plan. It may be that we no longer need a Parish Administrator. In the meantime, Joyce, as treasurer you can easily write the checks. We'll just need to get the signature card changed. Herb has agreed, with the support of the vestry, to help out when we need another priest. He's still a Lutheran, but, as you all know, we're in full communion with the Evangelical Lutheran Church."

Herb nodded happily. Mother P continued, "Herb's is strictly a volunteer position and he's indicated that he's happy to help. Kimberly will still be in charge of the Sunday School curriculum and our Wednesday night programming, but she'll now also be in charge of the scheduling of the building. Hayden is in charge of the music. Nothing could be simpler."

No one said anything.

"I know what you're all thinking," said Mother P, "and you'll get the story from Bev soon enough, I expect. I did not fire her, nor give her any cause to leave. We sat down this morning and had a frank and earnest discussion about the role of a Parish Administrator, and Bev was forthcoming about her concerns about changes I've made since I've gotten here ... and will continue to make. That's my job as your rector."

Silence.

"Anyway, I'm sorry she felt the need to leave." Another pause. "I've invited the rest of the Worship Committee to come in just a few minutes. We need to think about the services through Lent and Holy Week. Let me get us some coffee." She got up and left the room followed closely by Herb.

"I guess she's letting us comment without her being here," said Joyce.

"I never thought we needed an administrator, anyway," said Kimberly Walnut.

"What do you think, Hayden?" Joyce asked.

"We certainly *did* need an administrator while we didn't have a full-time priest and Bev was good at keeping everything running smoothly. Rosemary's right, though. If she wants to do Bev's work, the transition probably won't be difficult." Well done, I thought. That wasn't too hard.

Mother P opened the door and came back into the conference room carrying two coffee carafes. Herb followed with a metal painted tray of coffee cups, a bowl of sugar and non-sugar packets, some spoons, and some of that white powdered creamer. Behind Herb was Elaine Hixon, Billy's wife. Shea Maxwell and Wynette Winslow brought up the rear.

"I've asked Fred May to be on this committee, since he's the Senior Warden," said Mother P, "but he can't meet with us during the day. We might decide to have a few meetings in the evening. We'll just have to see how that works." She looked around the room. "By the way, in my meeting with Bev, I asked her to join the Worship Committee since that is where her gifts lay, and she agreed, but declined, understandably, to attend this morning. She'll be here for the next one."

I poured myself a cup of coffee, then one for Marilyn. The other carafe was making its way around the table during these announcements.

"I've been wondering," said Mother P, "if the season of Lent might be a good time to experiment with some alternate forms of worship."

It wasn't a question.

"It seems like a good time, a new beginning, the start of a new season. I wonder if a 'blended' service might work and serve to bring back some of the people who find traditional worship a little too stodgy. Maybe even bring in some new folks."

Again, it wasn't a question. Everyone looked at me.

"I couldn't say one way or the other," I said. "We've never had a 'blended' service since I've been here. We've tried a lot of things, make no mistake: a Clown Eucharist, puppets, spirit sticks, shoe polishing, liturgical dance, musicals, you name it."

Mother P seemed to consider this.

I said, "If I may ask — and I mean this in the unsnarkiest way — what is it exactly that you want to do?"

This was a test, of that I was sure. An Ash Wednesday test. *Blessed is the man that endures temptation: for when he is tried, he shall receive the crown of life, which the Lord has promised to them that love him.*

"We want to blend the traditional and the contemporary," said Mother P, obviously ready for this question. "We'd like to have your choral music along with something in a 'Praise and Worship' style. No drum kits or guitars or anything like that yet, but I have some choruses that I brought from my previous parish and I've already signed us up for a CCLI license." She looked around the table. "I can't believe we've never had one. Every church does."

I gave her my second nicest smile, not failing to notice the reference to "*your* choral music," and the equally surreptitious "No drums or guitars *yet*." *Let no man say when he is tempted, I am tempted of God: for God cannot be tempted with evil, neither tempteth he any.* Forty days and nights. And to think I could have gone with giving up cigars.

"What's a CCLI License?" asked Joyce.

"It's a church copyright thing," answered Mother P. "It allows us to make copies of music for the congregation. Songbooks and things like that."

"Oh," said Joyce.

Mother P said, "Hayden?"

"Well," I said, choosing my words carefully, "choruses are not my favorite means of musical expression, but what would you like me to do?"

"First of all, I'm thinking we could use some new service music."

"I agree," I said. "You know there are some settings in the hymnal that we haven't done for several years ..."

"I was thinking," interrupted Mother P, "that you might write us something new. You're quite a composer and that anthem last Sunday was just beautiful."

This caught me by surprise.

"*The Transfiguration*, right? I was very moved."

"It was gorgeous," added Joyce.

"And fun to sing," added Elaine.

" Well ... thanks."

"You know, I heard something at another parish — a setting of the mass using English folk tunes."

"The *English Folk Song Mass*?" I said. "We have copies upstairs."

"No," said Mother P. "I meant that maybe *you* could compose us our own sort of thing. A setting just for St. Barnabas."

I thought for a moment, then said, almost to myself, "You know, there's plenty of historical precedent. In the Renaissance, the 'parody mass' — that's what it's called — was very popular. Composers used entire sections of other people's melodic compositions to compose their own masses." I was relishing my brief foray into the role of music history teacher. "Palestrina alone wrote some fifty-odd examples."

"Uh-huh," said Mother P, nodding and looking interested. "Why is it called a 'parody mass?'"

"Oh, the term 'parody' has nothing to do with humor, in the modern sense of the word. In this case a better translation would be 'imitation mass.' Composers might use anything, even bawdy secular songs." I paused, then said, "Sure. Why not?"

"Excellent!" said Mother P. "Not bawdy songs, though."

"Of course not."

"Something catchy. Something the congregation can latch on to. A tune they know."

"Absolutely."

Elaine and Joyce stared at me, their mouths slightly agape. Wynette had lost a good deal of color. Shea Maxwell and Kimberly Walnut looked like a couple of cats that just split a plate of canary.

A knock sounded at the conference room door, it swung open and Dave Vance peered into the room.

"Sorry to interrupt," he said, "but I need to see the Chief."

Rosemary looked a bit put out but didn't say anything as I pushed my chair from the table, excused myself, and followed Dave into the hallway.

"What's up?" I said in a low voice.

"We've got a dead body," Dave whispered. "Looks like a youngster. A boy. Right across the park behind the Beautifery."

"*What!?*" I said, then lowered my voice. "Are you kidding me?"

"Otto found him when he was picking up the trash this morning. He was sitting down, propped up against the back wall by the dumpster. Nancy was in Boone, but she's already on her way back."

"Hang on a sec." I stuck my head back inside the room. The Worship Committee had apparently decided to wait for my return and were all looking in my direction.

"Sorry, gotta go."

"This is an important meeting, Hayden," said Rosemary Pepperpot-Cohosh.

I ignored her and followed Dave down the hall toward the exit.

"What's so all-fired important?" I heard Rosemary ask in frustration. "We were just getting somewhere."

"Probably just another dead body," said Elaine. "Nothing to worry about."

Chapter 7

The alley behind the Beautifery was devoid of any of the charm for which St. Germaine was renowned. It backed up to three establishments in addition to Noylene's Oasis of Beauty: the Ginger Cat, the Bear and Brew, and Eden Books. It was long and narrow and smelled vaguely of garbage — that rotten odor that pervades the proximity of metal dumpsters. Utility lines crossed overhead at every angle, taking power, internet, telephone, and cable TV into all the buildings on this end of the square. The cracked and worn asphalt was dotted with brown weeds poking through in numerous spots and no signs except an old, hand-lettered "No Parking" directive, painted on a board and hung on the whitewashed wall above the lone, yellow dumpster. Standing in the alley, surrounded by three walls and the entrance, one could see neither trees nor mountains. It might have been any sad alley in any city in the country. Even the birds stayed away.

Dave and I entered from the back, walked around Otto's garbage pickup truck and saw him standing next to the dumpster. He hadn't emptied it yet, and although the large bin wasn't overflowing, it was full enough, being the only dumpster for all four businesses. The Beautifery and the bookstore probably didn't have much on a daily basis, but the Bear and Brew and the Ginger Cat more than made up the difference. We walked up to Otto and followed his gaze down the wall. Just as Dave had said, there, sitting on the ground, as though he were sleeping, was what appeared to be a teen-aged boy. His hands were in his lap, his eyes were closed, his long black hair dropped over his eyes and around his shoulders. His chin rested on his chest. I pulled his hair back off his neck and felt for a pulse. No need. His skin had a hard feel to it. He was stiff and cold as ice.

The strangest thing about him was his dress. He was wearing a black sharkskin suit, a black shirt, and a black string tie with a rattlesnake head on the slider. Not a facsimile of a rattlesnake head — the actual head of a good-sized black rattler with the mouth open in mid-strike, the eyes glaring, and two predominant, inch-long fangs almost dripping venom. Each end of the string tie, resting in the middle of the boy's chest, was decorated with the rattles from the other end of two snakes. Eight or ten rattles at first glance, and each was maybe a couple of inches long. On his feet were black dress boots, the toe of one of them decorated with a silver tip. The other boot was unadorned. He had a skull ring with a turquoise stone on the middle finger of his right hand.

The back door of Eden Books opened and Nancy came striding out with Georgia right behind her.

"Are you kidding me?" said Nancy, her shoulders sagging as she saw the boy in front of us.

"That's what the Chief said," said Dave sadly. "His exact words."

"Oh my!" said Georgia. "Oh no! This is terrible!"

"Georgia," I said, "would you mind terribly going back inside and calling the paramedics?"

"I already ..." started Nancy, then stopped as she caught my eye.

"Georgia?" I said again. She was frozen in place, staring at the body. Then at the mention of her name, she seemed to snap out of her daze and regain her senses.

"Of course. Of course, I will." She returned to the back door of the bookshop and tugged on it, but it had locked behind her. With a huff of frustration, she walked past us and the garbage truck to make her way around the block.

"And, Georgia," Nancy called after her, "don't tell anyone about this just yet."

"I won't," she answered, and disappeared.

"I already dialed the EMTs," said Nancy, once Georgia had cleared the alley. "They're on the way."

"I figured," I said, as I squatted down beside the boy to take a closer look. "Odd clothes for a kid."

"Yeah," agreed Dave, resting on his haunches beside me.

"Can I go?" asked Otto. "I gotta lot of garbage to pick up and I'm already behind."

"Yeah," I answered. "Leave this one, though." I pointed to the dumpster just behind the truck. "Come and get it tomorrow."

"Will do," said Otto, and climbed into the cab. A moment later, the truck rumbled off and we were left alone in the alley.

"This is no kid," I said, once Otto had left.

Nancy bent down and joined Dave and me in a closer inspection. I pulled the jet-black hair which was hanging over the face of the corpse back behind his ears — easy to do since the length was a good four inches beyond his shoulders. Although the person resting with his back against the wall was diminutive, once we could see his face clearly it was obvious that his age was more advanced than what we believed at first glance. He had a hooked nose, deep-set eyes, a dark, ruddy complexion, and the lined countenance of a middle-aged man. His cheeks were scarred with pock marks, acne scars maybe, or something worse.

"An Indian," said Dave. "Cherokee, I'll bet."

"Native American," corrected Nancy. "He's tiny. Can't be more than five feet tall. I wouldn't know if he's a Cherokee, though."

"It's a good chance," I said. "Cherokee is only a couple of hours away."

Cherokee, North Carolina, is about an hour west of Asheville. Once a tourist destination on the Great Smoky Mountain Parkway, now the town is better known for its casino. Like most of the Indian reservations in the country, the Cherokee tribe had decided to cast its fortune in with a gambling operation and open a series of casinos. Cherokee was a relatively small town, but the boundary of the Eastern Band of the Cherokee Nation comprised over fifty thousand acres.

"I don't see any blood," said Nancy.

"Be hard to see with these black clothes," I said. "Maybe some pooling underneath. We'll wait 'til the ambulance gets here to move him, then send him over to Kent." I looked over toward the dumpster. "See that?" I said. "Somebody's gotta go through the garbage."

I looked at Dave, Nancy looked at Dave and Dave looked at the dumpster.

"Aw, man," he said.

I said, "I'm just glad this isn't a kid."

"Hang on," said Nancy, studying the man's face. "Look at this."

She pulled the sleek hair farther away from his face, revealing the man's forehead. There, right between his eyes, was the unmistakable shape of a cross.

Ash Wednesday.

* * *

After we'd gone through the pockets of the victim and come up empty, the EMTs loaded him into the ambulance and took him down the mountain to Boone to be delivered to Dr. Kent Murphee, Watauga County's medical examiner. I'd already called Kent and, it being a slow day, he was waiting to get started.

"What do you think?" asked Nancy. "Murdered?"

"Hard to think he wasn't," I replied. "He probably didn't wander into this alley, sit down behind the dumpster, and have a heart attack."

"Probably not," Nancy agreed.

"What about this garbage?" Dave said, eyeing the yellow dumpster. "Are you guys going to help or what?"

"Yeah," said Nancy. "I'll help."

"Me, too," I said.

Two hours later we were sifting through the entire contents spread in piles across the ground. Georgia had made a couple of visits, and Pete had shown up once, bringing us some coffee. He'd gotten the word from Noylene, who'd heard it from Darla, who'd come out the back door to dump yesterday's hair clippings while the ambulance was still there, but Pete didn't stay, once he'd discovered that we were sorting garbage.

Not finding anything that might be remotely connected to our Native American friend, we shoveled everything back into the dumpster and walked back across the park to the station to see if there had been any reports of Ash Wednesday rioting and looting. Nothing on the answering machine, but Nancy, after listening intently, informed me that the rabid possum had been spotted again, this time in Mildred Kibbler's oak tree, but never mind now, because when Mildred went back out to poke at it with a broom stick, the creature had disappeared.

"Why don't you call her back and tell her to call Ruby next time?" I suggested. "She'll take care of that possum."

"I already told Mildred to do just that," said Nancy, "but apparently she's not on speaking terms with Ruby. Something about a dead tree that fell into her back yard. I went and looked, but there was no tree."

"That happened fifteen years ago," I said. "Longtime grudge. Anyway, that possum's not rabid. Just friendly, and possibly hungry."

"I know it," said Nancy. "If it were rabid, and it had been exhibiting symptoms the first time Mildred called, it'd be dead by now. She keeps feeding it garbage, so it'll stick around."

I got Dave started on the dead body paperwork and tried to summon up some enthusiasm for composing a new mass. Nothing. I called Kent Murphee and made an appointment for after lunch.

Chapter 8

The Ginger Cat was everything that the Slab Café was not, catering mainly to the uppercrusty sort of tourists that liked their delicate sandwiches made out of ingredients that would terrify most mountain folk. Capers, for instance, look way too similar to rabbit droppings to ever be put on a plate of lettuce and called "Fennel and Caper Pastiche."

Meg was saving me a seat. Bev Greene was sitting beside her. I spotted them near the back when I came in, waved, and took a moment to hang my coat on the rack by the front door before making my way past the little store that made up the front half of the restaurant. Anne Cooke, the proprietress, had locally-made jams, jellies, quilts, knickknacks, geegaws, and gimcracks just waiting for the tourist with a few extra bucks burning a hole in his or her pocket. Mr. Christopher met me halfway to the table.

"Good afternoon, Sheriff," he said. "I believe you'll be dining with Miss Meg?" He extended an arm in the direction of the table. His other arm was bent at the correct angle and had a white, starched dishtowel draped over it.

"Indeed I am. Thank you kindly," I answered.

"Any news on the deceased visitor in the alley?"

"Does everyone know?" I asked.

Mr. Christopher nodded in the affirmative. "Pretty much," he said.

Mr. Christopher Lloyd was the current head waiter at the Ginger Cat. He had owned the premiere home design business in Watauga County for a number of years, being both an excellent floral arranger and a decorator. This was back before cable TV had all the home shows and Mr. Christopher was the man to hire if you needed some help furbishing or festooning. He was also in demand as a wedding planner, covering everything from flowers to music to receptions — soup to nuts as it were. This all came crashing down quite tragically.

Mr. Christopher had given all this up to become a TV star on HGTV. His show, The Fourteen Layers of Style, was supposed to be a big hit. He sold his business to his arch-rival, Dukota Squeeque, owner of Squeekie's, and poised himself to become a millionaire celebrity designer. It didn't work out.

Unfortunately Mr. Christopher had a thing for one of the cameramen, and they'd left a camera on in the studio one night after the shooting had finished. Entertainment TV somehow ended up with the tape and even HGTV couldn't keep him on the air, even though the ratings had been more than promising. So after four episodes Mr. Christopher found himself unemployed and unemployable. He was told by his agent that these things pass, and to just be patient for a couple of years. Hard to do when you've just bought a new house with a mountain gorge view and a late-model Jaguar. His wedding gigs were picking up, though, and he'd found work at the Ginger Cat to tide him over. As industrious people often do, he'd made himself indispensable to Anne, not only helping with the service aspect of the operation, but also creating new dishes, designing the menus, finding local sources of fresh produce, decorating — whatever it took. Now, a couple of years after his TV fiasco, there were also murmurings around town of a new cable deal.

I gave Meg a kiss on the cheek and pulled out the chair next to her. Bev was sitting across the table. I didn't know what to expect. Tears, maybe?

"Sorry to hear the news from the church," I said. "How are you doing?"

"Oh, I'm fine," said Bev. "And we have news as well, but first tell us about the dead guy."

"There's not much to tell yet. He appears to be middle-aged. Looks to be an American Indian, but there was no identification, and we didn't see any obvious cause of death. He did have a sign of the cross on his forehead."

"Ashes?" said Meg. "Like from a church service?"

"Looked like it to me," I answered.

"Then he didn't get it done here," said Bev. "Mother P decided that she didn't want to have the Imposition of Ashes at the morning service." There was no keeping the bitterness out of her voice. "Too much trouble, I guess." She brightened. "Anyway, I have a new job."

"Doing what?"

"Working with Meg. I'm the new secretary for her downtown office."

"Partner," corrected Meg. "You're the new *partner*."

"You have a downtown office?" I asked Meg, confused. "Do I know you? Have we met? My name's Hayden."

Bev laughed and said, "We just finalized the plan. It's good. It's an investment counseling service, mostly for old folks who can't afford one, or don't know where to go, or what to do with the assets they have. But we'll also show young people just starting out how to set up IRAs, investment accounts, that sort of thing."

"Free, of course," added Meg.

"Of course," I said.

Mr. Christopher showed up at my arm and looked down at me expectantly. He didn't say anything. That would be too obvious. The ladies were sipping tea. Something exotic and unpronounceable, no doubt.

"Coffee," I said.

"We have twenty-seven kinds of coffee, sir. May I surprise you?"

"You may." He disappeared and I turned back to the conversation.

"I've been wanting to do this for a while," said Meg. "It'll be fun. We'll set up a non-profit organization, rent an office, and work one or two mornings a week."

"And you know all this stuff?" I asked Bev.

"Not yet," she admitted. "But I can learn fairly quickly."

"We'll do a couple of week-long seminars," Meg said. "I'll walk her through. Most of it is pretty basic, but there are some tax laws we need to keep current on."

"Sounds like you guys have a plan," I said. "Who's funding this endeavor?"

"Why, you are, my sweet," said Meg.

"Excellent. I shall expect monthly reports."

I wasn't in the least worried. Meg had grown the family fortune by a substantial amount in the last two years and we were in no danger of financial exigency. "I presume this will all be tax deductible?" I asked.

"Of course," said Meg. "Now to the matters at hand." She narrowed her eyes. "St. Barnabas."

Just then Annette Passaglio appeared at the table. "Hayden," she said breathlessly, "sorry to interrupt, but we just heard about the dead boy found behind the restaurant."

"Hi, Annette. He wasn't a boy, first of all, and second, we have matters well in hand, so please do what you can to squelch the rumors before they get out of control."

"Really? I heard he was a boy." Annette was old money in St. Germaine, and her husband was an orthodontist in Boone. Once her children had grown and moved out of the house, she'd become a reporter for the St. Germaine *Tattler*, our semiweekly equivalent of the hometown newspaper, specializing in who was in visiting for the weekend, school awards, local history, local for-sale ads, and the like. A dead man in the alley adjacent to the square might be big news, especially if there was foul play involved, and Annette fancied herself to be the Geraldo Rivera of St. Germaine.

"No, not a boy," I said. "Closer to forty probably. He may have just suffered a heart attack. We don't know who he was or why he was in the alley. We'll know more this afternoon and I'll be sure to let the newspaper know. Right now we're doing everything we can."

"Including sitting down to a nice lunch?" Annette said sweetly.

"On the other hand," I said, "maybe I'll have Nancy call the *Watauga Democrat* and make sure they have the story first."

"Don't you dare!" hissed Annette. "I was just kidding! You call me immediately! No. Never mind. I'll call *you!*"

Annette disappeared and was replaced by Mr. Christopher, who placed a steaming cup of black liquid in front of me. "Brazil Zinho Esperanza," he announced. "Crisp, rather than bright. An excellent choice for those who enjoy a quietly complex, medium-roasted coffee with natural sweetness and low acidity. No cream or sugar required. I shall be back momentarily to take your lunch selections."

"Don't you just love this place?" said Meg.

I tried a sip of the coffee. Mr. Christopher was right. No cream or sugar required. I dumped in a packet just for spite. Then added some cream.

"So tell me what happened with the priest?" I asked Bev. "Rosemary?"

"Nothing much. I voiced some displeasure over the way she'd decided to change things. She told me that she appreciated my input, but as I was only the Parish Administrator, the worship service was not in my *preview*. That's exactly the way she put it.

'Not in my preview.' I said, thanks very much, but I really didn't want to be Parish Administrator any longer and that was it."

"She obviously meant to say 'purview,'" I said. "Or perhaps she meant to say 'sphere of influence,' or perhaps 'dominion.' To indicate that the worship service was 'not in your preview' would mean that ..."

"Shut up, Hayden," growled Bev. "I know what she meant. Anyway, I was getting tired of it. That Kimberly Walnut was driving me crazy. Now I can just sing in the choir and gripe."

"But you're on the Worship Committee," added Meg. "*She put you on the Worship Committee.*"

"I *know*," said Bev, raising her hands. "What's that about? Doesn't she know I'm going to be the fly in the ointment?"

"You may have my proxy when I'm not there," I said.

"Oh, good," said Bev, sarcasm apparent.

Mr. Christopher appeared. "Are we ready to order? You'll be gratified to know that Pat Strother has come over from Blowing Rock for the week. She's the sous chef over at Chez Nous, but they're closed for renovations. Annie's trying her out." He lowered his voice. "Just between us, I think she's *faaabulous!* Maybe we can get her full-time."

"I *am* gratified to know that," I said. "Deeply gratified."

"What is the special, again?" Meg asked, pretending to glance at the menu. She was getting the special. We all knew it. Mr. Christopher took a long, patient breath.

"Fresh salmon tartare with marinated cucumber and aged citrus vinegar. That's served with Maralumi milk chocolate parfait, a pear sphere, and cinnamon caramel for dessert."

"I'll have that," said Meg, closing her menu decisively. "No chocolate, though. I've given it up for Lent." She handed the menu to Mr. Christopher who turned to Bev. He didn't write anything down. No need.

"I'll have the duck salad, please," said Bev. "And could you substitute the black truffle Carbonara sauce for the red-wine grape Mostarada dressing? And put it on the side?"

"Certainly," said Mr. Christopher.

"I'll have a fried egg sandwich," I said. "Extra ketchup."

* * *

Lunch was delicious, or so Meg and Bev exclaimed to each other over and over, almost between every forkful. My sandwich was good, too. Mr. Christopher dressed up the fried egg with home baked sourdough bread, a creamy mayonnaise sauce that tasted vaguely of horseradish and parsley, grated Manchego cheese, and something he called "rocket," more commonly known as "a bunch of nettles that the cook found growing in the ditch out back." The plate was garnished with charred octopus *a la plancha,* on a bed of watercress. Well, of course it was.

"Tell us about this play we've been hearing about," said Meg, when Mr. Christopher came to whisk our plates away. "The Little Theater Production."

Mr. Christopher struck his theatrical pose. "*Welcome to Mitford,*" he said. "It's about the fictitious town of Mitford, North Carolina. One of your choir members, I believe, is playing the leading lady."

"Muffy LeMieux," I said.

"She's playing the character of Cynthia Coopersmith. I'm portraying Father Tim Kavanagh and directing. It's quite a large cast, thirteen men and ten women."

"I've read a few of the books," Meg admitted. "Kinda unbelievable, but sweet."

"Not like real life," added Bev.

"We open next week," said Mr. Christopher. "I still haven't finished the sets, but we're almost there."

"You're building the sets, too?" said Meg.

"Well," he said, modesty creeping into his voice, "I designed them of, course, and they have to be good. The cast is helping out, but most of them aren't skilled in stagecraft, so there's a lot for me to do. I'm making a trip over to Costco in Winston-Salem tomorrow to finish getting the set dressing."

"Speaking of sets," I said, "how's the TV business coming?"

"Still waiting for the new cable network to get the final okay on their broadcast license. Should be any day now, but it's brand new and doesn't have much programming. They're going head-to-head with DIY."

"And HGTV?" I asked.

"Oh, no. Not yet. Maybe in a few years. DIY, sure, but they're on the upper cable channels."

"I haven't ever seen DIY," said Meg. "What is it?"

"The Do It Yourself channel," said Mr. Christopher. "They have *The Vanilla Ice Project, I Hate My Kitchen, Man Caves* ... shows like that."

Bev asked, "And what's the new network called?"

"HHN. The Home and Handgun Network. It's based out of South Carolina. I was down in Columbia all day yesterday talking with the executives. I didn't get home 'til close to midnight."

"Sounds like a winner," I said. "And this time you'll be more ... circumspect?"

Mr. Christopher glowered at me. "I know *exactly* who was responsible for the last unfortunate incident. Religious bigotry will not be tolerated."

"Ooo," said Meg, who loved gossip as much as she loved unpronounceable lunch. "Do tell? Was it Raoul?"

"Let's just say that he'll be helping me this time around. He'll be on 'Team Christopher.'"

"Excellent," I said. "Will you be pitching your show, *Fourteen Layers of Chintz*?"

"*Fourteen Layers of Style*," corrected Mr. Christopher. "A variant. I've gotten it down to nine layers. The problem is that this new network wants shows already in the can. *And* they want their stars to be partners in the network. It's a significant investment." He looked positively glutinous with self-approbation. "Not a problem. I'm going to form a production company, buy my way in, and do the shows myself. Muffy and Varmit have volunteered some space, so I'm setting up a studio out at Blueridge Furs. There's a warehouse they're not using. After this play, I'm taking all the sets out to the farm and repurposing them for the studio. That's why they have to be good."

"If anyone can do it," said Bev, "you can."

Mr. Christopher eyed me with that look that I've come to dread. "Hey, Chief, you don't want to invest, do you? I can offer you a twelve percent share, *and* I'll come to your house and do a complete redesign for free. Only seventy-five grand."

"Alas," I said, "if you'd just offered me that deal a half hour ago, I'd have taken you up on it. But now, I'm the wealthy patron of a nonprofit financial advisement company for low income investors."

"Alas, indeed," said Mr. Christopher. "I'm charging you double for that egg sandwich."

Chapter 9

"He certainly was killed," said Kent Murphee. "No doubt about it."

Dr. Kent Murphee was the Watauga County Medical Examiner and Coroner. He was in his late fifties, although he looked quite a bit older, due to his dress (the same tweed jacket and vest he'd worn every day for the twenty years that I'd known him) and his penchant for starting his drinking as early as eight in the morning. Not today, though. Today he was sucking on his briar pipe and studying his victim carefully.

I looked at the naked body stretched out on the examiner's table.

"Of course, it probably wasn't first-degree murder," he said. "Manslaughter, maybe. He wasn't *intended* to be killed."

"Is he a midget or something?" I asked. "He's tiny. Look at those hands. Like a child's, really."

"No signs of dwarfism," said Kent, blowing some smoke out between his clenched teeth, "although I'd have to do some tests to find out for sure. Since the affliction has to do with a genetic mutation of the fourth chromosome, and there's no real evidence, technically he's just a very small person. He's right at four feet ten inches tall. That's generally considered the cutoff. He's just, well, small."

"What's he weigh?" I asked.

"One hundred four pounds."

The hair of the victim was wet, obviously rinsed by Kent, and was spread out on the table in a fan behind his head. The lights on the office were unsympathetic fluorescent bulbs, and it was the first time I had a really good look at the dead man. We were right about him being a Native American. Everything about his countenance bespoke the characteristic look of the Native American. He had black, shiny hair, and olive skin with a slightly yellow undertone. His cheek bones were prominent, giving him a wide-looking face, and he had very broad, straight teeth. There was a fold of skin by the bridge of the nose that gave him the appearance of having small, narrow eyes as well as a flatter nose bridge. He was well muscled and had very little body hair.

"Time of death?" I asked.

"He arrived here at 10:30. I'd say he'd been dead for twenty hours, give or take a couple. Let's say between noon and four, yesterday."

"That's a pretty wide margin," I said.

"Hey! This ain't *CSI Miami*. He was sitting outside all night. Cool temperatures, lividity, blah, blah, blah."

"Okay," I said, "tell me about the cause of death."

Kent took the pipe out of his mouth and dropped it into the breast pocket of his jacket, something I'd seen him do so often that I didn't comment on it anymore. The pipe would continue to smoke in his pocket for a few minutes, then it would go out of its own accord. His jacket never seemed to catch fire.

"He died of a heart attack," Kent said.

"Really? You know that? You haven't even cut him open yet."

"Don't need to," said Kent. "I checked his blood. The enzymes were off the chart. Heart attack."

"You know what caused it, I assume."

"I can't know for sure, but I can make a good guess."

"Well?"

"Look here," said Kent, pulling a pen out of his pocket and tapping between the man's eyes. All of a sudden it occurred to me that if Kent had washed the body, why was there still an ashen cross smudged on his forehead?

"The cross. It's not ashes, is it?"

"No, it's not," said Kent, "although I can see why you might have thought so. With the coloring of the man's skin, it might be an easy mistake to make. No, they're burn marks. I'm pretty sure they're from a taser."

"I've never seen a taser leave marks like that," I said. "Usually it's two burn marks about an inch apart."

"Yep. But I looked this up on the internet. An amazing thing, the internet. Did you know that you can find almost any information you want?"

"Yes, yes," I said impatiently. "So this taser ..."

"It's made in Germany," Kent continued, "and it's much more effective than the older models, recharges faster, and gives a bigger jolt. It also leaves this particular kind of a mark because the electrodes are connected with a tungsten wire rather than needing two independent points of impact."

"And you think that this caused a heart attack?"

"I think it *probably* did. Like I said, I can never tell you for sure. But what I do know is that he got a jolt, and then he had a heart attack, and then he died. I suppose he could have had the heart attack first, then someone tried to restart his heart by tasing him on the forehead." Kent looked thoughtful, then said, "No, I don't think so. You might tase him in the chest to restart his heart. But not on the forehead."

"Why would anyone tase him in the forehead in the first place?" I asked.

"Well, think about it for a minute," said Kent. "If I stick out my hand with a taser and you're only four feet ten inches tall, where is it going to hit you?"

"Good point," I said. "Did you take fingerprints?"

"In the file," said Kent.

* * *

I filled Nancy and Dave in on Kent Murphee's findings. "Let's run the prints," I said. "We don't need to advertise all of it. Not just yet. Everyone knows by now that we found a body, but he died of a heart attack. That's our story and we're sticking to it."

* * *

Five o'clock comes early and so does death; this is the motto of the alcoholic mystery writer. Friends? Sure I had friends. Gerunds were my friends. Reciprocal pronouns were my friends. I could conjugate verbs in seven tenses and dangle a participle like Kurt Vonnegut might dangle a wiener in front of his beloved Welsh Corgi, Sprinkles, until he lost that pinkie finger. I sent my metaphors Christmas cards, I called my analogies on Mother's Day, but my similes ... my similes I took dancing, bought flowers, and sent to community college, which is a real college, no matter what your Uncle Ollie says; besides, he's not even really your uncle, just some guy who moved in with your grandma. I slugged down a shot of rye and considered the matter.

This sheila's story stank like a walrus in a school bus, which was a timely analogy because Pastor Hank Langknecht, my Lutheran friend and confidant, had just told me he'd seen one, but Hank was prone to take a nip or two early in the day and what he'd probably seen was just a smelly kid with a glandular problem.

Suddenly a pigeon smacked into the window, a shot rang out, and Carrie Oakey jumped out of her chair like she was shot, which she was, a fact that made this particular simile all the more bittersweet, like chocolate. I smiled. That was it. This simile was chocolate, which actually made "simile" a metaphor, a "simiphore" if you will, but that sent up a red flag, so it was more like a conundrum. The pigeon was lagniappe.

"Ahhh ..." Carrie cried whimperously. Then cried again, one "h" longer, "Ahhhh ..."

"Hang on," I said. "I'm figuring out this grammar thing."

* * *

"I heard that you're writing us a new service music setting," said Martha Hatteberg, one of the altos. She was sitting in her usual place on the back row — one of the Back Row Altos, or BRAs, as they preferred to be known.

"I heard that there was a dead body behind Noylene's," said Rebecca Watts.

"I heard that Bev got fired," said Phil Camp. Bev walked in right behind him but didn't say anything.

"It's been a busy day," I said.

Our Ash Wednesday service had gone according to plan, and the choir had sung an anthem by William Bradley Roberts, *Prayer of John Donne*. I was planning on this anthem doing double duty and using it again on the Fourth Sunday of Lent a few weeks from now. It wasn't easy, but we'd been practicing it for a few weeks now. Rosemary gave a brief homily, and we all received the imposition of ashes. Kimberly Walnut couldn't find the ashes from the year before — it was our tradition to save a few palm branches from the previous year's Palm Sunday, burn them, and use the ashes for the Ash Wednesday service — so she manufactured some from somewhere. I didn't ask where. I just hoped she hadn't called the funeral home. Now, with the Ash Wednesday congregants dispersing, the choir members who had just been ashed were making their way back up to the loft.

"There was a man who died of a heart attack in the alley behind Noylene's," I explained. "We don't know who it was yet because he had no identification."

"I heard that he was a leprechaun," said Marjorie.

"He was a Native American," I said, then turned to Martha. "And I am composing a new setting of the mass. How did you hear about it?"

"I heard from Joyce. She seemed a little alarmed."

"Alarmed at what?" said Tiff St. James, coming into the loft and not wanting to be left out of the conversation. "The dead guy?" Behind her, following like a baby duck, was Dr. Ian Burch, PhD. They both had the smudges of repentance on their foreheads.

Tiff had been our alto section leader during the years she'd been a voice major at Appalachian State. She'd received a small stipend and a scholarship — well worth it, in my opinion. She had a beautiful voice and was a great sight reader. After she graduated,

Tiff took a job in Boone teaching music in one of the elementary schools, but she still came over to St. Barnabas to sing with us. She was a looker — thin, but quite beautiful — with dark hair and a model's eyes and cheekbones.

Dr. Ian Burch, PhD, fell to the other end of the "attractiveness" spectrum. Some might blame his small, flat head, his long, Ichabod Crane nose, his beady eyes, or maybe his ears that stuck out like two open doors on a VW beetle. In my opinion, it wasn't any one of these, but the effect of the whole. Added to this was a personality that gave the word "irritating" a whole new meaning. This personality was the product of an incredibly high self-esteem, a PhD in musicology, and an intimate relationship with the music of Guillaume Dufay (1397-1474) that he would be happy to share with anyone who made eye contact with him. He'd been smitten with Tiff St. James for a year and a half, and, although he had no contact with her during the week, Ian was happy to bask in her presence during choir rehearsals and Sunday services. Tiff got used to it and now shrugged it off, hardly even seeming to notice him. Dr. Burch owned and operated an early music emporium in St. Germaine called The Appalachian Music Shoppe, specializing in Medieval and Renaissance instrument reproductions — shawms, hurdy-gurdys, sackbuts, flatulenzas, and the like. Most of his business was conducted on the internet, and he made a good living.

Dr. Ian Burch, PhD, took off his cape and draped it over his chair, then sat down in the alto section, his cross-sectional casting due to his freakishly high countertenor voice, and patted the seat next to him so Tiff would know where she was supposed to sit. She looked heavenward, sighed and sat down.

"What was Joyce alarmed at?" asked Tiff again. The rest of the choir was pouring into the loft.

"I think she's a little scared that Hayden has been asked to compose our service music for Lent," said Martha.

"Oh, no!" said Sheila DeMoss. "Who asked him?" She took a seat next to Tiff.

"Mother P asked him," said Elaine Hixon. "I was there. I heard it."

"Didn't anyone tell her?" asked Steve DeMoss, Sheila's husband, and a bass.

"Hey!" I said. "I think I'm offended."

Mark Wells ticked off a list on his fingers. "*The Mouldy Cheese Madrigal, We Three Queens, the Pirate Eucharist ...*"

"*The Weasel Cantata*," added Bert Coley with a laugh. "*Crown Him You Many Clowns, The Banjo Kyrie ...*" Bert had been another of the ASU music students who had stuck around after graduation. He was currently a police officer in Boone.

"Don't forget *Elisha and the Two Bears*, the unknown Purcell masterpiece," said Bob Solomon. "My personal favorite."

Rhiza Walker chimed in. "*We All like Sheep*, the alternate aria from Handel's *Messiah*, found at the bottom of a chamberpot." She'd just come in and had skipped the imposition of ashes, judging from her clear complexion. Rhiza was a friend from way back. It was she and Pete who were responsible for my coming to St. Germaine as police chief. Rhiza was a soprano and a darn good one. She sat down next to Muffy LeMieux, joining Meg, Elaine, Georgia, and Bev. The only empty seat in the soprano section was Goldi Fawn Birtwhistle's.

"I don't know that one," said Martha. "Is it good?"

"No, it's baaaad," said Rhiza. "A lot of cadenzas on the word 'baa.' He wrote it for me specially, many years ago."

"How about that hymn you wrote for Brother Hog's Service of Re-Virgination?" said Meg. "Only you could rhyme 'liturging' with 're-virging.'"

I sighed.

"*The Living Gobbler!*" said Marjorie.

"Okay, okay, I get it," I said. "But I've also written a few nice things."

The choir loft was full. We had a good deal of room, but twenty-some-odd folks filled it up.

Joining Burt and Marjorie in the tenor section was Randy Hatteberg. Varmit, Fred May, and Phil Camp filled out the basses. Usually we had a few no-shows. This evening, only Goldi Fawn.

"Okay, let's get started," I said, and played a big chord on the organ to quiet everyone down. "We need to work on the offertory anthems, communion anthems, and the Psalms through Palm Sunday."

"How about the *Great Litany in Procession*?" asked Phil. "This is the First Sunday of Lent, right?"

The *Great Litany in Procession* was a tradition at St. Barnabas that usually happened either on the First Sunday of Advent or the

First Sunday of Lent, and we'd skipped it in December. But fifteen minutes of chanting prayers while processing through the church behind a billowing incense pot didn't have many fans.

"I have a note here on the organ from the rector saying we won't be doing it this year."

"Praise the Lord!" said Marjorie. "Finally, a voice of reason."

"Hang on," said Elaine. "Back to the mass you're writing. If we're supposed to sing this new thing Sunday, shouldn't we be looking at a copy tonight?"

"It's not quite finished," I admitted. "Never fear. It will be easy enough. Rosemary wants the mass based on a well-known tune that the congregation will be able to pick up quickly."

The choir groaned.

"Now, now," I said. "I'll have it Sunday morning and we'll go over it before the service. It's no problem."

Dr. Ian Burch stood up. "Are you planning a parody mass or a *cantus firmus* mass?"

"An interesting question," I said. "Probably neither, as you know them. It'll be a tune that we all know with some sort of paraphrase of the texts. All the texts except the *Sanctus*, that is. The *Sanctus* has to contain the exact words, in either the Rite 1 or Rite 2 versions."

Holy, holy, holy Lord, God of power and might,
heaven and earth are full of your glory.
Hosanna in the highest.

"Ah, a *cyclic mass* then, or some variant," said Ian Burch PhD. "The cyclic mass is a setting in which each of the movements shared a common musical theme, thus making it a unified whole. The cyclic mass was the first multi-movement form in western music to be subject to a single organizing principle. The period of composition of cyclic masses was from about 1430 until around 1600, although some composers, especially in conservative musical centers, wrote them after that date. In the first half of the sixteenth century this style was the dominant form. Then the Council of Trent, in a document dated September 10, 1562, banned the use of secular material stating 'Banish from church all music which contains the profane, whether in the singing or the organ playing, things that are lascivious or impure.'"

He paused a moment and leered at Tiff, followed by, "However, the reforms were most carefully followed only in Italy. In France, tastes had already changed, and, in Germany, the edict was ignored."

Ian sat down, placed his hands in his lap, and looked around the choir with a huge grin on his face.

"Thank you, Dr. Burp," muttered Tiff.

"Burch," corrected an oblivious Ian. "Dr. *Burch*."

"You better watch out for the Council of Trent," said Mark Wells. "I hear those guys are tough."

"I have an announcement," Muffy chirped.

My shoulders slumped. "Yes?"

"As many of you know, the Little Theater is putting on their spring production and we open a week from Friday. The play is *Welcome to Mitford*. I have plenty of tickets for all y'all here in my purse. They're fifteen dollars apiece."

"Tell 'em about Sunday!" said Varmit.

Muffy managed, to her credit, to look a little embarrassed.

"Go ahead!" insisted Varmit. "Tell 'em."

"Yes," said Bev, just a tad too brightly. "Tell us."

"Okay, I will," said Muffy excitedly, starting to wriggle like a puppy. "Mother P asked me to sing a solo during communion this Sunday. She wants me to sing *On Eagle's Wings*. It's based on Psalm 91, the Psalm for the First Sunday in Lent. It's my favorite! I'm adding a verse about coming to the Living Water. Mother P says it ties in with her sermon."

I watched Meg's eyes go wide, then I looked at Muffy and said, "Do you have some music for me?"

"Don't worry about that," crowed Varmit, having waited for Muffy's chance at solo stardom for five long years. "She's singing with an accompaniment track. Muffy's gonna have the whole Nashville symphony backing her up!"

"That'll be great," I said, after a hard swallow — *God is faithful, and will not allow you to be tempted beyond what you are able, but with the temptation will also make the way of escape, that you may be able to bear it* — then added, "I'll be looking forward to it."

* * *

"I think your detective story is going well," said Meg, busy chopping onions and dropping them into a cast iron frying pan. "Or as well as might be expected." The onions joined a couple of red and yellow peppers that were already sectioned and seasoned.

I was in the kitchen with my lovely wife, doing my grilling thing. This had become our pattern after choir rehearsal on Wednesdays. We'd go to church early, I'd do a little music planning, then rehearsal, followed by a late supper at home. Two rib eye steaks sizzled on the gas grill that was part of our monster stove. In addition, I had an outdoor charcoal grill — a taste I preferred — but with the temperature still in the upper 30s, I bowed to convenience.

"I think so, too," I replied, prodding the meat with a long fork. "I may even come up with a plot before long."

The phone rang and I paused in my steak poking to answer. It was Pete.

"What's the word on the stiff?" he asked.

"Kent says it was a heart attack. We still don't know who it is, but we have finger prints, so if they're in the system we'll know something soon and find his next-of-kin."

"Okay, I'll tell Cynthia. You doing anything tomorrow morning?"

"Nothing pressing," I answered. "Why? What's up?"

"We need to go over to Tri-Cities Airport. Our pig is here."

"Really? Excellent!"

"What's up?" asked Meg.

I put a hand over the mouthpiece. "Our truffle pig is here," I told her. "Tri-Cities Airport."

Pete said, "The terminal where we're supposed to pick her up opens at eight in the morning. I have the paperwork all filled out. You want to pick me up about seven?"

"Can do. Where are you going to keep her?"

"Out back of the house," said Pete. "I built a pen with a little heated pig barn and everything."

I put my hand over the phone again and said to Meg. "He built a pig pen behind the house."

"Does Cynthia know about this?" asked Meg.

"Here," I said, handing Meg the phone.

"Does Cynthia know you've built a pig pen behind your house?" Meg asked into the phone, then listened to Pete's answer. "Really?" she said. "I think you might want to tell her. Uh-huh ... uh-huh ..."

I went back to the grill, flipped the steaks over, and put on some mushrooms that I had marinating. Meg talked with Pete for a couple more minutes, then handed me the phone.

"Tomorrow morning," Pete said. "Come by the Slab at seven."

"I'll be there."

"He hasn't told Cynthia that there's a pigpen in the backyard," said Meg, when I'd hung up the phone. "She's been gone all week. Some kind of mayor conference."

"I wondered why I hadn't seen her at the Slab. It shouldn't be a problem, though. They live outside the city limits. There's no zoning out there."

"You're right about one thing. Zoning won't be the problem."

"What then?" I asked. The steaks were almost done. I pulled them to the bottom of the grill, then pushed the mushrooms around a bit, rolling them with my fork.

"Have you ever lived next to a pigpen?" asked Meg.

"No, but there are many people who keep pet pigs. I'm sure there's a way to keep everything ... umm, fragrant. Besides, we can't just put a six-thousand-dollar pig on somebody's farm. I expect she might be sleeping in the family bed before too long."

"Yikes," said Meg, then asked, "What kind of beer would suit you this evening?"

"Hmm. Let's see. Steak, roasted potatoes, grilled and sautéed vegetables ... a couple of bottles of Pliny the Younger should be just perfect. I got some bottles in yesterday from the west coast. Back of the fridge."

"Sounds great."

"You having one, too?"

"Absolutely."

Baxter the Wonder Dog had risen from his slumber in the den, smelled the steaks, and sauntered happily into the kitchen. He sat down beside the table and looked at us in expectation, first me, then Meg, his eyebrows moving up and down, independent of each other, as he considered his chances of getting lucky. A moment later, the electric window next to the sink slid open and

Archimedes the owl stepped across the sill and onto the counter. We were all here.

"I'll get Archimedes a treat," Meg volunteered, setting two bottles of suds on the table. "You start the vegetables. They won't take a couple of minutes."

"Got it," I said. I put the frying pan onto the stove top, then lit the burner.

"Bacon grease?" I asked.

"Olive oil," said Meg.

"It won't taste as good," I said.

Meg opened the refrigerator again and rummaged in the lowest crisper drawer, the one reserved for Archimedes. "Squirrel or rat?" she asked, her head hidden behind the door.

"Rat," I said. "He likes rats when we're having steak."

"Hey, there are still some mice in a shrink-wrap pack here in the back."

"Let's pull one of those out, too. He might be hungry. He hasn't been around for a few days."

"So one rat and one mouse?"

"A big rat," I said.

Baxter was now watching me exclusively, as I pulled the steaks off the grill and onto our plates. "You want me to cut Baxter a piece of your steak? I know you'd want him to have it."

"No, *your* steak."

"We'll split the difference. A bit of both."

Meg held a deceased mouse by the tail in one hand and a large rat in the same manner with the other. She pushed the door of the fridge closed with her rear end, then walked across the kitchen floor toward Archimedes. She offered him the mouse first and he took it in his beak, flipped it up and swallowed it in two gulps. His large, yellow eyes closed slowly, then opened, and his head swiveled around as he surveyed the kitchen. He took a moment to preen the white feathers on his breast, then reached up slowly with one talon and took the rat gently from Meg's extended hand. He hopped up onto the sill, the window slid open, and he disappeared, without a sound, into the night.

"I never get tired of watching him," said Meg. "And I don't even mind the dead rodents anymore. What are we listening to, by the way?"

"*Mass for Double Choir* by Frank Martin. It's part of my Lenten discipline."

"How about some Carmen McRae instead? You might get lucky later …"

"Lucky, you say."

"Well, you know what smoky jazz does to me."

"Carmen McRae it is."

* * *

The blood that was pooling underneath Carrie Oakey resembled a Rorschach inkblot test, invented in 1921 by Hermann Rorschach, and Detective Jack Hammer, who was not a fan of the test ever since the time he had identified image number 3 as "Me and my pet monkey, Cashmere, kissing," and the psychologist's secretary tweeted about it (OMG!), and once the squad found out, the teasing was merciless, poked at the body with the toe of his new brown wingtips that he got from Zappos on a really good sale.

"You ice her?" asked Hammer.

"Nah."

"Harrumph," he harrumphed. "I had to ask. Police procedure. Know who she is?"

"She said her name was Carrie Oakey."

Hammer nodded. "I've heard the name. Shot came from outside, I'm guessing."

"Good guess."

Hammer pulled out a hanky and wiped a face that was glistening like a quail's egg, either one fresh out of the quail but with most of the bird gunk scraped off, or one popping in a frying pan, covered with just a soupçon of oil, a smidgen of rosemary, and a niggle of white pepper; the point is that his face was moist, shiny, and just that color. "You got any thoughts on this?" he asked.

"Nope." I had thoughts, all right, deep thoughts that hung on the mustard-colored wall like a case of false teeth, but none I was going to share with this dumb button.

"Case of false teeth, eh?"

I shrugged.

"All right with you if I ask Marilyn some questions?" he said, looking out the door. She was sitting primly at her desk reading a romance novel and eating a radish.

"Be my guest," I said.

I needed to talk with Pedro and I knew just where to find him.

* * *

On Thursday morning, I rose early, dressed, and pointed the old truck toward town in the predawn darkness that was 6:30 a.m. I couldn't even budge Baxter from in front of the fireplace, giving him a nudge with my foot, and a quiet whistle as I walked by. Not interested. Too early and too cold. This time last week, I would have had an easy drive in the early morning light. Sunday, though, had marked the beginning of Daylight Saving Time, and we were now cultivating the afternoon and evening hours.

I put the Frank Martin Mass recording into the player — the one I'd begun listening to last evening, before I was so delightfully interrupted. Meg hadn't been bluffing. Smoky jazz was just the ticket.

It was still too frigid for any of the foliage to begin breaking out, even though the beginning of spring was right around the corner. The snow was gone, at least, but the mountains were cold and sere. I drove carefully, watching for patches of ice that might appear around a switchback, unseen until too late.

Coming into town, I slowed, then stopped and parked in front of the Holy Grounds Coffee Shop. I got out of the truck and walked in. Kylie Moffit, the owner, was working behind the counter. She and her husband, Biff, bought the coffee shop about three years ago. The original owners of the shop had renovated the old McCarty house just a year before and transformed the old American four-square into a thriving business: their Christian Coffee Shop occupying the bottom floor, and a wellness center specializing in massage and aroma therapy on the top floor — *The Upper Womb, a place of healing.* The design of the house was very popular at the turn of the century. Two stories tall, each floor contained four rooms — square, of course. A broad porch stretched across the length of the front of the house. When the Moffits bought the business, they converted the upstairs into their living quarters. The downstairs had tables, coffee stations, many cases of pastries, and a large counter, behind which Kylie was making pots of coffee in steaming, hissing machines that looked like gleaming, stainless steel, submarine apparatus, what with their knobs, dials, pipes, and gauges.

"Good morning, Hayden. You're up early!"

"Yes, I am. Pete and I are making a morning run to the airport."

"Coffee?"

"Yes, please." I looked around the shop. Six of the tables had people sitting at them, all with at least one open laptop adorning the tabletop — wireless access, obviously. A couple of customers had newspapers out. They all had coffee.

Kylie pushed a strand of dark hair away from her face, then wiped both her hands on a dish towel. Kylie Moffit was a girl who took fitness seriously. She could be seen out jogging around town on most afternoons, and, since she lived in the downtown area, everyone knew her enough to wave and shout a hello as they drove by.

"I heard about the dead guy," she said. "Wow! He just, like, died of a heart attack?"

"That's what the coroner says."

"And after he'd been to church and everything," she said. "Well, at least he had time to repent. Ashes to ashes, dust to dust, and all that. I'm more of a New Testament believer, though. I don't need to repent all the time, because I'm saved once and for all." She smiled at me. "Now, what kind of coffee would you like?"

"Hot."

She laughed. I'd been in before. "How about our house dark roast?"

"As long as you don't tell me the name of it."

She laughed. "Fair enough. You want room for milk?"

"Please. Give me two, if you don't mind. Big ones."

"Two *ventis*," said Kylie. "That's a twenty-ounce coffee. I could put a shot of espresso in them, if you like."

"Sure," I said. "Let's do that."

* * *

Two blocks down, I stopped in front of the Slab Café. It was full of people. I never ceased to be amazed at how many people got up this early in the morning and stopped for breakfast. Pete was ready and watching for me and, when I drove up, he didn't even wait for me to get out of the truck. He opened the passenger side door and climbed in.

"We don't have to listen to any of that churchy music this morning, do we?" he said. "It's a long drive."

"Nope." I handed him his coffee and switched off the CD player.

"What's this?"

"Coffee from Holy Grounds. Shot of espresso, cream, and three sugars."

"Ahh," he said, then took a long, slurping sip. "I've already had two cups this morning, but this is good. What kind is it?"

"No idea," I answered. "You have our pig papers?"

"Right here," said Pete, patting the left breast pocket of his olive-green army coat. "Everyone in the Slab wanted to know about the dead Indian. You have any more scoop yet?"

"Not yet," I said. "We should get something off the prints if he's in the state system. If not, and he's in the national data base, it'll take longer. If he's not there either, we may never know."

"Did you guys call down to Cherokee?"

"Nancy's checking on it, and she emailed a picture down to the Cherokee police, but it's a long shot."

We drove through town and out Old Chambers Road heading for Highway 321 toward Elizabethton. The airport was about sixty miles away, but in mountain miles that was an hour and a half, maybe a little more. Old Chambers was a torturous drive with a speed limit of forty, but we wouldn't be on it long. It intersected with the highway just past old Camp Possumtickle. We all still called it Camp Possumtickle even though it had been purchased and transformed into a Christian Nudist Camp at the same time, and by the same people who opened Holy Grounds. They had changed the name of the camp to "Camp Daystar," home of the Daystar Naturists of God and Love (DaNGL), but everyone who grew up around here knew the landmark as Possumtickle. The camp had been around since the 1940s, and almost all the kids had attended it in some form or fashion — Girl Scouts, Boy

Scouts, Brownies, Cub Scouts, Indian Guides, 4-H, church camps. They all knew it and loved it. Few went out there now. There were naked people everywhere. It just wasn't safe.

We headed up 321, around Lake Watauga, through Elizabethton and Blountsville, and pulled into the Tri-Cities Airport at 8:15. The airport served Kingsport, Johnson City, and Bristol, and was the only Tennessee airport of any size on this side of Knoxville. We looked for the freight signs and followed them to a large hangar some distance from the passenger terminal. The sign out front said "Air Cargo Logistics Center." Pete and I got out of the truck, walked in the front door, and Pete presented his papers to a tall, heavy man wearing light-blue coveralls and a white baseball cap with ACLC embroidered on the front. He had a day's worth of beard stubble, and hair that hadn't seen shampoo for several days. An unlit cigarette hung from his lips. He spread the papers across the counter and pretended to understand what they said.

"We're here for my pig," Pete said finally, helping him along.

He looked up. "That pig is yourn?" he asked, eyeing Pete's ponytail and earring suspiciously.

"Yessir," said Pete. "That's my pig. Or *mon cochon*, as we say in Gascony." He tapped the papers. "Says so right there. All in order with proper stamps and such. Approved by the FDA, the SPCA, the FBI, and the King of France."

I gave a snort.

"It's stinkin' up the place," said the man.

"No doubt because my pig has been quarantined and probably hasn't had the straw changed for about a week."

"Yeah, that's prob'ly it," he said, then gave a nod toward the side of the building. "Pull your truck around there. We'll put the crate in the back."

The crate was made of oaken boards six inches wide and an inch thick. The gaps between them were enough for the truffle-pig to stick her snout through and grunt at us when we walked up. She seemed to be in good spirits, although the man was right. The crate *was* stinkin' up the place. One of the sides of the crate was fastened with two heavy iron hinges and a padlock held the door closed. There was an envelope fastened with duct tape to the top of the crate. Pete pulled it off, opened it and scanned through a set of papers before dumping the envelope into his hand. A key fell out.

"There's another key stapled onto one of the back boards," said one of the air cargo men. "Just in case, I guess."

"Should we open it up?" I asked. "I'd like to get a look at her."

"Nah," said Pete. "She seems healthy enough. Let's wait 'til we get her home. I'd hate to have a six thousand dollar pig run off and get hit by a plane or something."

"Six thousand!" exclaimed another cargo man. "Man, I'll bet that's one tasty pig."

"She'd better be," I said.

Chapter 10

We drove up to Pete's house after a long trip home. We'd managed to get behind a farm truck whose top speed was thirty-five miles an hour for almost all of the trip back along Highway 321. The passing opportunities were few and far between and my old truck didn't have that burst of speed that drivers of more modern vehicles equipped with fuel injectors were used to, especially when traveling uphill. So it was close to eleven thirty when we arrived in St. Germaine.

I'd given Meg a call when we were a few miles out, and when I pulled the truck into Pete's drive, Meg, Nancy, and Dave were all waiting for us.

"How come you didn't call me?" asked Nancy when Pete and I disembarked. "I have a stake in that pig, too, you know."

"Someone has to watch the town," I said. "Besides, we haven't even unlocked the crate and looked at her yet. We didn't want her to go running off."

"Can we lift her off the truck?" asked Dave. "How much does she weigh?"

"Bill of lading says one hundred and eighty pounds," said Pete. "That's pig and crate combined. She's probably one fifty. Four of us should be able to get that crate off the truck."

"Let's do it," said Nancy.

We dropped the tailgate and slipped the crate to the edge, then lifted it off the truck and set it on the ground. Dave dropped his corner a little early and the crate hit the gravel with a bump. The pig oinked.

"Let's take the crate back to the pen," said Pete. "Then we can let her out and she can explore her new digs."

"Do you have a wagon, Pete?" asked Meg.

Pete gave Meg a quizzical look for a moment, then nodded and said, "Yeah. Yeah, I do. Don't know why I didn't think of it before."

The wagon that Pete had was a utility wagon, a green and yellow heavy duty model that Cynthia used for gardening. We wrestled the wooden box up onto the bed, then Dave took the handle and dragged the load around the side of the house with Nancy and Pete supplying the stabilizing influence. Meg and I followed, and a few moments later we lifted the crate off the wagon and positioned it to let our truffle pig run into the pen. The lock came off, the door swung open and our six thousand dollar investment came trundling out onto the grass.

"That is one weird-looking pig," said Dave.

"She's a full-blooded Mangalitsa," said Pete. "The only remaining long-haired breed of pig in the world. She's a swallow-belly."

"What's that mean?" asked Meg.

"Swallow-belly? That's the color. It means she's got a blonde belly and feet, with a dark body."

"I think she's quite fetching," said Nancy.

The pig started snorting around the pen, gobbling up old acorns as she found them. There were plenty since a large oak tree stood just outside the fence. Our pig was hefty. She was covered with gray curly hair not unlike that of a sheep. She had large ears, a low slung belly, large jowls, and a relatively short snout. Her tail was straight and long and had a tuft of hair on the end. She looked more like a wild boar than a domestic pig. A gray, furry, wild boar.

"The breed is originally from Hungary," said Pete. "They're coming back into favor as eating pigs. They have more fat than modern pigs. The meat supposedly tastes delicious."

"Better and better," said Nancy, "if the truffle thing doesn't work out."

"How big will she get?" asked Dave. "I mean, is she full grown?"

"Nah. She'll get up to three or four hundred pounds if we let her eat like a pig, so to speak," said Pete. "But we want to keep her lean and hungry."

The pig found the water trough and was slurping her fill. There was a pan with some pig chow next to the water, but the animal was happy to quench its thirst before diving into the yellow meal.

"Does she have a name yet?" asked Meg.

"How about Snouty," suggested Dave.

"You see, Dave," said Nancy, "this is why you'll never have a pet."

"I have a fish," said Dave. "Her name is Swimmy."

"I vote to name her Truffles," said Meg. "It's what she does, and she looks like a Truffles."

"Too confusing," said Pete. "What if I said, 'Where did we put Truffles?' Would we mean the pig or the funguses?"

Nancy laughed. "Really? Where did we put Truffles?"

"How about Portia then?" Meg suggested. "Or Phoebe?"

"Portia from *The Merchant of Venice*?" said Pete.

"Shakespeare's always good," said Meg.

"The quality of mercy is not strained," I said. "It droppeth as the gentle rain from heaven upon the place beneath. It is twice blest: It blesseth him that gives and him that takes."

"Huh?" said Dave.

"Portia to Shylock," I said. "Last act, I believe, if I remember my high school drama class."

"Okay, Portia then," said Pete. "Unless you have any other quotes by women with pig names that you can remember."

"How about 'I modeled my looks on the town tramp.' Dolly Parton."

"Portia it is," said Nancy.

"Oink," said Portia.

* * *

The Beautifery was situated between the Bear and Brew and Eden Books on the north side of the square. I was on my way to see Georgia at the bookstore when I spotted Goldi Fawn Birtwhistle busily administering beauty to a customer seated at her station in the front window of the beauty shop. Doing my sworn duty as choir director, I opened the door and went in.

"You see, honey," Goldi was saying to Lucille Murdock, "throughout the Bible — both Old and New Testaments — the number twelve is a prominent number. The twelve Disciples, the twelve sons of Jacob, the twelve layers of precious stones in the foundation of heaven or the New Jerusalem. Astrology has the twelve signs of the zodiac, and there are twelve houses to a horoscope, or, as we astrologers call it, a star chart."

Goldi Fawn Birtwhistle was a Christian astrologer and saw it as her gift to help people understand what the stars had to say to them. She had many scriptures to back up her claims, each of them written on a Post-it note and thumb-tacked to the walls around her station. She had a constellation map on the wall and a Jesus fish on her hair dryer. "A woman's hair is her crowning glory," Goldi Fawn would say to whoever would listen. "First Corinthians 11:15. My first duty is to the hair. Then, if someone wants her stars done, I'm happy to read them while she gets her nails buffed. It's only five dollars more. Most Christian astrologers charge *twice* that much."

Lucille Murdock was ninety years old and, although now an Episcopalian, grew up in a Baptist church and was dubious of Goldi Fawn's doctrines. She did, though, like the way Goldi Fawn did hair. She was sitting in the styling chair, her hair covered with pieces of what looked like tin foil. I saw a piece of flowered fabric peeking out from under the apron that covered her from neck to knees. Her hands were folded in her lap and her froggy eyes blinked at me from behind big, thick glasses that looked like fishbowls. She gave me a wan smile when she saw me and fluttered her fingers in greeting.

"Hi, Goldi Fawn," I said. "I just dropped in to say that we missed you at choir practice last evening."

"Thanks, Hayden. Sorry I didn't make it. I got tied up with a dye job that went bad. Noylene and me both had to pull out all our tricks to save that one. I was afraid for a while that we were going to lose her."

"She came through all right?" Lucille asked nervously.

"Oh, sure," said Goldi Fawn, as she rolled another piece of foil onto Lucille's scalp and slathered it with some lamp black. "Of course, some of that hair may fall out after a while. We had to use a lot of chemicals. Never fear. It'll probably all grow back."

"I just wanted to say hello. Is Noylene in the back?"

"Nope. She hasn't come in yet. She sometimes doesn't schedule appointments 'til the afternoon. She's a woman of leisure, that's what she is. Darla's in the back if you want a quickie."

That caught me by surprise. "A quickie?"

"A quick cut," said Goldi Fawn. "A walk-in."

"Oh," I said. "No, thanks. I'm good."

"You coming to the play next week?" Goldi asked. "I'm in it, you know, so I'll miss rehearsal next Wednesday, too. I'm playing the elderly heiress, Miss Sadie Baxter."

"I believe we already have our tickets," I lied.

* * *

Georgia — I was told when I went into Eden Books — was across the square at St. Barnabas. I exited the bookshop and cut across the park. I crossed the lawn, walked past the white wooden gazebo, past the statue of Harrison Sterling, and as I neared the church I saw Georgia come out of the red front doors. She didn't look happy.

"Georgia!" I called out, giving her a wave. She spotted me, returned the wave and crossed the street to meet me.

"What's up?" she said. "Do you have news on the guy in the alley?"

"Nope," I said with a shrug. "I thought *you* wanted to talk to *me*. That's what your message said on my voice mail."

Georgia looked at me in mock-disgust. "Hayden, that message was from last week sometime. I had a question about the setup for the Ash Wednesday service."

"Oh ... everything seemed to go fine."

"Kimberly Walnut couldn't find the palms from last year. You know where she got the ashes?"

"Nope."

"She burnt a couple of Palm Sunday bulletins on the kitchen stove. Said that was close enough."

I laughed. "We thought she might have tried the crematorium."

"Don't give her any ideas. Now," said Georgia in a serious voice, "let's talk about the altar guild."

"It's not in my preview," I said.

"Purview," said Georgia. "Doesn't matter. You have to help."

"What's Rosemary done now?"

Georgia took a deep breath. "Mother P ..." She paused and gave me a long look. "Hey, you don't call her Mother P."

"Can't do it."

Georgia gave me a smirk. "Rosemary has decided that during Lent she herself will be in charge of decorating the altar. Mr. Christopher has agreed to help her along with a couple of others. They don't want flowers or plants. Rather, it is her plan to use objects that will enhance the congregation's appreciation of her sermons."

"Sort of like a 'theme' altar," I said.

"Exactly," said Georgia. "Now what are we going to do about it?"

Another test. *Consider it pure joy, my brothers, whenever you face trials of many kinds, because you know that the testing of your faith develops perseverance.*

"Not my preview."

* * *

That afternoon I went into the church to practice. I planned to play the Bach Little Fugue in D minor at the end of the service, a short piece, only about two minutes long, but one I needed to play through a few times. Also on the practice schedule was my prelude, Johann Adam Reincken's *By the Waters of Babylon* (another Baroque favorite), and the hymns for Sunday. I'd picked the hymns and they were of a sombre nature. It was Lent, after all. The way things were going, I had a feeling that I wouldn't be picking the hymns for too much longer. Maybe, I thought, I could also come up with an idea for the mass I had been "commissioned" to write.

I went in the front doors and up the steps to the choir loft without going through the double doors that divided the nave from the narthex. I was surprised, therefore, to see Varmit LeMieux and Bear Niederman down front, busy putting up a large projection screen off to one side of the chancel steps, just above the hymn board. The screen looked to be about ten feet across and five high. I sighed heavily, decided to ignore them and concentrate on my work.

I'd started on the second hymn when Varmit appeared at the top of the stairs. I stopped playing and looked over at him.

"Could you give us a hand?" he asked. "We need someone to hold the other side of the screen while Bear puts the screws in."

"Sorry, Varmit," I said. "I haven't got time right now. How about Rosemary or Kimberly Walnut? It can't be that heavy."

"Nah, it's not. I can get one of them. You were just handy."

"I can't do it just now. How's Muffy's solo going? Have you guys rehearsed yet?"

"I've got the mic hooked up. She doesn't want to use one of those wraparound headphone mics and we don't have a wireless handheld, so she's going to have to use the one with the cord. It won't matter. She's great! You know, ever since she's been in this play, her stage presence is just *awesome*. I hooked the CD player up to the sound system, so all I've got to do is start the track and my baby'll be stylin' to *Eagle's Wings*. She's even working with an acting coach."

"That sounds fine, Varmit," I said.

"Muffy went to the Costco in Winston-Salem this morning. Mother P sent her over to get some stuff to decorate the altar during Lent, so we haven't tried it yet."

"Why are you putting the screen up? I mean, if Muffy's singing a solo."

"It's for next week," said Varmit. "We're not going to use it yet. Mother P thought it'd be a good idea to let everyone *see* the screen and get used to it for a week before we start putting the words to the choruses up there. She says she wants to get the congregation out of their comfort zone."

"Ah," I said. "If that's her plan, she's right on track."

* * *

"His name," said Nancy, "is Johnny Talltrees."

"You're kidding," said Dave. "Talltrees?"

"He was in the system?" I asked.

"He's in the system, all right," said Nancy. "He has a rap sheet taller than he is. Assault, extortion, illegal selling of alcohol, racketeering, illegal gambling, drug possession, you name it. He did some time in north Georgia."

"Where's he from?" I asked.

"Cherokee. You were right about that. I also got an email from the Cherokee police. They have him down as extremely dangerous. He's known to carry a box cutter and a small caliber pistol. He'll also kick you with those silver-tipped boots."

"Quite the little banty rooster," Dave said.

"Someone caught him by surprise," I said. "So what was he doing around here?"

Chapter 11

Pedro LaFleur would be holding court at Buxtehooter's, a pipe-organ bar in the Village that collects the beautiful people the way Russell Crowe collects Precious Moments figurines. The beerfräuleins, buxom, bewitching, and beautiful, were busy sloshing suds across the bar, singing Tyrolean Himmelfahrt carols, and playfully snapping each other's dirndl straps. The organist, a bird named Twelve-Fingered Teddy, was cutting loose on a Gottlieb Muffat toccata as the crowd started the two-step. I elbowed my way past a couple of passacaglia groupies, slugged a gink who was trying to pick a pocket, and pulled up a chair at Pedro's table.

"You want some wine?" Pedro asked with a belch. "I'm laying off the beer. I heard it was fattening."

"Sure," I said.

Pedro was my right-hand man, a countertenor with high notes that would make Beverly Sills blush and a repartee that rivaled Sylvester Stallone's cocktail banter. He was mean as a bull snake, chewed coal tar instead of breath mints, and had a face like a snapping turtle wearing a goatee. He dribbled me a glass from a bottle of Rosé that poured pinkly, like a stream of urine five hours after eating a beet salad.

"You want half of this beet salad?" he asked.

"Nah. Listen, we got trouble."

"Big trouble?" he interrogued.

"Yeah. A dame just got shot in my office."

"So what else is new? That happens every other Thursday."

"This is different. It was ... Carrie Oakey."

Pedro stopped eating his beets in mid-mastication and they fell from his lips like half-chewed pieces of raw liver. I didn't blame him. The mere mention of Carrie Oakey made my own head spin like a coconut when it's being spun by one of those island guys who spins coconuts for cruise ship tourists, the fine hairs of which (the coconut's, not the tourist's) were standing on end in fear, as if the coconut had been reading Stephen King.

"You sure?" he said, his mouth half-full of beets, or half-empty, depending on one's personal philosophy. "Carrie Oakey is dead?"

"Dead as that pet hamster I was keeping for you," deciding to break all the bad news at once.

"What happened?" said Pedro, sadly.

"Wet tail," I said, "and a bullet."

* * *

"How about a dramatic reading?" asked Meg. "You could do one for Mother P's Wednesday night Lenten program. You know, right before choir practice. They start next week."

"I think they're doing a Bible study, if I'm not mistaken. Will you be in attendance?"

"They are, and no, I shall not be in attendance. They're watching a video series and answering questions from a workbook. Not my cup of tea."

"It's a new world," I said.

"I'm sure they could make room for a well-known author such as yourself."

"You are being sarcastic," I replied. "In point of fact, some of these chapters have found their way onto Al Gore's international interweb. I am becoming very well known in some circles."

"Probably not circles I would brag about, if I were you," Meg warned. "Where are they showing up?"

"Mostly on my Facebook page."

"You have a Facebook page? When did this happen?"

"This afternoon," I said smugly, "and I have three friends already. You're not the only interweb genius in this household."

* * *

"We gotta go see the Big Brickle," I said. "Brickle. That's the way in."

Pedro nodded.

"You know what happens if all this gets out?" I said.

"Holy crap, it's the end of the world," Pedro said, missing yet another chance to demonstrate that he could differentiate between scatology and eschatology.

"Yeah," I agreed. "Riots in the streets. Total anarchy."

"2012," said Pedro. "We knew it was coming."

* * *

Friday morning at seven o'clock the phone rang. I was awake, trying to psyche myself into enjoying my run, and it was Meg who answered it. She talked for a moment — I couldn't hear what she was saying — then came dashing onto the back deck and handed me the receiver.

"It's Noylene."

I took the phone and put it to my ear.

"Morning, Noylene," I said.

"Rahab's been kidnapped!" Noylene shouted into the phone.

"Hang on. Calm down a minute and tell me what's happened."

Noylene was frantic. "I got up this morning and got ready for work. I didn't bother the baby 'cause I thought he was still asleep and Rosa has the Slab covered until seven thirty. Then I went in to check on him before I left and he was gone! *His bed was empty!*" She was almost screaming now.

"Calm down. Calm down," I said into the phone, hoping she could give me the story. "You said 'kidnapped.' Maybe he just wandered off. I've heard of toddlers doing that."

"He did *NOT* wander off!" She broke down into sobs.

"Where's Hog? Maybe Hog has him."

"He doesn't. He's right here."

The next sound I heard was the voice of the Rev. Dr. Hogmanay McTavish. He sounded scared. Very scared. "Hayden," he said, his voice breaking, "there's a note. A ransom note!"

"Put the note back where you found it," I said. "Don't touch anything else. I'll be right there."

* * *

    Meg called Nancy while I quickly changed clothes, jumped into the Chevy, and headed down the mountain at a dangerous clip. Noylene and Hog lived up on Quail Ridge, five miles on the other side of town from our place. There was no easy shortcut. I had to do the ten miles into town, then the five miles up the ridge on the other side. It'd be a half hour before I got there. Nancy was closer and could get there quicker. I tried to call her as I came flying down the two-lane road, but, like I figured, there was no service. Sometimes I can pick up a signal if I'm lucky. Not today. Nothing about this felt like a lucky day. Meg had yelled to me that Nancy would meet me there as I was climbing into the truck. I'd waved and floored it all the way up the long drive, not taking my foot off the gas until I'd nosed onto the highway.
    Noylene's place on Quail Ridge, as I remembered, was about a hundred and thirty acres. It wasn't uncommon for fourth or fifth generation mountain folk to have huge tracts of land. Land had been cheap, very cheap, and, if the land had stayed in the family, many of these families were land rich and cash poor. That is to say that they lived a hand-to-mouth existence, sometimes living on welfare checks and food stamps while they sat on several hundred or sometimes thousands of acres that, under different circumstances, might afford them comfortable sustenance. But, for these people at least, the land was the thing. Quail Ridge had been in Noylene's family for a long, long time, but unlike many of these mountain families, Noylene had money. How much, I didn't know. What I did know was that she didn't spend any of it on a fancy house.
    I sped through town, considered stopping at the station, but thought better of it, then continued through St. Germaine and took Highway 184 up toward Quail Ridge. When I saw her drive, I braked hard, turned and spun my tires on the gravel, then tore up the mile-long trek to her home. She, Hog, and little Rahab lived in a doublewide trailer set on concrete blocks about halfway up the ridge. I skidded to a stop behind Nancy's Harley and got out of the truck. Noylene's little, red 4x4 Toyota pickup was in the drive next to Hog's big, white Cadillac. Both of the vehicles were older, Hog's being a vintage '94 model, bought back when the Caddy was the choice of evangelists everywhere. Now, I supposed,

preachers gravitated toward a Lexus SUV or a Land Rover, but in Hog's heyday the white boat was the thing.

The doublewide mobile home was anything but mobile. It sat securely on blocks and had eighteen-inch skirting around the bottom. It had recently been painted a powder-blue color. The trim was white and provided some contrast. White plastic shutters had been applied to the vinyl siding on each of the windows that faced the front. The trailer was sixty feet long and thirty feet wide. Eighteen hundred square feet of living space and that didn't include the screened-in porch that Noylene had added to the back. I walked up the front steps and knocked on the door. It opened almost immediately.

I looked into the face of Brother Hog and was struck immediately by how old he appeared. His color was bad. His usually carefully-coiled coif was stuck in a haphazard way onto his head. He had a day's-worth of white stubble and his eyes were bloodshot and unblinking.

He opened the door and stood to one side. "Come on in, Hayden."

Nancy was with Noylene in the living room. I looked around. The layout of the trailer was what designers call "open concept." The kitchen was open to the living room with an island separating the two spaces. A dining table with four chairs sat beneath a glittering crystal chandelier. There were no dishes on the table, but the kitchen sink was full of dirty dishes. I noticed a dishwasher, but it was closed. The living room was carpeted. Nancy and Noylene sat on a green and brown plaid sofa. Perpendicular to the sofa was a matching love seat, and a leather recliner occupied the other corner, all facing a large, flat-screen TV. A wide hallway headed toward the far end. Another, narrower hallway led off the kitchen to the near end of the house.

"Tell me again what happened," I said, sitting down on the love seat and facing Noylene. Hog walked over and sat down on the edge of the recliner and leaned forward, his feet planted on the floor.

"Like I told you," said Noylene. "I got up at six and got ready for work. I thought that Rahab was asleep and I didn't want to wake him and I didn't have to be at the Slab 'til seven thirty. Around seven, when I went to check on him and kiss him goodbye, he was gone. The bed was empty."

"This was on the pillow," said Brother Hog. He held out a piece of paper.

"I told you to put it back where you found it," I said, looking at Noylene. She shrugged.

"We'd already handled it and read it," said Hog. "Didn't seem smart to put it back."

I pulled a pair of latex gloves out of my pocket, took a minute to snap one on, and took the note from his hand.

We have your boy. We want $75,000 in non-sequential hundred dollar bills. We'll contact you this afternoon. If you involve the police or fail to follow our instructions, we will dispatch the boy. We care nothing for him and are already killers. We have nothing to lose.

It was obviously written on a computer and printed out on any one of a million generic laser printers that almost everyone had in their homes. The font was a san-serif, nondescript choice that could be found on everyone's computer. Arial or something like that. I turned the paper over. Nothing on the back. Twenty pound copier paper found in every printer in America.

"Why seventy-five thousand?" I asked.

Hog shook his head and said, "No idea."

"Would these people know how much money you have?" asked Nancy.

"I don't know how," answered Noylene. "They obviously know we have *some*."

"You have this much?" I said. "I mean, that you can get your hands on today?"

Noylene glanced over at Hog, then said, "Yeah. We can get it."

"It's buried in the backyard somewhere, isn't it?" I said.

"We ain't saying," said Hog.

"Somebody knows about it," said Nancy. "They know you. Think! Who did you tell?"

"We didn't tell anybody anything," Noylene growled. "Did we, Hog?"

"Not a word," said Hog. "You *know* we didn't."

"Yeah, I know," I said. Nancy nodded her agreement. They wouldn't have told a soul. It wasn't the mountain way. I was pretty sure that Noylene didn't even tell Hog everything. And Hog probably had a few financial secrets of his own.

"Let's look in the bedroom," I said.

"I looked when I got here," said Nancy and we walked down the narrow hall. "Nothing but a broken window."

Rahab's bedroom was behind the kitchen. It and a bathroom were the only rooms on this side of the trailer. It was a nice large room, with windows on two sides, one facing the driveway, one facing the backyard. It was carpeted in the same beige stuff that was in the living room, and the walls were painted a bright yellow. It was a toddler's room — lots of toys scattered around, a small bookshelf, and a set of wooden bunk beds. Rahab's bedding was unmade on the bottom bunk. A book was next to the pillow. The blue letters on the cover said *Baby's First Old Testament*. The top bunk was made and had a few stuffed animals on it.

"Our bedroom's on the other end," said Hog. "Across from the guest room. D'Artagnan stays in the guest room when he's around." D'Artagnan was Noylene's son by a previous marriage. Currently in his thirties, D'Artagnan was a sometime bounty hunter and full-time ne'er-do-well.

"You don't think that D'Artagnan had anything ..." I started, but Noylene cut me off.

"No, he did not!"

"Is he around where we could talk to him?"

"I'm telling you he had nothing to do with it," said Noylene. "He knows that if he did something like this, it'd be the *last* thing he ever did." This was not an idle threat from Noylene, and I'd bet that D'Artagnan knew it. "Besides," she continued, "D'Artagnan's been in Tucson since last week."

"You sure he's there?"

"That's what the Pima County assistant district attorney said. Asked me if I wanted to post his bond. I said no, thanks, let him stay in there for a while."

I grunted. Noylene said, "The note was there on the pillow," then pointed to the window on the back wall. "That window's been busted. Last night, I guess. The glass is okay, but the hatch has been sprung. Somebody busted it, slid it open, and took Rahab. There's a bottle missing, too." She started crying.

"Let's see if we can get some prints from the window," I said to Nancy. "And call the FBI. They've got more experience and resources than we do."

"Don't you dare!" barked Noylene, her tears drying up as quickly as they started. "No FBI! I only called *you* by mistake. I panicked."

"They said they'd kill the boy," said Brother Hog. "You read the note."

"They always say that," said Nancy. "Our best bet is to find them and find them fast, and the FBI can help us with that."

"No!" said Hog. "No FBI!"

Noylene looked at me, a pleading look coupled with great sadness. She started chewing on her bottom lip, then said, "I don't want anyone to know about this. You tell Meg that she is not to tell anyone. We'll wait and hear what the kidnappers have to say."

"Can we tap your phone at least?" Nancy said. "We might get a trace we can use. Maybe a location if we're lucky. It'll take me a couple of hours to get it set up, but I can do it from the office."

Hog nodded, but didn't say anything.

"You'll let us know as soon as they call?" I asked. "We're involved now, whether you like it or not, but we don't have to call the FBI unless Rahab's taken across state lines."

"Yeah," said Noylene with resolve. "We'll let you know."

"It would be good to copy the serial numbers of all the bills. It won't take two of you a few hours. Seven hundred fifty hundred dollar bills. You want some help, I can get someone over here. Dave, maybe."

"No, thanks," said Noylene. "We can do that ourselves."

"Call when you hear from them," I admonished again. "We can help you."

"We'll call," said Noylene. "I'll tell you this. The first thing we're going to do is get Rahab back. The second thing is to find whoever did this. When we do, they won't be doing it again."

* * *

Nancy went back to the office to set up the phone tap. I stayed and dusted for prints. There were none. None, as in *not any*. The window had been completely wiped down. I got in my truck and headed home for a shower thinking that this was not going to end well.

Chapter 12

It took Nancy about forty minutes to set up the tap with the telephone company and she was finished by the time I showed up at the station. Now she could log in to her computer or iPhone and trace the call in real time. We could also listen in and record the call. If the phone used to call Noylene was on a land line, and if an address was attached to it, the trace was easy and she'd have the address in short order. If the phone was a mobile and had a GPS chip, she could get an exact fix on the location, then follow it if it moved.

"Do you want Dave to go babysit the Faberge-Dupont-McTavishes?" she asked. "I called him and he's coming in, but he could just as easily go on up to Quail Ridge."

"I don't think it'd do any good, and probably just make them nervous," I answered. "I'll drive up and check on them around noon and see how they're doing with those serial numbers."

"You think this is connected to Johnny Talltrees? It'd be a heck of a coincidence if it wasn't."

"Yeah," I answered. "We operate under the assumption that there are no coincidences. But right now we have to concentrate our efforts on getting the boy back safely."

"I agree," said Nancy.

Meg opened the door to the station and walked in. She looked worried.

"What's the news?" she asked.

"No news," I said. "All we have is the ransom note. No prints, no identifying marks, no bad grammar, nothing. The kidnappers say they're going to call this afternoon with instructions."

"Oh, I hope he's okay," Meg said.

"I'll bet he's fine," said Nancy, taking the note from my hand and reading it again.

We have your boy. We want $75,000 in non-sequential hundred dollar bills. We'll contact you this afternoon. If you involve the police or fail to follow our instructions, we will dispatch the boy. We care nothing for him and are already killers. We have nothing to lose.

Nancy said, "This is a close job. Somebody who knows the family."

"I agree," I said. "Noylene and Hog don't live like they have money, but they do. Someone had to know that."

Nancy said, "The window hasp was busted, but the glass wasn't broken. It was the only window in the back. Rahab's room. That trailer has four bedrooms so the kidnappers had to know where the kid slept."

"So at least one of them has been in their house," said Meg.

"I think it's just one person," I said. "The note says 'we,' but why would 'we' ask for only seventy-five thousand dollars? If they thought that Noylene and Hog had seventy-five thousand, why wouldn't they think they had a hundred? Or two hundred? 'We' is always more greedy than 'I.' He wants a specific amount, and it's not that much in the grand scheme of things. Rather, it's an amount that the kidnapper knows they can get their hands on, and fast."

"Agreed," said Nancy. "Also, he says 'we' five times in this note. Overkill."

"Non-sequential bills," said Meg, looking over Nancy's shoulder. "I would have said 'unmarked.' That's what they always say on the cop shows — unmarked bills."

"Good point," I said. "I'd say that whoever it is is educated. Also, notice that the kidnapper says 'dispatch.' He can't bring himself to contemplate the word 'kill.' Can't even *write* it. Not since they're talking about a child." I thought for a moment. "You know what? ..."

"It's a woman!" interrupted Meg. "I know it."

"I think you're right," I said.

"Yep," agreed Nancy. "If it is, I don't think a woman will hurt that baby, especially if she knows him."

"Someone at the Beautifery?" Meg said.

"Yeah," I said, and mentally ran through Noylene's Purveyors of Beauty. Goldi Fawn Birtwhistle, Darla Kildair, and Debbie Understreet. I didn't know much about any of them. Goldi Fawn was a member of the choir, but other than the fact that she was a Christian astrologer, I had no knowledge of her personal situation. I knew Darla and Debbie even less.

"Want me to check on Noylene's employees?" asked Nancy.

"Yes, I do," I said, and named them. "We should probably look at Pete's employees, too. Noylene works at the Slab almost every day." I thought for a moment. "Let's review Hog's acquaintants, too. Could be that the link is Brother Hog instead of Noylene."

***

The next couple of hours passed slowly. At noon, I decided to drive back up to Quail Ridge and see if Hog and Noylene had recorded the serial numbers of the bills — this presuming that the two of them had seventy-five thousand dollars in hundred dollar bills stashed somewhere in or near the trailer. I was pretty sure they did. I'd talked to Meg a couple of times after Noylene's call early in the morning, filling her in on our progress, or rather, lack of it. Now, driving back up the mountain, I called her again.

"Anything?" she asked, worry clouding her voice.

"Nothing yet," I said. "I wish we could call in some pros. I don't like this one bit."

"Let's just hope we're right and that whoever took him won't hurt him."

"Yeah," I said, then lost service as the road wound through a holler surrounded on both sides by sheer rock faces. I called back a couple of minutes later, but the call went straight to voicemail.

The trailer was just as I'd left it. The Caddy and the Toyota pickup hadn't moved since we'd left. I glanced at the tire tracks as I walked by to see if the vehicles had gone and come back. Nope. I walked up onto the porch and knocked on the door. Hog opened it almost immediately and beckoned me in.

"How's the recording going?" I asked as I wiped my feet on the mat inside the door.

"Takes longer than I thought it would," said Hog. "We're more than half finished, though. Noylene keeps getting up to have a smoke."

"Nervous energy," I said.

"Yeah," said Hog. "C'mon in."

He ushered me into the dining room, where stacks of hundred dollar bills were placed around the table. Noylene was sitting at a chair, a lit cigarette hanging from her lips, diligently copying the number of each bill onto a yellow legal pad with an old half-finished yellow pencil that had been sharpened with a penknife. The knife was on the table beside her, open, and a small trash can was at her knee. She saw me looking at it.

"Daddy gave me that knife when I was a knee-high," she said. "Mother-of-pearl handle. Taught me how to whittle. I couldn't give it to D'Artagnan. That boy would have cut his thumb off with it. I was thinking Rahab might like it someday. For just a little sprout, he's clever with his hands."

I took the chair next to her. Hog sat down across from me. Noylene finished copying the serial number from the bill in her hand, placed it in a stack to her left, and took a new bill from the pile in front of her.

"Thought you gave up smoking," I said.

"Yeah, well, I've taken it back up," Noylene said.

"Want me to help with this?" Not waiting for an answer, I reached for another pad on the table.

She took a long drag. "Sure," she finally answered, then blew a puff of blue smoke up into the ceiling fan.

* * *

An hour later, we'd finished. I looked at my watch. 1:28. "Want me to stick around?" I asked.

"We'll call you," said Hog. "Soon as we hear from the scum that took our boy."

Noylene was bundling the bills back into fifty-bill stacks using thick rubber bands that had been piled up in the middle of the table. Fifteen stacks. The entire amount would fit in a small plastic grocery bag and wouldn't even weigh two pounds.

"Not to be nosey," I said, "and this is just for the sake of the investigation, but how much could you two have come up with if you had to? Cash, I mean."

"Why do you want to know?" asked Noylene, her eyes narrow.

"If the kidnappers asked for a specific amount, maybe they knew how much you had on hand."

Noylene looked over at Hog and he nodded. "Makes sense," he said. "This is just between us?"

"Of course."

"This about taps us in the cash-on-hand department. There's more in a few banks around the area, but it would take us a day to round it up. And we have some gold … "

I held up a hand to stop him. "That'll do. Can you think of anyone who might have known or found out how much y'all had on hand?"

Noylene shook her head. Hog looked thoughtful, then said, "Nope."

"We don't tell our business," Noylene said. "Don't talk about it, don't cogitate, don't speculate."

"I get it," I said, "but it sounds as though someone found out."

* * *

I left the property and took some time driving the roads that fringed Quail Ridge. There weren't many, and I didn't see anything that might be considered out of the ordinary. Feeling dumb as a stump and saying a silent prayer for Rahab, I went back to town.

Chapter 13

"Meg's called three times," said Nancy. She was sitting at her computer, monitoring Noylene's phone. Dave was sitting at the other desk chair, the one that might fall over backwards if you leaned the wrong way.

"I've been out of range," I said. I shrugged off my jacket and laid it on the counter.

"No, your ringer is off," said Nancy.

"How do you know?"

"Check it," she said.

I pulled out my phone, looked at it, then surreptitiously clicked the mute button back to ring.

"Nope, it's fine," I said.

"Slyly done," said Nancy. "You know, you should be a spy or something."

"Any news on Rahab?" asked Dave.

"No contact since I left the trailer. I helped them finish copying the serial numbers. That was about forty-five minutes ago. I was hoping the kidnapper would call while I was there. No luck."

"Maybe they're watching the place," said Nancy. "Could do it from almost anywhere up there. You know, the note said don't contact the police. Maybe they saw your truck."

"Maybe," I conceded. "I doubt it, though. We think it's just one person and, if we're right, they're going to have their hands full with a two year old."

"Call Meg back, will you?" said Nancy.

"I'll do it right now."

But I didn't. The door to the station opened and Muffy LeMieux came in, her light green angora sweater in full bloom.

"Hi, Muffy," I said, forgetting about the phone call.

"Hi, Muffy," echoed Dave.

"Aren't you cold in that outfit?" asked Nancy, when she saw her.

"Oh, no," said Muffy, then added, "Well, these stretch pants are a little chilly."

"You look *wonderful*," gushed Dave, then realized what he sounded like, and said in a serious tone, "I mean, that sweater really suits you, Miss LeMieux."

"Thanks, Dave. You're a real sweetie!" Muffy squeaked, then turned her attention to me. "Hayden, can I talk to you for just a minute? You know, alone?"

"Hang on!" barked Nancy, typing furiously on her computer keyboard. "Noylene's phone is ringing!"

Dave and I quickly huddled over her shoulder and peered at the monitor.

"Someone answered it," said Nancy. Her fingers flew over the keys. "The call's coming from a cell phone," she said, scrolling down the page, looking at screen after screen quicker than I could make heads or tales out of any of it. "Dammit! No GPS chip. Must be one of those cheap, disposable ones."

"Can we listen in?" I asked.

Nancy hit a button and Hog's voice came across the computer speakers. "Yessir, I have the money. Let me talk to Rahab."

"I'm recording the call," hissed Nancy.

A moment later a baby's voice came jabbering across the lines. I couldn't make out anything he said, but apparently Hog was satisfied and gave a nine digit number to the caller.

"Oh, jeeze!" I said. "Did Hog just give the kidnapper a cell number?"

"Sounded like it," Nancy agreed. "Wait. They've hung up."

"Bring up the recording," I said.

Nancy hit a few keys, then we heard a voice, a *male* voice, say, "Hogmanay McTavish, do you know why I'm calling you?"

"Yes."

"Give me your cell phone number."

"Not yet. I want to talk to my boy."

"You have the money?"

"Yessir, I have the money. Let me talk to Rahab."

A pause, then some baby talk, then Brother Hog repeating the nine digit number, then a click.

"Call them back," I said, but Nancy was already dialing. "Tell them to wait for us until we get there."

Nancy listened for a few moments. "No answer," she finally said.

"Oh, my God!" said Muffy, her mouth open in a little "o." "Is this a kidnapping?"

"Muffy," I said, "not a word to anyone."

"Of course not!"

"Let's go, Nancy," I said, pulling my jacket back on. "Dave, wait here. Call if you hear anything."

On the fast trip up to Quail Ridge, Nancy said, "That was a man's voice."

"Sounded like it to me, too," I said. "We'll listen to it again when we get back. Could have been a woman with a low range. Obviously, whoever it was would try to disguise their voice."

"Yeah. Especially if it was someone in town we might recognize."

We were back up at the property in fifteen minutes. I swung into the entrance, spraying gravel in all directions, then floored the old Chevy up the rutted driveway. When we were in view of the trailer, we could see that Noylene's truck was gone.

I skidded to a stop, and Nancy and I were both out of the cab and up the steps in two shakes. Nancy banged on the door with the flat of her hand. No answer. She banged again, hard.

"Noylene," I called. "Answer the door!"

We heard footsteps, then the door opened and Noylene looked out at us with red-rimmed eyes.

"Where's Hog?" I asked.

"He went to get our boy back."

"You know where he went, Noylene?" Nancy said.

"No, not exactly. Whoever it was called his cell and said for him to start driving. They'd call him again and give him directions."

"And he took the money with him?" Nancy asked.

"Yes, he did," said Noylene. A tear escaped and ran down her cheek. She brushed it away with the back of her hand. "Said I wasn't to come. Just Hog."

I said, "I'm sure everything will work out fine. May we come in and wait with you?"

Noylene stepped back away from the door and we went in. The house was the same as I'd left it, except for the dining room table. The cash was gone and the three yellow legal pads were stacked and pushed to the far edge.

"Y'all want some lemonade?" Noylene asked.

"I'll have some," said Nancy.

"No, thanks," I said, then pulled out my phone to call Meg. Voicemail again. I didn't leave a message.

"We'll take those legal pads, okay?" I asked, nodding toward the table. "We can put those serial numbers in the system and hopefully catch someone spending one of those bills."

"Sure, I guess." Noylene disappeared into the kitchen. We went into the living room and sat down, Nancy on the long sofa, me in Hog's recliner.

My phone rang and it was Meg. "I'm over at Noylene's," I told her. "Hog's taken the ransom money and gone to get Rahab. He didn't wait for us."

"Call me," she said. "Call me as soon as you know anything."

"I will."

***

An hour later we heard the little Toyota truck backfiring up the driveway. Noylene ran to the door, flung it open, and practically flew down the steps and into the driveway. A few moments later, before the truck had even fully stopped, she yanked the passenger door open, pulled little Rahab from his car seat, and began smothering him with kisses. He babbled happily and used both his hands to pull Noylene's hair.

Hog got out of the truck and smiled at Noylene, then at us, obviously proud of himself.

"You should have waited for us," said Nancy. "We might have caught the kidnappers if you'd waited."

"Couldn't chance it," said Hog. "But now that Rahab's back, you go ahead and catch them."

"At least find out who they are," said Noylene. "I'd like to speak with them." Her face was hard.

"You didn't see them?" I asked Hog.

"Nope. I dropped the sack of money in the middle of Turtle Branch Road like he told me."

"You had phone service?" I asked. "The whole time?"

Hog looked thoughtful. "Yes. Yes, I did. Never lost it, not even once, and I was on the phone with him the whole time."

Nancy and I looked at each other. "Must have plotted it out pretty carefully," she said to me, then to Hog, "Who's your phone service provider? I lose my connection up here all the time."

"Carolina West Wireless."

Nancy pulled out a pad from her breast pocket and jotted the information down. Noylene carried Rahab up the steps, onto the porch, and into the house, all the while talking softly into his ear.

"Tell us the rest," I said to Hog.

"Like I told you, I dropped the sack of money in the middle of Turtle Branch Road just where he told me to. There's hardly anybody that drives that road. It's a cut through. No houses on it."

"He?" said Nancy. "You sure it was a he?"

"It was a man, I think. Maybe not, but I think it was. So I dropped the bag and he told me to drive real slow and I would see Rahab sitting by the road in about a half mile."

"And he was?" I asked.

"Yes," said Hog, now with a tired smile. "He was tied to a tree, sitting on a blanket, and chewing on a carrot. He even had a little stocking cap on. The rope wasn't tight around him, but he couldn't just walk away. Took a couple of minutes to untie him. The rope's in the back of the truck, if you want it. The blanket and the hat, too. None of that's ours."

"Thanks," I said. "We'll take it all. I sure am glad you got Rahab back safe and sound."

"Me, too," said Hog. "Now you guys find out who did this. Rahab and I have a tent revival scheduled for next week at the campground in Valle Crucis. I don't want to have to worry about someone kidnapping him again."

* * *

On the way home Nancy said, "What do you think? A man?"

"My gut says it's a woman," I said. "Everything about it says female from the planning on down to the blanket and the stocking hat." I paused, then said, "Still, there could be two of them working together."

Nancy squinched an eye at me. "I don't think so. Plus, we still have the Talltrees case on our plate. Who uses a taser? A man?"

"No," I said.

Chapter 14

I'd heard the rumors. Carrie Oakey was going to shut down the Society for the Betterment of Choirs. The SBC had a dirty secret that had been kept by the Anglican Boys choirs for the better part of a century. Leprechauns. Leprechauns masquerading as boy sopranos. With their high, peepy voices and their creepy little fingers, they could go undetected for decades as long as they kept moving. After a few years in one place, it was a dye job, some liposuction, a quick shave, and a new pair of short pants, and they were off to a competing choir, a sack of coins and a gold watch for their trouble. The only time the choir director had to worry was when St. Paddy's Day fell on a Sunday.

The baby name grift was to keep me busy, out of the loop, while Carrie Oakey moved in and cleaned them out. And since I would be busy investigating the bishop, he wouldn't be able to call me in. But why now? Then it hit me like a cantaloupe thrown from an interstate overpass: the leprechauns were tied to the Mayan calendar just as surely as St. Lucy was the patron saint of optometrists, what with her eyeballs on that plate and everything, and 2012 was the end. The end of everything.

***

I kept thinking about the seventy-five thousand dollars as I drove into town on Saturday morning. It was Nancy's day off and Dave was working the station, but I thought I'd check in at least, then go over to St. Barnabas and practice a bit. I still had some work to do on the Reincken organ postlude and I had to come up with something for the service music. I'd told Rosemary that I was almost finished with it — no sense in panicking the priest unnecessarily — but couldn't get it into the bulletin for the congregation this quickly. We'd agreed that we'd let the choir sing it this coming Sunday, then have the congregation join in next week. All this, predicated on the assumption that I'd actually come up with something.

During the season of Lent, we didn't sing our customary *Gloria*, but substituted a more penitent *Kyrie* instead.

Kyrie eleison. Christe eleison. Kyrie eleison.
Lord, have mercy. Christ, have mercy. Lord, have mercy.

The *Sanctus* remained, as did the music sung at the breaking of the bread, known as the "fraction anthem." This anthem changed from week to week and was generally only sung by the choir, our usual text being the *Agnus Dei — Lamb of God, who takes away the sins of the world, have mercy upon us.* This being the case, I could get away with writing a *Kyrie* and a *Sanctus* for the congregation to sing, and then maybe a more elaborate *Agnus Dei* for the choir.

As I drove down the mountain toward town, I slipped the recording I'd been listening to out of the CD player and replaced it with one featuring Leon Redbone, entitled *On the Track*. In my opinion Leon Redbone was a genius, a one-man folk-jazz enigma. I clicked through the tracks, landing on a favorite, *Lulu's Back in Town*. Four songs later I was pulling into my parking place in front of the police station, when the last song on the album came up and a familiar tune floated through the cab of the pickup. It was a tune I'd learned as a kid, sung in music class in elementary school, figured out how to play on the harmonica when I was eight, and harmonized around every campfire since I could remember. I froze and listened to Leon warble through the old classic. Divine inspiration? Oh, yes! I bowed my head and offered a prayer of thanks for illumination, then a prayer asking forgiveness for what I was about to compose.

* * *

Dave was in the office, reclining in his swivel chair, his feet resting on the desk, eating a vanilla donut stuffed with Bavarian creme, judging from the yellow pudding gracing his chin.

"Morning, Boss," he said. "You want a donut? There're one or two left."

I opened the white cardboard box sitting on the counter and viewed the remnants of multicolored sprinkles, smears of chocolate, apple filling, powdered sugar, and white and yellow creme. Also in the box was a plain cake donut, no glaze, no sugar. I picked it up.

"This is it?" I asked.

"I ordered a dozen assorted. That's how they get rid of those plain ones I think. No one likes 'em."

I took a bite, then tossed it in the trash can. "Yeah," I said. "I can see that. I'll be at the Slab if you need me. After that, I'll be at the church."

"Nothing happening here," said Dave. "I'll stick around 'til two or so, then I'm heading home."

I left the station and crossed the side street, taking time to stop and wave to a couple of kids running through the park. It was still chilly, but the wind had stopped and the sun was out in full force. The Slab was just on the next corner and it was, as I expected it to be, full of customers. Saturday mornings were always good for a big breakfast crowd. I opened the glass door and the cowbell tied to the crossbar jangled my arrival. Pete had three waitresses hustling the food and drinks and so, content to watch over his empire, was sitting at our table in the back of the restaurant. Cynthia Johnsson, Pauli Girl McCollough and Rosa were scurrying to and fro with full and empty plates, baskets of biscuits, coffee pots, and menus. I hung my coat on the rack by the door and Pete waved me over as soon as he saw me.

"Sit down," he said. "Have some breakfast."

"Don't mind if I do."

"I heard about Noylene and Hog's baby boy. I guess everybody has by now."

The small town grapevine was nothing if not efficient. "What did you hear?" I asked.

Pauli Girl was at my elbow a few seconds after I'd sat down, filling my coffee cup. Pauli Girl McCollough was the middle child of Ardine and PeeDee McCollough, although PeeDee had been absent for most of the children's lives. The word in the wind was that Ardine had taken care of the problem of an abusive husband in the way that many wives had in the long history of the mountain folk. It was not a scenario I cared to contemplate professionally, knowing full well that PeeDee had been perfectly happy getting drunk and beating not only his wife, but also his young children. I had heard, through the same St. Germaine grapevine, that Ardine took it when it was just her, but when her husband started on the kids, enough was enough.

Ardine earned her living working at a Christmas tree farm and making quilts that she sold in gift shops around the area. The Ginger Cat, for example, had a couple on display. I'd seen them the last time Meg and I had lunch. She and the kids lived in a single-wide up in Coondog Holler on about a half-acre that sidled up to the Pisgah National Forest. There was an old spring box on the property where they got their water, and a septic tank that may or may not have been constructed from a 1945 Studebaker with the windows rolled up.

One thing PeeDee had insisted on when his progeny appeared on this earth was to name them after his favorite thing next to himself, his dog, and his truck. Hence, the children were all named for beers: the eldest, Bud, the middle child, Pauli Girl, and the youngest boy, Moose-Head. Moosey for short.

Bud was twenty years old and finishing his last year at Davidson. He was majoring in business, but his real passion was wine. The fruit of the grape had been his singular focus since he was twelve years old. If all went according to plan, he'd graduate in May and set up his wine shop in St. Germaine. I was his business partner. Bud had landed us in the catbird seat when he discovered, at a farmhouse auction, three cases of wine that he had me buy. Thirty-six bottles of Chateau Petrus Pomerol 1998, that would reach maturity sometime in the next few years. According to Bud, who knew a thing or two about wine, these bottles would be worth somewhere in the neighborhood of a quarter million dollars when we were ready to cash them in. For the past few summers, when not attending wine courses, Bud had spent his time at the Ginger Cat, offering his expertise to Annie and her customers. Bud was the youngest of the seventy-five Master Sommeliers in the United States and had already been contacted by several New York restaurants with offers of employment. Bud's nose for wine, and his penchant for the lingo of wine-speak, made him a natural. It wasn't uncommon to find him holding court in the Ginger Cat expressing his opinion on a young cabernet: "an astonishing marriage made in heaven and hell; of richness and decay; chocolate and schoolgirl's uniforms with a flare of cream cheese; a cigar box containing a Montecristo, a single yellow rose and a hot brick sitting on top of a saddle."

Bud would turn twenty-one in April and could legally sell wine the day after. I'd already gotten our license and lined up a building. We'd start renovations around Easter and be ready to open for the summer tourist season.

"How about the breakfast special, Chief?" Pauli Girl asked.

"What is it this morning?"

"*Machaca con huevos* and jalapeño corn cakes."

"I recommend it," said Pete, sipping his coffee. "Manuel is on his game this morning."

"Sounds good," I said to Pauli Girl, then added, "How's school going?"

Pauli Girl gave me a smile that would melt anyone's heart. A year younger than Bud, she was the prettiest girl in town and, once she'd finished high school, had taken a path pointing her towards a nursing career. Even with the rigors of studying, she still worked weekends and holidays in St. Germaine when she wasn't busy with her nurse's training.

"I'll be finished with my LPN certification this spring, but now I'm thinking about going on and getting my RN," she said. "I can make more money, that's for sure. A Registered Nurse can get a job about anywhere."

"Are you thinking about staying at Appalachian State?" I asked.

"Till I graduate," she said. "Then I'd like to move somewhere with, you know, a little more action."

"I know exactly."

"Let me get this order turned in. I'll have it up for you in a jiff." She turned on her heel and disappeared into the kitchen.

"At least she didn't call you 'Hon,'" said Pete. "Yesterday she called me Hon. I hate to be called Hon by someone that young. I have corns older than she is." Pete shook his head in disgust. "Now tell me about the kidnapping."

"You probably heard all there is to tell. Rahab was stolen out of his bedroom. The kidnappers left a note and Hog and Noylene paid the ransom. The whole episode lasted less than six hours."

"Seventy-five large is what I heard," said Pete.

"The grapevine is very effective. When did you hear about it?"

"Hannah, Amelia, and Grace came by this morning for breakfast on their way to the Piggly Wiggly. It seems that Roger makes them all work on Saturday now. They were filling Cynthia in on all the details while they ate."

"How on earth? ... "

"I don't know," said Pete, raising his hands in consternation, "but they had all the facts, or seemed to, right down to Nancy tracing the phone call, and Rahab found beside the road chewing on a chicken leg."

"Carrot," I said.

"Huh?" said Pete.

"It was a carrot, not a chicken leg."

"Oh. Anyway, you have any suspects?"

"Not a one."

"Grapevine says it's a gang of kidnappers and they're liable to strike again at any time. Lock up your babies."

"That's a relief," I said.

"What? That there's a gang of kidnappers?"

"No, that the grapevine is wrong for once."

Cynthia walked over to the table and plopped down in the chair next to me. "I'm exhausted," she said. "Get me a cup of coffee, will you Pete?"

"Get back to work," said Pete.

Cynthia glared at him. I laughed. "I'll get it," I said, and started to get up.

"Never mind," said Cynthia. "Here's Rosa." She turned an upside-down coffee cup right side up as Rosa walked by and Rosa was happy to fill it for her. "I tell you, I'm beat!" Cynthia said. "I didn't get home 'til late last night, then up at five to get ready for work." Cynthia didn't look as though she got up at five o'clock. A tall, willowy blonde, she was wearing very little make up, or so it seemed to me, and didn't look as though she needed it. Belly dancing kept her figure in great shape. She was wearing an old pair of faded jeans that fit snugly, a pair of Nikes, and a sweatshirt that advertised North Carolina State University. Her hair was tied back into a ponytail.

"Did you make the acquaintance of our pig?" I asked.

"Alas, I did not," said Cynthia. "Our pig ... that is, *your* pig, was fast asleep in the hay of her comfy, heated, little pig house."

"Heated?" I asked.

"Of course, heated," said Pete, looking at me with astonishment. "I told you that before. You want Portia to get cold?"

"No, I guess not."

"I heard about the kidnapping," said Cynthia. "Not to mention the dead, heart-attack guy in the alley. Sheesh. I can't even leave town for a couple of days before everything goes to heck." She sighed heavily. "The Town Council is going to want updates on your progress. We can't have a band of baby kidnappers roaming the hills looking for children to abduct. Is the dead guy connected to the kidnapping?"

"No proof of that," I said. "We shall keep your council well informed. As mayor, you are privy to all our investigative secrets."

"What about me?" asked Pete. "As a truffle pig owner, I have a right to know."

"Well, of course," I said. "I'll send you hourly peeps."

"What's a peep?" asked Pete.

"It's a Twitface thing. I don't know for sure. I just know that you'll be getting peeped."

"Tweets," said a young man at the next table. "You get tweets. From Twitter."

I snapped my fingers. "That's it," I replied. "Twitter. I have an account now, you know."

"What's your user name?" asked the man, pulling out a phone, then punching in information with both thumbs. He was obviously adept at social media and looked the part. His light brown hair was cut short except for his front bangs that had been waxed up into a comb. He sported black, horn-rimmed Buddy Holly glasses and was wearing black jeans with a long-sleeved T-shirt that proclaimed that he was interested in saving polar bears.

"Umm ... I can't remember," I said. "I'll have to look it up." Mercifully, just then Pauli Girl appeared at our table with my breakfast.

"You should tweet that you're eating breakfast," said the man.

"Why would he do that?" asked Pete.

"People want to know," said the man with a shrug. "I'm tweeting it right now. Eating breakfast with a couple of old guys who have a pig."

Cynthia laughed, drained her coffee cup, and got to her feet. "I have to leave here at one o'clock," she told Pete. "I have a Little Theater rehearsal this afternoon."

"You're in the Mitford play?" I asked. "When did this happen?"

"Mr. Christopher called me last week. Someone dropped out of the production, so he wanted to know if I could do it. I'm a trained thespian, you know."

"I can vouch for that," said Pete, then dropped his voice to a conspiratorial whisper. "In fact, this one time ..."

"Quiet, you!" Cynthia said, then turned her attention back to me. "I haven't been to a rehearsal yet, but I've learned all my lines. I'm playing Aunt Rose."

"Aunt Rose?" I said.

"Uncle Billy's lovable but dotty wife. She likes to direct traffic wearing a military trench coat and rubber boots."

"Ah, yes," said Pete, closing his eyes and stroking his chin stubble. "I have fond memories of that trench coat."

"Hush!" shooshed Cynthia. "I'm the mayor! Don't be blabbing all over town!"

The young man at the next table tweeted for all he was worth.

* * *

After breakfast I said my goodbyes, then walked across Sterling Park to St. Barnabas Church. The day was warming up as the sun rose in the sky. A few more days of this weather and we'd all forget winter like it was an unwelcome relative, visiting too long, but once gone as forgotten as a bad dream. The dark red front doors of the church were unlocked and I pulled one of them open, walked into the narthex, then up the stairs and into the choir loft. There was some activity happening down at the front by the chancel. I looked down from the back balcony and watched as Rosemary Pepperpot-Cohosh, her husband, Pastor Herb, Muffy LeMieux, Bear Niederman, and Mr. Christopher — all new members of the Altar Guild — were discussing the placement of decorations. The projection screen was hanging to the left of the chancel steps about ten feet above the floor, right above the hymn board, as obvious as a front gold tooth on a Lutheran.

The committee was gathered around the altar, chattering away, when I played a chord on the organ, startling them. They stopped talking and looked up at me.

"Sorry to bother you," I said. "You don't mind if I do a little practicing, do you?"

"Of course not," said Rosemary. "You go right ahead. You won't bother us a bit."

"Before you start," said Mr. Christopher, "could you come down and give us your opinion on something?"

"Sure. Be right there."

As I walked down the center aisle, I was conscious that the group had formed a semicircle in front of the altar, blocking my view.

"Okay," said Mr. Christopher. "Stop right there and tell us what you think."

I stopped and watched as the members of the guild parted in the middle and stepped away from the altar, revealing the decorations for the First Sunday of Lent.

I was aware of Muffy LeMieux's solo, *On Eagle's Wings*. I might even go so far as to say that I had prepared myself to hear Muffy sing it in church. What I wasn't prepared for was the three-foot-tall, full-grown, stuffed bald eagle standing atop the altar with a squirrel in one, raised talon. The squirrel's glass eyes were wide with terror, and its lips were pulled back over its teeth in what can only be called the genius of the taxidermic art. The wings of the great bird were spread to their full eight-foot span, and its hooked, cruel beak was partially open in a defiant, soundless screech. It was something straight out of the Smithsonian Institution's exhibit on giant North American raptors, that is, if the Smithsonian still had any stuffed and mounted bald eagles. They might have some in the back, I thought, hidden away in a crate somewhere. If they did, the birds would have to be pre-1940 eagles or else accompanied by a permit from the Secretary of the Interior. This much I knew. There was something called the Bald and Golden Eagle Protection Act of 1940, and it didn't do to get caught with one of these endangered birds. The Smithsonian probably had hundreds of legal specimens, but none, I'd wager, mounted like this one.

"Wow," I said. "Where did you get the eagle?"

"It's mine," said Bear proudly. "I didn't shoot it though. I hit it with my Jeep."

"Ah," I said.

"I did shoot the squirrel, then I worked it into the tableau. The eyes were the hardest."

"It's a nice touch," I admitted.

"Mother P said she needed an eagle, so I donated it to the church for a tax write-off. I figure it's worth maybe a couple of thousand."

"Of course you can!" said Mother P happily. "I'll give you a receipt."

"I think you might find," I suggested, "that a stuffed bald eagle might be a bad choice for an altar decoration. An 'ill-eagle,' if you will." I chuckled at my own wit. "You could get into plenty of trouble."

"Pish-tosh!" said Mother P. "Bear didn't shoot the thing. You heard him. He hit it with his Jeep."

"Yes, but ..."

"What we want to know," said Mr. Christopher, "is whether you think it would be better to have an American flag draped over the front of the altar or just go ahead and use the white linen cloth?"

"But isn't purple the color of Lent?" I asked.

"Purple don't work with the eagle," complained Muffy. "The feathers are too dark. They sort of blend in. We really want the eagle to pop!"

"Not to mention that my sermon has an element of patriotism," added Rosemary.

I took a deep breath. *My brethren, count it all joy when ye fall into divers temptations; Knowing this, that the trying of your faith worketh patience. But let patience have her perfect work, that ye may be perfect and entire, wanting nothing.*

"The flag, then," I said. "Definitely the flag."

Forty-five minutes later, I didn't feel the least pang of guilt as I finished up my mass.

* * *

It was mid-afternoon when I decided that it would be a good thing to talk to Cynthia alone. She was, after all, the mayor. I climbed into my truck and made the ten minute drive up Oak Street where the Little Theater was putting the final touches on its production of *Welcome to Mitford*. With less than a week to go, dress rehearsals were imminent and imminently terrifying. Over the years, the St. Germaine Footlight Club had occupied many venues, the most famous of them being the second floor of the courthouse, where they performed for thirty or so years back in their heyday. There had been a raised stage area, a huge velvet curtain, room for flats, props and backstage paraphernalia, pretty good theater lighting, a couple of small dressing rooms, and seating for about one hundred seventy patrons. In the 1960s, the Town Council deemed that the second floor of the courthouse was needed for office space, and so the Little Theater raised enough money to build a performing space at the top of Oak Street, and had been there ever since. It was a block building and owed its charm to the architectural style known as "bad," but had a nice little lobby, a box office, a good-sized stage, dressing rooms, and seating for about two hundred. There was also fly space, another story above the stage to hang backdrops and set pieces — something that the courthouse never had.

I walked into the theater and saw Cynthia up on the stage, chatting with Muffy LeMieux. The set was the interior of a house with two doors and a window. One of the doors was shut; the other one, obviously the front entrance, was open, and there was a bit of set dressing to depict the outdoors just beyond the threshold. The window was festooned with drapes and ties and the walls were covered in some sort of textured wallpaper with a light pink pattern. A couch was set at a theatrical angle down center. Two upholstered chairs flanked it on either side, and a small drum table acted as a stand for a lamp and a few random books. All of this, decorated with Mr. Christopher's signature Fourteen Layers of Style.

Cynthia was standing behind the couch and had a cup of coffee in her hand. Muffy was reclining in one of the chairs taking a slurp out of a plastic water bottle. Break time. I walked down one of the side aisles and up to the lip of the stage.

"Hayden!" said Muffy when she saw me. "We were just talking about you!"

"All good, I hope."

"Of course! Did you come to watch part of the rehearsal? We're about to do the scene where Father Tim neglects his diet and exercise and goes into a diabetic coma while driving and wrecks his car. I'm just waiting on Mr. Christopher."

"It sounds scintillating," I said, "but I think I'll wait to see the show. I don't want to ruin any of the surprises." I turned my focus to Cynthia. "Would you have a minute to chat?"

"Sure. Let me come around."

Mr. Christopher came out onto the stage from one of the wings. "Hayden, I thought I heard you. Do you think you can do something about these chainsaws going day and night? It's incredibly difficult to rehearse with all this racket."

I listened for a moment. Nothing.

"Well, of course they stopped as soon as you came in," huffed Mr. Christopher, then perked up as he heard the buzz of a nearby weed-whacker. "There! There it is!"

"I'll see what I can do," I promised.

"Try it now," hollered a voice from backstage. Mr. Christopher walked over to the front door and flipped the light switch. Then walked over to the side table and clicked the lamp off and on a few times. Nothing.

"Did you connect the hot wire to the common terminal of the first three-way?" Mr. Christopher yelled.

"I think so," the voice came back. "Which one is that?"

"The black one. Oh, for heaven's sake! Connect the black one to the black one, then the white one to the white one, then the black load wire to the common terminal of the opposite three-way switch. Then you can connect the travelers."

"Which screws do I attach 'em to?"

"Doesn't matter! There's no polarity. Oh, never mind. I'll do it myself." He flounced off stage and we heard some muffled growling.

Muffy giggled. "I think he has a crush on Varmit," she whispered.

A moment later Cynthia appeared from one of the exit doors located on the floor beside the stage.

"What's up?" she asked. She still had her coffee cup and took a sip.

"I thought I should fill you in on a few things, you being the mayor and all."

Her eyes widened slightly. The table lamp blinked on, then off, then on again.

"It works, Sweetie," Muffy yelled.

"Let's go outside," I said, then added in a whisper, "I'd like to keep this confidential."

Chapter 15

Moosey McCollough was the youngest of the McCollough children. He was eleven years old, almost twelve, but small for his age. He had a mop of unmanageable straw on his head, freckles, and bright blue eyes that peered out from behind oversized wire-rimmed glasses. He wore blue jeans, summer or winter, and the fact that he had worn holes through both knees didn't warrant, in Ardine's opinion, throwing them away. They had been patched multiple times. He usually sported a striped T-shirt and was rarely seen without his high-topped Keds, although lately he had switched from red to black, a sign of his coming-of-age. His best friend was Bernadette Kenton.

When I drove up, they were both waiting for me outside Bernadette's house sitting on the stoop, wearing light coats against the cool weather we'd had all week.

"Can we ride in the back?" hollered Moosey.

"Nope," I said. "It's against the law. You're not eighteen."

"Aw, man," answered Bernadette, as she and Moosey clambered into the cab of the truck. "My uncle lets us ride in the back of his."

"He's not a cop," I said. "I'd have to give myself a ticket. Besides, it's dangerous."

"You used to let us do it," complained Moosey.

"Children don't bounce as high as they used to."

It was a ten-minute drive to Pete's, Moosey and Bernadette chattering all the way. We pulled up at the curb in front of the house and the two kids slid out of the cab in a jiffy.

"Now where's that pig?" asked Moosey.

"In the back," I said. "Don't scare her, though. She may not be used to us yet."

"Is she really from France?" asked Bernadette.

"Yep," I said.

"There's a place in France, where the alligators dance," sang Moosey.

"And one wouldn't dance, so they kicked him in the pants," joined in Bernadette. They howled with glee. I was used to this from these two.

Pete was at the Slab for the afternoon, so we walked around the side of the house, through the back yard, and found the pig pen. There was our truffle pig, rooting up something or other beside her pig house and oinking to her heart's content.

"Wow!" said Bernadette. "I've never seen a pig like that. She's beautiful."

"She's a long-haired Mangalitsa pig. Very rare. Her name's Portia."

"It sort of looks like a sheep," said Moosey. "With that hair and all."

"A little bit," I admitted.

"Can we go in and pet her?" asked Bernadette.

"Yeah, can we?" added Moosey.

"Sure," I said, then unlatched the gate and opened it. "Be careful, though. Don't chase her, and don't go into that corner of the pen." I pointed to the corner where the pig had obviously decided to do her business.

"Pew!" said Bernadette, making a face. "Don't worry!"

The two kids went cautiously into the pen and walked slowly up to the pig, who looked up at them, grunted a greeting, and went back to snouting up the soil. A moment later, Bernadette and Moosey were scratching the pig's back, tickling her under the chin, and feeding her an apple that Bernadette had smuggled in by way of her coat pocket. At a hundred and fifty pounds, Portia wasn't a huge pig, and her belly probably counted for half of her weight. She was a little over three feet long, I'd say — maybe about forty inches, nose to tail — and stood two feet high at the shoulder. Her head then sloped downward, in the manner of pigs, and large jowls framed her short face and snout. Her ears were large and hung forward, shading her eyes. The porcine mouth had a bow-like quality that made her appear as though she were smiling, and her eyes, beneath long, black lashes, were the most startlingly blue. She was, of course, covered with long, gray, curly hair.

Our pig was obviously used to children, or else just glad for the company, because she gave up her hunt for grubs and began frolicking with Moosey and Bernadette, chasing them around the pen, then being chased by them. She oinked happily and gave out a couple of squeals that first startled the kids, but then made them break into peals of laughter.

"When can we take her out for ruffles?" asked Moosey. He was kneeling beside the pig and hugging her around the neck.

"What's a ruffle?" asked Bernadette.

"Truffle," I said. "Truffles are like underground mushrooms. A pig can find them because their noses are so much more sensitive than ours. They can smell them under the ground. We might take her out next week. We're letting her get used to the place."

"Can we come?" asked Bernadette. "Hey, look at her tail!"

Like any happy dog, our Mangalitsa's long, straight tail was wagging back and forth to beat the band.

"She really likes us," said Moosey. "That's why she's wagging her tail."

"I think she does," I said. "It'd probably be good to take you two on our truffle hunt. She might find us what we want just to make you guys happy."

"Excellent!" said Bernadette.

* * *

"Any ideas on who kidnapped Rahab?" Meg asked as she whisked the dishes off the table and into the dishwasher.

"Not yet," I said. "We have this other thing, too. The dead Indian. We're operating under the assumption that they're connected somehow." Meg already knew about Kent Murphee's findings, and during a lovely meal of lamb curry, we'd dismissed the unpleasantness and talked about her upcoming business venture with Bev Greene — the nonprofit financial advisement company that she was very excited about starting.

We finished clearing the kitchen and repaired to the den, where I opened a bottle of Pinot Grigio that Bud had recommended and poured us each a glass. Then, as Meg curled up on the sofa with her book to the sounds of a Vivaldi violin concerto, I sat at my desk, pulled the chain to illuminate the green glass of my banker's light, and prepared myself for another foray into the world of noir wordsmithing.

"Is your mass finished?" Meg asked, suddenly looking up from her reading. "You need to finish your mass before you write any more of your detective story. It's due tomorrow."

I felt like I was back in junior high school. "Yes, ma'am," I said. "It is finished."

"All of it?" asked Meg.

"Well, the *Kyrie* and the *Sanctus*. The fraction anthem for tomorrow is Muffy's solo. *On Eagle's Wings*."

"No *Gloria*?"

"We don't do a *Gloria* during Lent," I reminded her.

"Yes, now I remember. Can I hear it?"

"No, you may not," I said. "It's a surprise."

Meg's face fell. "Oh, *no*."

"Have no fear," I said. "It is a work that is worthy of the Rev. Dr. Rosemary Pepperpot-Cohosh."

"Oh, *NO!*" Meg said. "What about your Lenten discipline? I'll win our bet. You'll have to go with me to the Catawba Colonic and Detox Institute for a week."

"Is that the name of it? No way! This *is* my discipline," I replied. "No snarky comments. No criticizing the sermon. No snide remarks about the liturgy or lack thereof. I shall go along with the church program, whatever that may be. I will not say anything negative and will be supportive in so far as I can. And I have been."

"So what is this mass, then? The one that's so awful that you won't let me see it?"

"I was asked — nay, almost commanded — by the Rev. Mother to compose such a mass. A musical setting on a common, well-known tune which the congregation will be familiar with. And I have done so."

"And you think that this won't come off as snarkiness? Your deliberate attempt to make Mother P eat her words?"

"It may well," I said. "But let me point out to you that, number one, this was not my idea, and, number two, since no one has actually seen the mass, especially you, it cannot be assumed that it is anything but genius."

"We'll all see it tomorrow," said Meg. "Then your discipline is broken. I'll win the bet!"

"Au contraire. Tomorrow is Sunday and Sundays are excluded from Lent."

"*What?*" Meg said. "I don't believe it."

"Look it up yourself," I said, "or better yet, count it up on your fingers. Forty days from Ash Wednesday to Easter. That doesn't include Sundays. If you count Sundays, it's forty-six."

"Well, who forgot to tell me that?" asked Meg. "You mean I could have been eating chocolate?"

"You still can. The first Sunday in Lent is tomorrow. You haven't missed anything."

"Wait a second! Now I get it. You won't let me see your mass because tonight it's still Lent. Tomorrow is Sunday and you're off the hook. I'm not sure God would like this. You're using a Lenten loophole."

"It's not a loophole. It's been this way for hundreds of years."

"Well, I rebuke it!"

"Rebuke away, my darling," I said. "I'm secure in my absolution."

"Harrumph!"

I smiled and turned to my typewriter. My only friend.

* * *

The Big Brickle had an office in the Goree Building on the thirteenth floor. Big had agreed to see me and Pedro, and, even though the henchman was holding a heater on us, I knew that a gun was nothing more than a two-edged sword liable at any moment to turn its back on the very hand that was biting it.

We were ushered into an office that looked as though it had been decorated by Martha Stewart's prison roommate, then thrown up on by the cast of "Hoarders." The Big Brickle was wallowing on her overstuffed couch, one hand clutching a crate of bonbons, and the other pushing the delicious morsels, interminably, into her gaping maw.

"Hi there, Big," said Pedro. "Haven't seen you in a while."

That was an understatement. Pedro had been avoiding the Big Brickle ever since he dumped her on Valentine's Day. To his credit, he did leave her a note tied to a barrel of chocolate syrup as a parting gift.

The Big Brickle looked around, saw us, and delicately belched a hairball into her silk hanky. She made a move to get up. The room was hot and the humidity made her massive thighs, under her lightweight cotton dress, stick together like two manatees in heat. They came apart with a smacking sound that gave me the shrieking willies.

"Long time no see, boys," said the Big Brickle in a voice like flat Guinness. "Seems like you only call on a girl when you want something."

To describe the Big Brickle as a "girl" would be like calling a musk ox "Betty." Her given name was Peanut — Peanut Brickle — and the last time I'd seen her, she was as mad as Jimmy Dean's pet pig, Flowerpot, when the pig inadvertently discovered the source of Jimmy's wealth by snouting open the secret door to the sausage factory, but Flowerpot's anger only lasted a few unkind, if ultimately life-changing moments, unlike the Big Brickle who really could hold a grudge, and if she was still carrying this particular grudge, I just hoped she'd take it out on Pedro. I was too pretty. Everyone said so.

Chapter 16

The choir was gathering in the loft for our pre-game rehearsal. Since we weren't doing the Great Litany in Procession, Mother P, obviously not a fan of the penitential rite, had seen no reason to change the service other than substituting the *Kyrie* for the *Gloria*. In other years, years when the Great Litany was relegated to Advent, we might have begun the first Lenten service with the Penitential Order that included a confession of sin and absolution. We had in past years included the decalog — a reading of the ten commandments — or else a summary of the law found in the Gospels of Matthew or Mark. Music for the occasion had always been fairly somber. But this year we were "blending." I wouldn't even be surprised if a forbidden "Alleluia" snuck in here or there.

"Are we singing the Psalm this morning?" asked Meg. She was the first soprano robed and in her seat by virtue of being married to the organist. The rest of the sopranos were filling in the section as they arrived.

"We are not," I said. "I was informed this morning that, during Lent, Rosemary would like to have the Psalms read antiphonally by the congregation. The text is in the bulletin."

"Then I'm singing it at communion!" added Muffy, who had found her seat. "Psalm 91. *On Eagle's Wings*. That's why I'm not wearing my choir robe." Muffy was in a lavender angora sweater that wouldn't have been out of place in a 1940's Jane Mansfield film. It was a tight fit, accentuating her curves, and she had demurely accented the look with a strand of pearls. She had on light-gray stretch pants and high heels. Her dark red hair exhibited a touch of Lenten restraint, seemingly not quite as teased, nor piled as high as usual.

"Varmit's downstairs," she announced. "He won't be singing this morning. He needs to run my mic and the CD player."

"Back to the Psalm," Elaine interrupted. "Antiphonally. How does that work?"

"I'm sure that Rosemary will give us direction," I answered. "But that's what it says in the bulletin. 'Antiphonally.' I presume that the right half of the congregation says the even verses and the left hand side does the odd ones."

"What do *we* do?" said Mark Wells. "We're in the back."

"Your choice," I said. "Now take out your anthem for the offertory and let's go through it. *Lord, For Thy Tender Mercy's Sake* by Richard Farrant."

"What the hell is *that* thing?" asked Marjorie, pointing down at the altar. Marjorie had found her chair and just noticed the new sanctuary decor.

"I believe it's a bald eagle," I answered. "And a squirrel."

"I know it's an eagle! *Why is it on the altar!?*" Marjorie was incensed. As a thirty-year member of the Altar Guild, although now long retired, she had standards.

"It's there because Mother P is preaching on Psalm 91," said Muffy. "The new members of the Altar Guild thought that it would help the congregation visualize the promise. For He will command His angels to guard you in all your ways. On their hands they will bear you up, so that you will not dash your foot against a stone. Also, there's eagles in there somewhere."

"So what?" said Marjorie. "When she preaches on Abraham and Isaac, is she going to throw a slaughtered goat up there?"

"Now, Marjorie," I said. "I believe that was a ram."

"Where's the squirrel come in?" said Randy.

"It came with the eagle," Meg said.

"Well, I don't like it!" spat Marjorie. "Not one little bit!"

Muffy pursed her lips and didn't comment further.

Joyce Cooper's face appeared at the choir loft door. "Hayden," she called. "I really hate to interrupt, but you need to come down here for a minute."

The look on her face told me she wasn't joking. I got up from the organ bench and wound my way through the sea of legs and billowing surplices, then descended the steps into the narthex. Joyce was waiting at the bottom of the stairs.

"Two Indians," she said and pointed through the door into the church. "Sorry. Native Americans. On the left side. See them? I went up and tried to talk to them. They stared right through me. Gave me the creeps. Something's not right."

"I'll talk to them," I said, moving into the church and making my way to the side aisle.

They saw me coming and both turned to face me, slowly, their hands coming to rest in front of them, hands clasped just above their belt buckles. They were both dressed in black, the taller of the two wearing a black suit, black silk shirt with no tie and black dress cowboy boots. He was a shade over six feet and powerfully built, heavy shoulders and a thick middle. Glancing at the hands in front of him, I saw large, calloused knuckles and several gold rings. He had on a gold necklace as well, a chain with a golden arrowhead that dangled onto his hairless chest. The shorter of the Indians was not that much shorter, but he was slighter. His face was meaner and his small, black eyes followed my movements with intent. He was wearing black, skinny jeans and a black turtleneck, and dress cowboy boots with silver tips on the toes that looked exactly like the one I'd seen decorating the boot of Johnny Talltrees. Both men had long, black hair, slicked, and tied back in ponytails. They looked dangerous. They were dangerous.

"Gentlemen," I said as I approached. The church was empty except for the choir, watching from the loft, and Joyce, who was standing nervously by one of the back doors leading to the narthex.

One of them, the smaller one, nodded at me but didn't say anything.

"My name is Hayden Konig. I'm the Chief of Police." I held out my badge, then slipped it back into my pocket. "I also work here at the church. Is there anything I can do for you?"

"No, Chief," said the smaller one. "Thanks just the same. We were looking for someone. We heard he might be here."

"Johnny Talltrees?" I asked.

The smaller Indian's eyebrows went up a hair, but other than that his expression didn't change. "You know Johnny?" he said.

"I'm afraid I have some bad news for you. Johnny's dead. We're looking into the circumstances surrounding his death. I'm sorry for your loss."

The smaller Indian gave a shrug. The taller one stood stock still. Then the small one said, "No loss to me. We wondered what happened to him."

"We?"

"We, his employers. We represent the Friendly Gaming Club in Cherokee."

"And your name is ..."

"I am called George Gist." I had no doubt he was making that up.

"And you aren't looking for Talltrees?" I asked.

"Not particularly," he said. "We are looking for someone else."

"Someone in particular?"

George Gist shrugged.

"Well, this is a church and we will be having a worship service here shortly. If you're not here to join us in worship, I'll have to ask you to wait elsewhere."

George Gist considered this for a moment, the gave a small nod. "We will wait for him elsewhere."

"If you mean anyone harm," I said, "it might be best if you go on back to Cherokee." I gave him a hard look, then shifted my gaze to the tall Indian. He hadn't moved. Hadn't blinked as far as I could tell.

"We just need to have a word. As I said, we'll wait for him elsewhere." George Gist glided past me and was followed by his confederate. They walked to the door, looked back into the church one last time, then disappeared outside. I followed them back down the side aisle at a reasonable distance and looked out the front doors. They were both standing in the park, facing the church, hands clasped in front of them, watching.

I started to climb the stairs back into the loft when Joyce grabbed hold of my coattail.

"What did they want?" she asked.

"They were looking for their friend," I lied. "You know, the one that we found in the alley."

"Oh," said Joyce, and considered my answer. "They certainly look scary."

"Yes, they do," I replied. "But looks aren't everything."

* * *

"Back to work, everyone."

"Who were those guys?" Rhiza Walker whispered. "Are they still here?"

"They've left," I said, then gave the choir the same story that I'd just given Joyce. Friends of Johnny Talltrees. "Now let's get to the music, shall we?"

By the time we'd sung through the short offertory anthem, corrected a few mistakes, then sung through it again, our jollity had returned and the visitors were forgotten. Since we had no

Psalm to practice and no communion anthem to contend with, we were through in record time.

"Now," I said, "it's time to rehearse our new service music." I took a stack of photocopied music off the top of the organ and passed it over to Bev Greene, who handed it down the rows of singers. As they looked at the title page, their mouths dropped open, and more than a few snorts and coughs uttered forth from the ranks.

"Since this is new," I said, "the choir will be singing it alone this morning. Then next week, we'll have congregational copies as well, and they can sing along."

"Has anyone seen this yet?" asked an incredulous Fred May, our Senior Warden. "And by 'anyone,' I mean Mother P?"

"That's a good question," I said. "I admit that Meg made me feel a bit guilty about writing this. So, in a spate of Lenten remorse, I called Rosemary in this morning and played it for her."

"It's true," said Meg sadly. "He did. I was there."

"And?" said Fred.

"She loved it," said Meg, and crossed herself. "God forgive us."

"It's full steam ahead," I said. "*Missa di Poli Woli Doodle* with a tip o' the hat to Leon Redbone. Let's sing through it, shall we?"

I played an introduction and the choir entered in four parts. It was a composition worthy of the best of the bad Renaissance composers. It began with a homophonic, or hymn-like, section, all the parts moving together, and then a lovely polyphonic ending of each stanza reminiscent of Palestrina. As in all traditional *Kyries*, there were three sections: *Lord have mercy, Christ have mercy, Lord have mercy*. The choir sang:

Lord have mercy, now we pray,
Singing Poli Woli Doodle, Kyrie;
Lord have mercy, now we pray,
Singing Poli Woli Doodle, Kyrie;
Kyrie, Kyrie, Kyrie, I've gone astray;
Hear my reverent confession,
and forgive me my transgression,
Singing Poli Woli Doodle, Kyrie.

The second verse was the same, but now in a minor key and a little slower.

Christ have mercy, now we pray,
Singing Poli Woli Doodle, Kyrie;
Christ have mercy, now we pray,
Singing Poli Woli Doodle Kyrie.
Kyrie, Kyrie, Kyrie, I've gone astray;
When I hear my Lord a-calling,
then I find my sins appalling,
Singing Poli Woli Doodle, Kyrie.

I had to stop playing at this point because several of the altos had succumbed to attacks of laughter and had fallen out of their chairs. "Very nice," I said as they struggled back into their seats. "Let's do this last verse unaccompanied, please."

Lord have mercy, now we pray,
Singing Poli Woli Doodle, Kyrie;
Lord have mercy, now we pray,
Singing Poli Woli Doodle, Kyrie;
Kyrie, Kyrie, Kyrie, I've gone astray;
And at last I know I'm shriven,
and my sins have been forgiven.
Singing Poli Woli Doodle, Kyrie.

"Ow, ow, ow!" yelped Martha. "My side hurts! Stop singing!"

"I like it," said Muffy. "It has some bounce to it and it's easy to learn."

"You will have a lot to answer for on the Day of Judgement," said Bob Solomon. "I'm not sure even Jesus can get you out of this one."

I bowed my head and placed my hand humbly over my heart. "Only doing my job." I looked across the choir and returned their collective smiles with one of my own. "Now let's sing through the *Sanctus*."

* * *

The service began, and the choir processed to our opening hymn, as per usual, and then climbed the stairs to the loft and found their seats. Mother P read the collect.

"Almighty God, whose blessed Son was led by the Spirit to be tempted by Satan; Come quickly to help us who are assaulted by many temptations; and, as you know the weaknesses of each of us, let each one find you mighty to save; through Jesus Christ your Son our Lord, who lives and reigns with you and the Holy Spirit, one God, now and for ever."

"Amen," answered the congregation.

The choir sang the new *Kyrie* to stunned silence.

"Now, will the children please come forward for the Children's Moment?" said Mother P, smiling happily.

Children's Moments had never gone particularly well at St. Barnabas. In fact, we'd done away with them, sending the kids out to their own service in the chapel during the second hymn and having them return in time for communion. This seemed to work well for our previous rector and had been Mother P's practice during her first few months in residence. Now it seemed that Kimberly Walnut, an outspoken proponent of the Children's Moment, had persuaded the rector to give it a go once again.

Ten or so preschool and kindergarten children wandered haplessly up to the front of the church and stood in front of Mother P. When Moosey and Bernadette and their crew were young enough to take part in the Children's Moment, every Sunday was a new exercise in terror for the priest and an opportunity for hilarity across the congregation. Now that those kids had graduated to the upper grades, and not having had a "Children's Moment" for a number of years, we didn't know what to expect. Still, the congregation was hopeful, and all leaned forward in their seats, vying for a good view of the festivities.

"How many of you know what this is?" said Mother P, pointing at the giant bird on the altar.

"Well, duh!" said a towheaded kid whom I recognized as Charlie Whitman. I knew his mother and father quite well. "It's a squirrel, of course."

At this the other kids giggled, and the congregation sat back in their pews, content in the knowledge that this was only going to get better.

"No," said Mother P, "I mean the eagle."

"An eagle got my kitty, I think," said a little preschool girl whom I didn't know. She was dressed in a light-pink pinafore over a white dress with loads of ruffles. "That's what Daddy said."

"Yes, well, eagles are large birds, and they sometimes do catch ... um ... smaller animals ... er ... for sustenance."

"To *eat* them?" asked the little girl in horror.

"Of course to eat them!" said Charlie, pointing at the eagle. The raptor's white-tipped wings spread across the entire width of the altar. Its white head was horrifying, and its eyes and beak bespoke metaphoric death to anything that might fall into the grasp of its fearsome talons, from America's most powerful enemies to rodents with dental issues.

"Look at that squirrel!" Charlie continued. "That eagle's not takin' him to a picnic, y'know!" The little girl started to whimper.

"Wait," said Mother P, trying to salvage her story. "God is like an eagle. He'll carry you up ... "

"Like *that?*" interrupted another little boy, pointing at the taxidermied rodent, its terror so vividly and excellently interpreted by Bear Niederman: eyes wide, lips peeled back in a horrific grimace. "*No, thanks!*"

"Daddy says that my kitty went to heaven," sniffed the little girl. "Will I see her when I get to heaven?"

"Yeah," said another, younger boy. "What about my dead gerbil? Will I get to see my gerbil? It wasn't an eagle that got him, though. Mom said it was parasites."

"Well, we don't believe that animals go to heaven," said Mother P, now looking around but unable to escape. "Heaven is just for people." This was a theological can of worms that she didn't want to open, not during the Children's Moment. "But let's get back to the eagle ... "

"So my kitty's not in heaven?" sobbed the girl. "Daddy told me the eagle took her to heaven."

"Just like God'll do," said Charlie, nodding grimly. "He'll swoop down and snatch you up when you least expect it."

Mother P glared at Charlie, then turned back to the girl. "No, sweetie, your kitty's not in heaven. And God won't take *you* to heaven either." She looked confused for a moment. "No, wait," she said. "He will, someday. What I mean is ..."

"If that cat's not in heaven, then it's in hell, right?" said Charlie, coming to the obvious conclusion and willing to pin down the rector on the unshakable tenets of her faith. He spun on his heel, pointed at the younger boy and yelled, "Along with your stupid gerbil!"

"My gerbil is *not* in hell!" yelled the boy. "You take that back!" He lunged across the carpeted aisle at Charlie, his fists clenched and murder in his eyes. The other boys chose sides in a heartbeat and didn't hesitate to leap into the fray in support of their comrades. By the looks of it, this was a long-standing feud between the two boys and any excuse to renew their animosity would be acted upon.

"Waaaahhh!" cried the kitten girl, and the other three girls in the group loudly joined her in loud pangs of sympathetic grief for the poor cat, forever doomed to scratch in the flaming litter-box of eternal damnation. "Waaaahhh!"

As soon as Mother P had pronounced that all pets would, in fact, *not* be going to heaven, a couple of mothers had begun moving unobtrusively to the front of the church via the side aisles, sensing that this Children's Moment, like so many others, was not going to end well. Now, with Mother P frozen in disbelief at the sobs and at the brawl in front of her, the two parents waded into the mob and separated the warring youngsters. Julie Whitman, Charlie's mother, grabbed Charlie and the other boy both by an ear, pulled them apart, and marched them down the center aisle to the youngsters' squealing protests.

"You just wait until I get you home, Charlie Whitman!" she hissed. "And you, too, Howard! Your mother is going to hear about this!"

The girls and the other combatants were corralled, pacified, and herded out the side door into the choir robing area, finally heading, we presumed, back to their classrooms. Mother P stood at the top of the chancel steps. She raised her arms in a sort of pathetic gesture and muttered, "God is like this eagle."

"Nice!" said Bev, crossing her arms and giving herself a little hug.

* * *

It was during communion that the unspeakable happened. Muffy had disappeared from the choir loft during the Prayers of the People to ready herself for her Special Music. *On Eagle's Wings*, written by Michael Joncas, had been around since the 70s. It is now considered a "standard" in most Praise and Worship services. Muffy and Varmit had no trouble in procuring the accompaniment track recorded in the correct key by the Nashville Philharmonic Digital Orchestra and backed up by the Holy Faith Word of God Tabernacle Choir.

The communion elements, the bread and wine, had been placed in front of the eagle — the only place for them, really — and this meant that Mother P had to do her celebrating in front of the altar with her back to the congregation, rather than vice-versa. It wasn't difficult to hear her — she had a loud and authoritative voice and the flat mic on the altar had been turned around to accommodate her — but it was a bit disconcerting nevertheless and reminiscent of the old pre-Vatican II days. The choir sang the *PWD Sanctus* at the appropriate spot and headed down to take communion. I stayed up in the choir loft, noodling around on the hymn tune *Aberystwyth*, planning to play until Muffy was ready to begin her tribute. I did notice that neither the children nor Kimberly Walnut had come back in for communion. As the choir came back up the side aisles toward the loft, Muffy stepped up beside the eagle, took the microphone from where it had been hidden under the tail feathers, draped the black cord artistically around her other hand and waited for the music to begin.

It was a sound that hadn't been heard in St. Barnabas for twenty years, at least as far as I knew. We didn't sing with taped music, and we didn't sing with microphones. The rector and the lay readers did use mics and they were placed where they'd do the most good: on the two lecterns and on the altar. We'd had a clip-on mic for the priest at one point, but it went horribly wrong in a bathroom incident when the priest forgot to turn it off. Since then, and because St. Barnabas is fairly small and acoustically well designed, the stationary mics have been more than adequate. Our architect, however, did allow for the fact that we might want other mics on occasion, and so jacks had been placed in auspicious points in the chancel. Varmit had plugged Muffy's mic cord into one of these. She clicked the microphone on with an audible pop that echoed through the building as the music swelled. The speakers that had been put in the church were first rate. The amplification was state-of-the-art. Unfortunately, the orchestra was a bad imitation done with computer generated sounds, and the excellent sound system did nothing to disguise that fact.

The performance was something that Muffy had obviously rehearsed. It was staged as well as any country music video choreographer could have done. Muffy waited for the introduction, then sang the opening verse, all her choral training thrown to the wind, her Loretta Lynn twang echoing forth in all its rural splendor.

She closed her eyes in prayer, both hands clasping the microphone in front of her, then she opened her eyes and moved slowly down left, away from the altar and toward the baptismal font.

And he will raise you up on eagle's wings,
Bear you on the breath of dawn ...

Mother P's sermon did have something about Living Water in it. I wasn't sure of her point or what it had to do with the eagle and the squirrel, but it was my Lenten Discipline to give her the benefit of the doubt. Besides, she had more than enough explaining to do to the vestry after this service was over. It didn't occur to me that anything was amiss as Muffy went over to the font and began another verse, the one that she'd written to go with the sermon.

For to his people he's given a command
to walk in his footsteps always:
Come to the Living Water,
Come and be restored.

She closed her eyes again, this time holding the mic in her right hand and reaching into the font with the other.

And he will raise you up on eagle's wings,

She dipped into the water and raised a handful of liquid grace shoulder high, letting it spill dramatically from her fingers back into the font. She reached down into the pool again.

Bear you on the breath of dawn ...

That's as far as she got. There was a loud, horrible buzzing sound followed by a loud *bang*, a bright flash that silhouetted Muffy for a split second, and then the lights in the sanctuary went dark. Although there was daylight coming in through the stained glass, the sudden change in the ambient light inside the church made it difficult to see. The emergency lights popped on a second later and the fire alarm started buzzing loudly. Some smoke was visible in the front of the church, by the chancel steps.

"Everyone outside!" shouted Fred from the balcony. "Don't push. Leave by the nearest exit."

I was already down the stairs and racing for the baptismal font.

Chapter 17

Muffy was dead.

Kent, the coroner, put the cause of death as electrocution. I contacted my electrical contractor that Sunday afternoon and had him come and look at equipment. Terry Shager had been doing electrical work all his life. He'd lost all his left toes and the hair on the left side of his head to a high voltage accident a decade ago, but he was the best electrician in town. Terry came in the front door of St. Barnabas wearing his faded blue bib overalls and a button-down, long-sleeved white shirt with a yellow tie. He listed slightly to the left as he marched down the aisle in his heavy, rubber-soled work boots. His gray hair was cut short on the right side of his head and he was still hopeful, after these ten long years, that the missing hair might grow back on the left. In anticipation of this, and under Noylene's supervision, he rubbed his scalp every night with a healthy dose of Italian vinaigrette salad dressing. His blue eyes twinkled and he was usually smiling, although his walrus mustache hung down past his lower lip so sometimes it was tough to tell.

"Hayden," he said as he limped in. "How you doin'?"

"I'm okay, Terry. Did you hear what happened this morning?"

"Sure did. Sorry about Muffy. I worked for her and Varmit over at the fur farm when they were setting up."

"Yeah," I said. "Terrible thing. Could you take a look? Be careful, though."

"I'm always careful," Terry said, "these days. Only a year 'til retirement, and I need all the hair I've got left. There's this woman I'm thinking about asking out. Stacey."

"Stacey down at the Ag Center?"

"Nah. Stacey down at St. Germaine Federal Bank." He got a sly look in his eye. "Gives me a lollipop every time I come in."

I nodded. "I know Stacey. Redhead, right? Want me to put in a good word for you?"

Terry's shoulders shook with an embarrassed chuckle. "Well, okay. If you wouldn't mind." He looked around the church and said, "So what's the deal?"

I pointed toward the baptismal font. "Muffy was singing into the microphone, then dipped her hand in the water and that was it." I thought for a moment. "She didn't get the jolt until she dipped her hand into the water the *second* time."

"I'll find out what happened," promised Terry. "Gimme a half-hour or so."

He was as good as his word. Terry's verdict was that the wiring in the amp was improperly done: one extraneous wire that should have been grounded, providing an energized connection to the mic cable shielding, and since we hadn't ever used the amp with a corded microphone, no one had any idea of the problem. Because the outer casing of the mic was hard plastic, it was the metal on/off switch that got all the juice. When Muffy reached into the font the second time, her thumb came in contact with the switch and the electrical circuit was complete. It was a terrible accident. The amp hadn't been plugged into a GFCI plug — a ground fault circuit interrupter — because the electrician hadn't seen the need to install one. Not his fault, said Terry. The outlet was nowhere near any water and the building code didn't require one.

"Any chance of foul play?" I asked him.

"Sure," replied Terry thoughtfully. "Always a chance." He showed me the offending ungrounded wire. It didn't mean anything to me.

"Lookee here. If someone moved this ground from this here screw over to this one, that'd do it."

"Does it look tampered with?" I said.

He squinted hard at the components in front of him. "Nah," he said. "I don't guess so."

After Muffy's accident, Varmit was beside himself. He'd made it to the baptismal font before I had, knowing something had gone horribly wrong when the amp had shorted out. The flash that we'd all seen in the sanctuary had been duplicated at the sound system console in the sacristy where Varmit had been monitoring Muffy's performance. He burst through the side door, saw the lovely Muffy laid out in her lavender angora sweater and gray stretch pants, and almost leapt upon her. She looked utterly beatific in repose, the one exception being her carefully-coiffed hairdo that had become unstrung and was standing on end like a bright-red version of Buckwheat's bouffant in the *Little Rascals*. The only reason that Varmit hadn't leapt upon her is because I arrived at the scene a half-second later and yanked him back, then performed CPR on Muffy for the next ten minutes until the ambulance arrived. I had been hoping that someone, anyone, had called 911, since I didn't take the time to do so. I needn't have worried. Forty people reported the incident.

The CPR was a vain hope and I knew it about three minutes in. There was no pulse, no breath. I kept it up for Varmit's sake and let the EMTs carry her out with an oxygen mask over her mouth. They took her to the hospital to have her pronounced. Varmit rode along in the back, holding Muffy's hand, the picture of a grieving husband.

The two Indians had watched in stony silence from the middle of the park as Muffy was loaded into the ambulance and her husband climbed in beside her. If Varmit noticed them, he gave no indication. They watched the ambulance drive off, then stared at me for a long moment, turned and walked off in the direction of the courthouse.

Chapter 18

The Slab Café was busy on Monday morning and the breakfast talk was about Muffy LeMieux.

"It was the most gruesome thing I've ever seen," said Annette, holding court at the table by the front window. "Muffy was singing one minute and the next minute she was lit up like a Christmas tree. Bizuurp! Bang! That was all she wrote."

I sighed. Nancy and Dave were both at the table with me in the back. We could hear Annette from there and we were doing our best to ignore her. Pete came out of the kitchen and plopped down in the fourth chair.

"Did you get any details from Terry Shager?" he asked.

"Yeah," I said, and filled him in. "It looks like a freak accident," I concluded. "We hadn't ever used that mic jack because we never needed to. Plus, who knew she was going to stick her hand in the water? It was a series of unfortunate events culminating in tragedy."

"Will the funeral be at St. Barnabas?" Dave asked.

"I haven't heard," I said.

Cynthia, seemingly tired of filling Annette's coffee cup, put the pot back on the warmer, untied her apron, took it off, and slung it over an empty chair. She dragged up a chair from an adjacent table and sat down.

"Okay," she said, "I've heard the story five times now. I don't want to hear it again."

"She has a new audience every ten minutes or so," Nancy observed.

"Is that it for the Hootenanny service?" asked Pete. "It's over?"

"I seriously doubt it," I replied. "Probably just a setback."

"Might this be construed as God not being in favor of blended worship?" said Pete.

"There are two schools of thought on such Divine Intervention," I said. "Yes, there are those who point out that maybe God doesn't care for blended worship at all and that's why this happened. Holy retribution, if you will. Then there are those who hold that no, it was Satan that did it, because Satan knows that God *loves* blended worship and this was a way to sabotage it."

"Wow," said Dave. "Really?"

"You'd be amazed," I said. "Of course, it could have been an accident."

"Any progress on the Rahab Fabergé-DuPont kidnapping?" asked Cynthia. "Or how about the murder of Johnny Talltrees? There's a City Council meeting tonight, you know. I thought I might fill them in on your progress."

"No news," said Nancy. "No clues. Rahab's safe, though."

"Oh, by the way," said Dave, "that reminds me. Brother Hog is requesting police protection at the tent revival on Thursday in Valle Crucis. I got the call this morning. He's afraid that the kidnapper might try it again since it went so well the first time."

Nancy snorted. "Police protection?"

"Little Rahab is preaching his first sermon," I said. "North Carolina's premiere Baby Evangelist. That's what the flyer says. They were all over town as of this morning."

"I've never heard of such a thing!" said Cynthia. "You can't even understand that baby. He can't talk yet."

"Brother Hog will be interpreting. Unknown tongues, you see. Very Biblical."

"It's a new world," Pete said.

"Cynthia!" called Annette. "May we get some more coffee, please?"

Cynthia growled, got back to her feet and disappeared into the kitchen.

"I happen to have something," said Nancy, "just so the morning won't be a complete bust."

She opened a leather folder and pulled out a piece of paper with a picture on it. "I did some checking on this George Gist."

"Not his real name?" I said.

"No, but he may not be as clever as he thinks he is. I did some checking on the internet and it turns out that George Gist was the name of an old Cherokee warrior. Actually, his name was Sequoyah. It turns out that there's a George Sequoyah who lives in Cherokee. So I checked with the Cherokee police and they emailed his sheet and picture. This him?"

She pushed the paper across the table at me. I spun it around and looked into the flat black eyes of the smaller of the two Indians I'd talked to in the church.

"That's him," I said with a grin. "Nice work."

Nancy smiled back. "He works for a two-bit casino that specializes in giving credit, then charging one hundred twenty percent interest on the debt. The other guy is probably Jango Watie. Big guy. Lots of muscle, doesn't say much. They work as a team."

"That sounds like the other guy," I said. "You have a picture?"

"They didn't have one," said Nancy. "Not yet. They're working on it."

"Isn't it illegal to charge that much interest?" asked Pete.

"Maybe here," said Nancy. "But the casino is on the reservation. Sequoyah's been charged with assault, battery, sexual assault, and solicitation. A murder charge is pending, although it probably won't stick."

"Has he done any time in the big house?" asked Pete.

Nancy perused her sheet. "Three years total. Mostly, though, no one testifies."

"Any idea who they were looking for here?" Pete asked.

"Nope," I said. "He didn't say."

My cell phone rang, and I looked at the display. It was Marilyn at the church.

"Hi, Marilyn," I said. "What's up?" Marilyn had my cell number. No one else at the church did and that's the way I wanted it. The only reason I'd given Marilyn my number is that she never called. Well, hardly ever.

"You'd better get over here right now," she whispered. "Something's up. There are a couple of goons standing outside Mother P's door."

"Are they Indians? Umm ... excuse me. Native Americans?"

"No. White guys. Green uniforms. And they have badges."

"I'm on the way."

***

By the time I'd gotten over to the church, Marilyn was flagging me down from the side door leading into the office complex.

"They went into the sanctuary," she said.

"Did they say what they wanted?"

Marilyn shook her head. "Nope. They just came in and got Mother P and marched her into the sanctuary. She looked pretty scared. Is this something about Muffy's accident?"

"I don't know. I can't see how it would be. I'll go check on her."

"Well, you'd better fill me in," she said, then disappeared back into the building.

I walked around to the front of the church and entered through one of the red double-doors. Red doors are a common tradition in the Episcopal Church. Historically the red doors of a church were a symbol of sanctuary. Those in need would not be captured or harmed inside the holy walls of the church, which offered physical and spiritual protection. People who passed through the red doors were safe. I wondered if this protection would extend to Rosemary Pepperpot-Cohosh.

Walking through the narthex and into the nave, I noticed all the lights on and remembered that Terry had promised to come in early this morning and reset all the breakers, making sure there were no more hazards. Mother P was standing in front of the altar with the two men. Both of them were tall and they turned when they heard me coming down the center aisle. They were both dressed in dark green, matching coats and trousers, with light brown shirts and black ties. The emblems on their left arms identified them as North Carolina Wildlife enforcement officers. They were both wearing silver badges and had handguns holstered on their hips. One of them had a Smokey Bear hat in his hand. "Ooo," I said to myself. I knew what was about to happen.

"Hayden!" called Mother P. "Thank God!"

"Good morning, Rosemary. Officers." They did not return the greeting.

"I'm Chief Konig. St. Germaine Police Department," I said to the agents. "You're here about the eagle?"

The bald eagle and its unfortunate-looking prey were still on top of the altar, sitting on the unfurled American flag.

"Yessir," said one of the agents. "My name is Bill Henderson." He indicated the other man. "This is Gary O'Shea."

"Tell them that this eagle is Bear Niederman's," gushed Mother P. "I have nothing to do with it."

"Mr. Niederman claims that he gave this eagle to the church," said Officer Henderson, "and that you accepted it willingly."

"But I didn't kill it!" cried Rosemary.

"Here's the receipt that Ms. Pepperpot-Cohosh gave to Mr. Niederman," the agent said to me. He reached into his breast pocket and produced a piece of paper that he handed across the aisle. I opened it and read it, knowing perfectly well what it said.

> *One bald eagle, stuffed, given to St. Barnabas Church, St. Germaine, North Carolina, by Bear Niederman.*
> *Value - $2000*
> *signed: The Rev. Dr. Rosemary Pepperpot-Cohosh, rector*

"I didn't kill it!" Rosemary wailed again.

"Doesn't matter," said Officer Henderson, who was doing all the talking. "The Bald and Golden Eagle Protection Act prohibits anyone without a permit issued by the Secretary of the Interior, from taking bald eagles, including their parts, nests, or eggs."

"Well, there you are," said Rosemary. "Obviously, I didn't do it. It's Bear you want!"

I was amazed at how quickly she threw her parishioner and cohort under the bus.

Officer Henderson went on. "The Act also provides criminal penalties for persons who take, possess, purchase, barter, offer to sell, purchase, or barter, at any time or any manner, any bald eagle, alive or dead, or any part, nest, or egg thereof. Bear Niederman is already under arrest and has willingly offered to testify against you as the instigator of the crime."

"What?" Rosemary's mouth dropped open.

"Of course, the church is liable as well, but we'll deal with that in due time. For now, you're under arrest. You'll have to come with us."

"*What!?*" Rosemary shrieked again.

"Do you have a warrant?" I asked.

"We don't need a warrant," said the silent agent, Officer O'Shea. "Public building. No search required. Admission of guilt right here on the receipt."

"Is that right?" Rosemary asked me, terror in her eyes.

"I'm afraid so," I said.

"What will happen to me?"

Officer O'Shea answered. "For a first offense, you're looking at a fine of up to one hundred thousand dollars, two hundred thousand for organizations, and that includes churches, imprisonment for one year, or both." He shifted his gaze to me and looked at me with the hard eyes of a fresh game warden carrying all the conviction of youth. "And you should be ashamed. You, an officer of the court. You know the law. You should have reported this as soon as you found out, or at least stopped this magnificent bird from being put on display."

I watched as Mother P's legs went to rubber. Officer Henderson had a hand under her arm and held her steady.

"I am sorry," I said to the officer. "Truly."

"The state will make an example of this," Officer Henderson said, and quickly snapped a pair of handcuffs on Rosemary. "And this is a federal offense as well, so I'm sure they'll be making their own case. Make no mistake: eagle poaching will stop in this part of the Blue Ridge."

He tugged Rosemary down the aisle toward the front doors, while his partner gathered up the eagle and the squirrel and followed them. The flag was dragged off the altar and dropped to the floor. I stooped to pick it up.

"Why didn't you tell me?" Rosemary cried. "Hayden! Why didn't you tell me?"

"I did tell you," I called after her. "Remember?"

"Why didn't you tell me louder?" she wailed.

Chapter 19

"Get this," said Nancy. "Varmit LeMieux came in this morning after you went over to the church and wanted to know where he could get his hands on Muffy's death certificate."

"That was fast," I said.

"I told him to go down to the coroner to get it."

"Did he say why he wanted it?"

"Only one reason I can think of," said Nancy.

I nodded. "Life insurance."

"Time to take a look?"

"Oh, yeah," I said.

* * *

"I suppose you're going to deny everything," said Meg. "I talked to Nancy this afternoon. Mother P is still in jail down in Boone."

Pete and Cynthia had come over for a late Monday night supper after the City Council meeting. Pete still went to the Council meetings, since they were open meetings, but sat in the back and hardly ever said anything. Also joining us was Meg's mother, Ruby. We were all sitting at the kitchen table enjoying a feast of pan-fried chicken, mashed potatoes, and all the fixin's.

"I heard about the priest!" said Cynthia. "I didn't know about the eagle. What was she thinking?"

"She's not from around here," said Pete, "or anywhere else that has eagles. She's from one of those flat, midwestern states, right?"

"Iowa," Meg said. "They have plenty of bald eagles in Iowa." Then she turned to me. "You called the game warden, didn't you? And remember, you can't lie during Lent."

"I can, too. There's no sanction against lying during Lent," I said. "My discipline is to go along with Rosemary's program, whatever that may be. I will not say anything negative about the liturgy, the sermons, or any other goings on, and I will be supportive in as far as I can. I believe that I have stuck to my discipline within the spirit, as well as the letter, of the law. You shall lose your bet."

"There!" Meg crowed. "You might just as well have admitted it."

"I admit nothing. In fact, it was I who gave Rosemary the name of a good lawyer, but Judge Adams is a hard case concerning eagles. He remanded her into custody until her hearing tomorrow afternoon. No bail 'til the hearing."

"No bail?" said Pete. "Really? No bail?"

"The last that I heard, Herb Cohosh was raising a big stink over at the county courthouse," I said. "I don't expect that it will do much good."

"What's the bet?" asked Cynthia.

"If Meg loses, she has to learn belly dancing," I said.

"I do not!" Meg answered. "Here's the deal. If I win, Hayden has to go with me on a health week. A week at a medical facility specializing in fasting and cleansing the body with colonics, stomach massages, aromatherapy — you know, stuff like that."

"Sounds heavenly," said Cynthia.

"You're kidding, right?" said Pete. "A week? That'll kill you."

"Exactly," I said, "but if I *keep* my Lenten discipline, then Meg loses and she has to cook hamburgers three times a week for seven weeks."

"Wow!" said Pete. "That sounds great."

I licked my lips in anticipation. "Buffalo burgers, Swiss cheese and bacon burgers, chili burgers ..."

"Lamb burgers, garlic and onion burgers ..." added Pete.

"Cream cheese jalapeño burgers, horseradish burgers, Cajun burgers ..."

"Oh, stop it," said Meg. "If you squealed on the priest, you lose."

"*If* I squealed, and I'm not saying I did, then I do *not* lose. I went along with her program. Not only that, but I tried, oh-so-nicely, to talk her out of it."

"He's right, dear," said Ruby. "Might as well face the facts."

"Fine," Meg huffed, then decided to change the subject. "Speaking of squealing, how's our pig?"

"She's great," said Pete. "Rooting around the yard to beat the band. I'll be taking her out tomorrow afternoon for a trial run."

"Excellent," I said, rubbing my hands together. "We just need two pounds of truffles to make our money back."

"Wanna come?" asked Pete.

"I don't think so. I have all these crimes to solve, you see."

"Yeah," said Pete. "When it rains, it pours."

We ate our fried chicken, finished the rest of our supper, then repaired to the living room. Meg filled our glasses with a nice Cabernet and we settled back into our chairs. Baxter had been relegated to the outdoors and was now sitting on the back deck peering at us through the plate glass window. Archimedes seemed to know when we had guests and had made himself scarce as usual.

"Have you seen that possum over at Mildred's?" I asked Ruby. "I figured you would have shot it by now."

"I was going to, but it had a collar on," said Ruby. "I swear. That Mildred Kibbler couldn't see a woodpecker tapping her on her nose. She's blind as a dang bat."

"So it was a pet possum?" said Meg.

"The possum's name is Possum Joe. He belongs to Penny Trice, who lives behind Mildred. He got out of his cage, disappeared, and Penny's been handing out flyers up and down the street. She's raised him from a pup."

"Did she find him?"

"He was sitting in Mildred's tree, pretty as you please. I reached up and plucked him out, then called Penny and she came and got him."

"Glad you didn't shoot him," said Pete. "That would have been terrible. That is, unless there was some kind of stew involved."

"Oh my gosh, Cynthia!" Meg said suddenly. "Don't you have play rehearsal tonight? I forgot all about it."

"There's no rehearsal. Mr. Christopher is meeting with the board of directors. With Muffy gone, I think we're going to have to postpone it a few weeks. Maybe cancel it altogether. She had the lion's share of the dialogue."

"Can't they get someone to step in?" Meg asked.

"I guess they could," said Cynthia. "But no one's heart is really in it at this point."

"Perhaps they could do a dramatized version of one of your stories?" Pete suggested. "How's the new one coming, by the way?"

"Splendidly," I said. "In fact, since St. Patrick's Day is on Wednesday, I've incorporated a little bit of Ireland into the narrative."

"Do tell," said Ruby with a laugh. "A reading, perhaps?"
"I'd be happy to," I said.
"Oh, *no!*" moaned Meg.

I walked over to my desk and picked up the stack of papers that were accumulating beside the typewriter. "Chapter One," I said, then proceeded to catch everyone up on the story before including my latest.

* * *

"Don't eat us, Big," I said. "I know Pedro did you wrong, but it ain't the end of the world."

"Yeah, it is," Big grunted sadly. "Apocalypto videre. I'm drownin' my sorrows in bonbons. We've only got a couple of months left."

"That's what I heard," I said. "You know why we're here? Carrie Oakey is dead."

The Big Brickle snorked another handful of bonbons. Bonbons were nothing to her. Big was known to gobble full-grown guinea pigs when she was in the mood, then wash them down with Diet Coke when she knew perfectly well that she shouldn't mix hairy products with artificial sweeteners.

"It was only a matter of time," she said. "The leprechauns are on the move. They're all heading to Sarsaparilla for the Feast of St. Quetzalcoatl. In another week or so there won't be a boys choir in the country that can sing "Missa di Poli Woli Doodle," much less "Ecce Uvulare" on Ash Wednesday. Not that it'll matter much, one way or the other," she added depressedly.

"So why would one of them winkles want to off Carrie Oakey?" I asked.

The Big Brickle shrugged. "No reason I know of. She's the one who wanted the leprechauns out of the choirs anyway. Maybe she knew something I don't."

"Maybe," agreed Pedro. "Thanks for not killing us, by the way."

Big waved at us absently, her arm wattles catching the breeze and waggling like one of those inflatable advertising tube characters you see at pawn shops, all the while making that disgusting flapping sound that one of those toy push-ducks with the rubber feet makes when you scooch it across the kitchen floor.

"So, what happens on the Feast of St. Quetzalcoatl?" Pedro said.

"Well, the Mayan calendar runs out, for one thing," she answered.

"Anything else?" I asked, setting my jaw and preparing for the worst, like that time in junior high when I was playing spin-the-bottle and the bottle pointed at Debbie who played clarinet in the band, but it really wasn't that bad, considering her mustache and all.

"That's not enough?"

"We don't buy into all that Mayan hooey," I said thinly. "What else?"

Big shrugged. "No one knows."

"Except the winkles," I said.

"Except the winkles," the Big Brickle agreed.

* * *

"My, but that was ... writing," said Ruby, searching for an appropriate word.

"Arm wattles?" said Cynthia. "Astonishing."

"I've never heard anything like it," agreed Pete.

"I told you," said Meg. "I told you."

Chapter 20

"Let's go over this stuff," I said. "This is not coincidence. The two Indians, for example, Jango Watie and George Sequoyah."

Nancy, Dave, and I were sitting in the police station on Tuesday morning. We hadn't seen the two men since Sunday, but that didn't mean they weren't around. We'd finally gotten a picture of Jango Watie and I'd identified him as the big fellow I'd seen in the church on Sunday morning. The Cherokee police had warned us about the two. Dangerous.

"We've got a dead Cherokee named Johnny Talltrees," said Nancy. "Killed in the alley behind the bookstore, or killed somewhere else and left there. According to Sequoyah, he also worked for the casino in Cherokee."

"Murder for sure?" asked Dave.

"Manslaughter, anyway," I said. "He was tased and his heart stopped. Whoever did it might not have meant to kill him, but they hit him between the eyes. Maybe because he was so short."

"Then panicked and dumped the body by the dumpster," suggested Nancy. "I can see it."

"It's a thought," I said, then continued. "Rahab is kidnapped, then the ransom paid, and the boy returned. Connection?"

"Probably," said Nancy.

"I agree," said Dave, "but what is it?"

"Don't know yet. We do think that the kidnapper acted alone, right?"

"And might be a woman," added Nancy. "I don't see these Indian guys doing it. Someone took care of that little guy. Dressed him in a hat. Gave him a carrot."

"Right," I said. "Sunday morning, Jango Watie and George Sequoyah show up. Two collection guys from the Friendly Gaming Club in Cherokee, which, by all accounts, is anything but friendly. An hour later Muffy LeMieux is electrocuted. Terry can't find anything amiss other than a faulty ground. An accident?"

"Maybe," said Nancy. "Maybe not."

"Then, yesterday morning, Varmit comes in here looking to get the death certificate."

"Man," said Dave, "he didn't even wait 'til she was cold. You think he's after some life insurance?"

"That's the only reason I can think of," I said. "Be good to know how much life insurance, if any, Varmit had on her."

Nancy jotted the information down in her pad.

"Also be good to know who exactly our Indian friends were looking for on Sunday morning."

"You think they might have killed Muffy?" asked Dave. "You know, as a warning, or something."

"How long were they down front before you saw them?" asked Nancy.

"I don't know," I said. "Joyce called me down when she spotted them. I can't imagine how they would have known that Muffy would be dipping her hand in the water, though, even if one of them had the where-with-all to rig the amp. First off, that baptismal font is kept covered and the wooden lid is heavy. It wasn't a spur-of-the-moment theatrical move. She'd staged the whole thing, all the way from the prayer she was saying between verses to dipping her hand into the water and letting it roll off her fingers."

"Are we now operating under the assumption that Muffy was murdered?" asked Nancy. "And that the kidnapping and the other killing are somehow related?"

"That'd be my bet."

"Did Varmit have the know-how to rig that amplifier?" Dave asked. "He wasn't an electrician."

"I expect he was competent. He was wiring the set for the Little Theater production."

"You saw him?" asked Nancy.

"No, I didn't. But I heard Muffy call out 'It works, sweetie' to someone working on the wiring behind the set. Unless she had another sweetie, I'm guessing that was Varmit."

"Ooo," said Dave, appreciably.

"Let's find out about that life insurance, if there is any. A call to the Friendly Gaming Club might be in order. I wonder if they know Varmit LeMieux."

* * *

Muffy LeMieux was due to be buried in Greensboro in the family plot. The funeral would be on Thursday morning at Second Baptist Church, Muffy's home congregation. This information was tweeted at me by Bev. At least, I think it was tweeted. It popped up on my phone, anyway. It was Meg who set up my Tweety account, so I can't be sure."

At two o'clock, Nancy and I met up at the Holy Grounds Coffee Shop for an afternoon espresso. She'd been doing some legwork on the casino connection. I'd been chasing down Varmit's insurance agent. It wasn't too tough. As part owner of a flourishing enterprise in St. Germaine, i.e., Blueridge Furs, his business license had the name of the liability insurance carrier. A couple of calls later and I was talking with Fiona Babcock of Babcock Insurance. Yes, they had insurance, Feona assured me. Yes, there were "key-man" life insurance policies on both Muffy and Varmit LeMieux, but she wasn't able to provide any other details. Another call to Judge Adams for a warrant and I had the information I was after.

Kylie brought our order to the table. Nancy had chosen one in the back, but it didn't matter. At two o'clock, we were the only ones in the place.

"Warming up," said Kylie. "Be spring soon."

"Feels like it," said Nancy, offering her a small smile, but nothing else. Kylie took the hint and disappeared into the kitchen.

"What did you find out?" said Nancy, taking a sip of the black, syrupy coffee.

"We were right about the insurance policy," I said. "Babcock Insurance is carrying a half-million dollar key-man policy on both Muffy and Varmit."

"What's a key-man policy?"

"It's insurance that compensates the business for financial losses arising from the death or extended incapacity of the member of the business specified on the policy. It's generally taken on an essential member. So, if that person dies, the business can either liquidate or have time to find a replacement."

"And Muffy was essential to the business?"

"Well, after Varmit and she bought Blueridge Furs from Roderick Bateman, I guess they're the ones who've been running it."

"Let me understand," said Nancy. "Blueridge Furs gets the half-million."

"Yep."

"And according to the business license, Blueridge Furs is now Varmit LeMieux?"

"Yep. No other partners, according to the license on file."

"Interesting," said Nancy. "I talked with the 'comptroller' at the Friendly Gaming Club. Comptroller. What a joke!"

"Did he offer any insight?" I asked.

"He did indeed," said Nancy. "He didn't even require a warrant. It seems that Mr. LeMieux owes the Friendly Gaming Club seventy-five thousand dollars."

"The exact amount of Rahab's ransom."

"Indeed," said Nancy. "So now we know why the Indians are in town and who they wanted to see."

"So why didn't Varmit just pay them the seventy-five grand? No need to kill Muffy for the insurance."

"He owes somebody else as well?"

"Maybe," I said, "but now I'm wondering about Blueridge Furs' financial position in this economy. It could be that they're in trouble."

"It could be," agreed Nancy. "Let's find out."

* * *

"Any word on the plight of the good reverend?" said Bev. I'd stopped by the new offices of Greene and Farthing, Financial Counseling. Meg had chosen her maiden name for the new business. The office was just off the square, behind the library in a small house that had been, in recent memory, a dentist's office, a TV repair store, and a pottery shop. Bev was cleaning and there was still a lot of work to do before they'd be up and running.

"I talked with Judge Adams a couple of hours ago on another matter, but he said that he wasn't inclined to let this go. She'll have her hearing late this afternoon, then bail will be set, and she'll be back home by dinner."

"Shame," said Bev absently, then, "Look at this mess! Once we get this all cleaned up, we still have to get the contractors in, take down a couple of walls, redo the bathroom and the kitchen. Paint, carpet, signs, computers, desks ... Who would have thought it'd be so hard?"

"Me, that's who!"

Bev laughed. "No sweat. This is going to be great. I can't wait to get started."

"Have we, umm, bought this building?" I asked nervously.

"Not yet," said Bev. "We're closing next week, I think. That ball's in Meg's court."

* * *

Stacey Lindsay was in her office when I arrived at St. Germaine Federal Bank. I'd called ahead for an appointment. She stood as I walked in and offered her hand.

"Hayden, good to see you again."

"Thanks," I said. "You, too."

"I checked on the Blueridge Furs account after you called, and normally I couldn't even speak with you about it, but since it's a matter of public record there won't be a problem."

"Public record?" I said.

"Their bankruptcy. Chapter 11. It was filed two weeks ago."

"Isn't that supposed to be in the paper?"

"No, not necessarily. Sometimes, if a reporter goes through all the recorded court documents, they'll find it and do a story. Most times not. Can you imagine what *The Tattler* would do with this?"

"So Blueridge Furs is out of business?"

"Oh, no," said Stacey. "Not yet, anyway. When a business is unable to service its debt or pay its creditors, the business or its creditors can file with a federal bankruptcy court for protection under either Chapter 7 or Chapter 11."

"What's the difference?" I asked.

"In Chapter 7, the business ceases operations, a trustee sells all of its assets and then distributes the proceeds to its creditors. Any residual amount is then returned to the owners of the company. In Chapter 11, the debtor remains in control of the business operations as what we call a 'debtor in possession.' Of course, he's subject to the oversight and jurisdiction of the court."

"And how is it that you found out?"

"The bank was notified as soon as Blueridge Furs filed with the bankruptcy court. We hold a note on the property."

"So Varmit hasn't been making payments?" I said.

Stacey flipped through some documents resting in front of her, then settled on one and read for a moment before answering.

"He's only a couple of months behind, and he's been making some minimal payments. We might not have said anything except that he has a balloon payment due on the first of April. It's a big one. A little over a hundred twenty-seven thousand dollars."

"So filing Chapter 11 bankruptcy was preemptive," I said.

"Yes, I believe it was. That doesn't mean that the debt is wiped out, mind you. Just that he has time to reorganize and come up with a plan suitable with both us and the court."

"What if he has other creditors?"

Stacey shook her head. "He doesn't. Not that this filing applies to, anyway. The bank is the only creditor listed."

"Thanks," I said, standing up to leave. Stacey had another customer pacing impatiently in front of her office door.

"No problem," said Stacey. She stood up to shake my hand again. "Like I said, it's all public record."

I opened the door to leave, then turned back. "Hey, do you know an electrician named Terry?"

Chapter 21

"Can you help us out?" asked Pedro, showing a lot of cojones, considering he was begging a favor from a jilted Amazon with enough attitude to put the squeeze on us (not to mention our cojones), but not literally showing them, because that would just be disgusting.

"Sure. No skin off my nose," said Big, peeling a big piece of skin off her nose. She lumbered over to her desk, opened the bottom drawer and pulled out a winkle, kicking and screeching. He was wearing a little, pointy, green hat, knee breeches, a brown coat, and shoes with buckles.

"Man," said Pedro, "talk about your stereotypes."

"Shut your yap!" screeched the leprechaun in fury. "She makes me wear this getup!"

"Cute," I said to the Brickle. "Will he help us?"

"He has to," said Big. "I sprinkled some salt on his tail."

"She did it to me, too," muttered Pedro, suppressing a grin at the memory. "And a little cinnamon."

"Them's the rules," said Big, "and he knows it. He either has to give me his pot of gold or serve me for a year. A winkle isn't going to give up the gold."

"Not at sixteen hundred dollars an ounce," grumbled the leprechaun.

"He used to sing with St. Bart's, the American Boychoir, the National Cathedral, who knows where else? ..."

"I was a soloist!" hissed the winkle. "A treble soloist! And you stick me in a drawer. Pah!"

"What's his name?" Pedro asked.

The Big Brickle smiled for the first time. "Fluffernutter O'Brannigan."

"Keeeee!" screeched the leprechaun at the mention of his name.

"Maybe we'll just call you Fluffy," I said.

"Pah!" said Fluffy with as much venom as he could muster, dressed in knee-pants. "I curse you and all your ilk. The leprechaun's curse!"

"Save it for Darby O'Gill," I said.

"Harken to me, Fluffernutter O'Brannigan," chanted the Big Brickle, "I hereby commend your servitude to Pedro LaFleur," she wiggled a wattle at the winkle, "with all the rights and privileges therefore appertaining, etcetera, etcetera."

"Pah!"

"This treble is gonna be trouble, if I have any sooth to say," prognosticated Pedro, forebodingly.

I nodded and fondled my gat.

* * *

Choir rehearsal on Wednesday night started slowly. The group came into the loft in relative silence, found their seats, and started thumbing through their music. Usually there was much jollity and fellowship to be enjoyed and it was tough for me to get them all focused. This evening, though, they were under a cloud, and allowably so.

"What's the news about the play?" I asked. "Anyone know?"

"Cancelled," said Goldi Fawn Birtwhistle, sadness written on her face. She'd been the last soprano to come in. "I talked to Mr. Christopher. He says that there's no way to do artistic justice to *Welcome to Mitford* without Muffy. I even offered to take the lead role, but he's already taking the sets down and moving them somewhere else."

"Well, let's go ahead and rehearse our music for Sunday," I said.

We sang through our anthem, *When Jesus Left His Father's Throne,* but didn't bother with the *Missa di Poli Woli Doodle.* No one seemed in the mood. After we were finished, we all sat in silence for a moment.

"You know who would have liked this story?" said Marjorie, waving my latest missive in the air. "Muffy, that's who."

"She really would have," added Tiff St. James. "She told me that she was Irish. This is St. Patrick's Day after all."

"You could tell that she was Irish by her hair," said Martha. "She was a lot of fun."

"She loved unicorns," said Goldi Fawn. "Leprechauns, too, I'll bet."

"I liked her sweaters," said Mark Wells. That brought a laugh.

"I can't make it to her funeral," said Elaine. "I feel like I really should go, but I'm behind at work."

"Well, it's in Greensboro," said Meg. "At eleven o'clock. That's a two-hour drive one way. Most of us can't make it."

"Hey!" said Randy Hatteberg, "What happened to Mother P? I heard she was arrested."

"She was arrested," I said, "for violation of The Bald and Golden Eagle Protection Act."

"Are you kidding?" exclaimed Burt Coley. "Everyone knows about that. I figured that the church had a permit. If that eagle was pre-1940, they're not hard to get."

"That eagle," I said, "wasn't even pre-February."

"Oh, man," said Burt, shaking his head. As a police officer in Boone, he knew the penalties. "That's not good. Who'd she draw?"

"Judge Adams," I answered.

"Oh, *man!*" he said again.

"She had her hearing yesterday," said Meg. "The trial date was set for May and her bail was set at one hundred thousand dollars. Cash bond."

"Are you serious?" said Fred May. "For having a stuffed bald eagle?"

"That's the maximum fine," I said, "for a first offense at least. It's federal court, not district. Judge Adams says he wants to send a message. Apparently the game wardens have found carcasses of three bald eagles with their tail feathers removed in the past few months. They'd all been shot."

"Did Mother P make her bail?" Fred asked.

"She had to come up with ten percent. The bond agent came up with the rest. She's no flight risk, so, to answer your question, yes, she did. She was released last night."

"My word," said Bev. "What a mess."

"Indeed," added Rhiza Walker. The rest of the choir made mumbling affirmations of agreement, then silence again.

"I wish there was something we could do for Muffy," Elaine finally said. "You know. Just us."

"Well," I said. "I thought maybe we'd sing something." I could see a few smiles. "Look in the back of your folders. This is the piece that we sang at last year's 9/11 Remembrance Service over at Sand Creek Methodist."

Smiles, broader now, as the choir flipped to the back of their folders. Muffy had made a big deal out of this choral number when we'd sung it last fall. It was the last Sunday afternoon before Mother P had arrived. *Sing Me to Heaven* was a piece that wasn't exactly liturgical, but would be just right for Muffy's sendoff. The fellow that composed it, Dan Gawthrop, was a friend of mine, and lived right up the road. Muffy had found out, somehow gotten his phone number and cajoled him into coming to our performance. Then she'd gotten him to autograph everyone's copy.

"Let's try it," I said. I gave a chord and played the opening melody line. The choir blended their voices as if they remembered the piece, something that this choir often failed to do.

> *In my heart's sequestered chambers lie truths*
> *stripped of poets' gloss*
> *Words alone are vain and vacant, and my heart is mute*
> *In response to aching silence,*
> *memory summons half-heard voices*
> *And my soul finds primal eloquence, and wraps me in song*
> *If you would comfort me, sing me a lullaby*
> *If you would win my heart, sing me a love song*
> *If you would mourn me and bring me to God, sing me a*
> *requiem, sing me to Heaven*

The chords were rich and lush and our voices moved as if another spirit were present. I'd stopped waving my arms somewhere on the first page. I wasn't conducting. We were just singing.

> *Touch in me all love and passion, pain and pleasure*
> *Touch in me grief and comfort, love and passion,*
> *pain and pleasure*
> *Sing me a lullaby, a love song, a requiem*
> *Love me, comfort me, bring me to God.*
> *Sing me a love song, sing me to Heaven.*

We finished the piece and the last chord echoed through the resonant building. There weren't many dry eyes, and I'd noticed that Dr. Ian Burch, PhD, had carried most of the alto part through the last half of the song, as the rest of the altos were gulping. As the sound died away, and silence returned, we heard an "Ahem" at the choir loft door. Standing there, framed in the light from the stairwell, was Rosemary Pepperpot-Cohosh. Mother P. Tears were running down her face.

"I had no idea," she said, then choked up. She gained control of herself a moment later and said, "Thank you for that. Do you think we could pray together?"

We all bowed our heads. The choir members reached for one another's hands without looking at each other, linking themselves in an unspoken bond, no one saying a word.

"O most merciful Savior," said Mother P, "into your hands we commend your servant Muffy." She took a deep, audible breath, as if to compose herself, then continued. "We humbly beseech you to welcome her, a sheep of your own fold, a lamb of your own flock, a sinner of your own redeeming. Receive her into the arms of your mercy, into the blessed rest of everlasting peace, and into the glorious company of the saints in light. Amen."

"Amen," said the choir.

Silence again, heads still bowed, then Bev said, "Our Father, who art in heaven," and the choir joined in. We finished, stood there for a long moment, and then the choir began to file out of the loft and down the stairs. Not a word was said.

Rosemary gave everyone a hug as they departed and soon she and I were the only ones remaining.

"I had no idea," she said again, then wiped some remaining tears from her face.

I looked at her. Her face was lined and she seemed older.

"Thanks for posting my bail," she said with a sigh. "I suppose you told the choir?"

"Nope. Not even Meg."

She cocked her head and studied me with a quizzical look. "I had no idea that this music could be so ... so ..."

"Yeah," I said with a smile. "We could have sung *Eagle's Wings*, I guess."

Rosemary smirked and then gave a small chuckle. "Don't be ridiculous." She hugged me and, not knowing what to do with my hands, I sort of hugged her back, just using my fingers. Then she said, "Would you have the choir sing that piece on Sunday morning for the congregation?"

"Nope."

"Why not?"

"It's not an appropriate anthem," I said.

She looked into my face, then down from the balcony over the empty church. "You'll have to help me, you know," she said. "I'm new at this."

"I'm happy to do it," I said.

Chapter 22

A sky the color of rotten eggplant hung low over the town as the rain splattered down like raisins sprinkled on the oatmeal of humanity by an angry God.

"Get me outta this weather," groused the leprechaun.

"Shaddap," said Pedro, then turned to me. "Don't I remember some rule about not getting your winkle wet?"

"Nah," I said. "That's them wicked witches you're thinking about. You want to kill a leprechaun, you have to roll him in a tortilla and cover him in chipotle."

We were in Sarsaparilla, Mexico, a little town that just about lived up to its motto: Este lema está en español.

"Where to?" Pedro asked the winkle.

"Try the church," was the grumpy answer.

"This one?" I asked, looking up at a mud-covered building with a bell tower. "Santa Hortensia Vaca Cara?"

"Pah!" said Fluffernutter. "How many churches do you see? It's the only one built over Mayan ruins. Besides, St. Hortense the Cow-Faced was born in Ireland."

"I doubt it," said Pedro. "I heard that you leprechauns lie like pixies."

"Nah, that's them mermaids you're thinking about," said the winkle. "Leprechauns are bound by Faerie Law never to tell a lie."

"Yeah?" I said. "Well today is the Feast of St. Quetzalcoatl, 2012. The end of the Mayan calendar. What's going to happen?"

"I can't lie, but I don't have to tell you, either. You must guess!" laughed Fluffernutter O'Brannigan, doing a little dance.

***

"I suppose that Varmit's down in Greensboro?" Nancy said. "The funeral's at eleven, I hear."

"Yep," I said. "I called him last night when I got home and told him to come in and talk with us when he got back. He said that he'd be back late this afternoon, but I don't really expect to see him until tomorrow."

"If then," said Nancy. "Are you going to Greensboro?"

"No. Rosemary and Herb are going. Some other folks from the congregation are taking the church van. I think that Martha Hatteberg is even skipping her Bible Study to take a carload of choir members."

"That's good," said Nancy. "Any sign of the Indians?"

"I haven't seen them since Sunday morning, nor heard any reports. You?"

"Nothing," replied Nancy. "I guess we wait on Varmit, then. He's our only suspect, as far as I can tell."

"Yeah," I said. "There're still a couple of things that bother me, though."

"Like why did he kidnap Rahab if he was going to kill Muffy anyway? The half-million would more than cover his debt to the casino and his bankruptcy besides."

"Like that," I said.

* * *

A police presence at a tent revival in Valle Crucis was certainly not called for. Even if it was, it was certainly not in our jurisdictional scope to provide it. Still, Noylene had cornered me in the Slab and made me promise to be there. She couldn't be there due to a conflicting date with the Carolina Neighborly Commission on Beauty, of which she was the chairperson. CarNCOB (as it was known) was a self-appointed group of Watauga County beauty stylists whose mission it was to inform the people who they felt needed their services as to their deficiencies. This was accomplished, in the most part, by standing outside the Walmart Supercenters and handing out "tickets" to the store's unfortunate customers. These tickets cited the offending shoppers concerning their transgression, and gave them a 50% discount at any one of the sixteen beauty and stylist shops to which the members of CaRNCOB belonged: one time, void where prohibited, good on a Tuesday from nine to eleven, by appointment only, color not included. Walmart did not care for the generosity bestowed upon its shoppers by the Commission, and more than that had summoned the police on several occasions. This meeting, called by Noylene, was to set up a more clandestine way of entering Walmart — maybe involving disguises or else hiring girl scouts — in order to present the more heinous of the offenders with said tickets.

Truth be told, I would be at Brother Hog's revival anyway. Baby Evangelists don't come around every day.

It happened, then, that on Thursday evening, Meg and I traveled the twenty miles or so to Valle Crucis in the late afternoon. We stopped in at the Mast General Store and did a little shopping, then found a nice place for a bite to eat, and finally made our way out to the meeting place.

Hog's old tent had been set up at the Valle Crucis Conference Center, and we could see at once that Brother Hog had lost none of his sparkle during his two-year hiatus from the tent revival circuit. The blinking, yellow arrow on the four-by-six-foot portable marquee standing perpendicular to the entrance of the Conference Center pointed the way, proclaiming in large, illuminated, clip-on letters, "Bro. Hogmanay McTavish's Gospel Tent Revival." I'd forgotten that Brother Hog had a following in these parts, and, when word had spread across the mountains of his return to preaching the Word of God and that his son was joining him, the faithful and the lost alike poured out of the hills.

We'd arrived early, around six, and the tent was still empty, most of the visitors choosing to have their supper picnic on the grounds before the service. It was like a tailgate party sans alcoholic beverages. There were cars everywhere, people were plopped into fold-up camp chairs, tables were set up and loaded with food, everything from fried chicken to prosciutto roll-ups. Sweet tea seemed to be the drink of choice and we were offered many a cup as we wandered through the fair-like atmosphere. Several ladies were handing out tracts and Meg politely took them whenever they were offered.

"Look at this one," Meg whispered, handing me one titled *The Passover Plot*. She was busy thumbing through *Here Comes the Judge*.

"Thanks," I said. "Look at this crowd, will you?"

"How many do you think?" asked Meg.

"Three or four hundred at least, and there's still an hour 'til show time."

"Standing room only, I guess," said Meg. "We'd better get a seat early."

Brother Hog had a couple of revival tents. His smaller one would seat about three hundred. This one was larger. I estimated about five hundred chairs plus a stage that had a large pulpit, room for a local, gospel-music group, and his electronic organ. Hog had a 1964 Hammond B3 and that's what he liked. He told me that it had that old-fashioned "come-to-Jesus" sound. He was right. The Hammond B3 had a very distinctive flavor, its sounds mixed by sliding drawbars mounted above the two keyboards. Add a couple of Leslie rotating speakers and you had an organ that could bring the flocks into the fold quicker than a sermon on the last days.

Contributing his reverent, jazz-gospel stylings to the service was Hog's old compatriot, Robert E. Lee. Robert E. was one of the best in the business, having provided the special music for the likes of the Letty Sisters, Bishop Daniel Nutt, the Amazing Ichthus and his Prophesying Fish, and The Chopping Team (lumberjacks with chainsaws and a Gospel message!). Like his namesake, Robert E. was a soldier, a Soldier for Christ, and when duty called Robert E. answered. This was duty.

"Hey," said Meg, "there's Pete!" She waved across the field toward the tree line and Pete, seeing us, waved back. Then from behind an oak tree appeared Moosey and Bernadette. Moosey had hold of a leash and on the end of the leash, strapped into a nylon harness, was Portia the truffle pig. She was circling the large tree, rooting here and there.

"They've got Portia with them," Meg said.

"Let's go see how they're doing."

"Fine with me. We've got a few minutes. I want to get a good seat."

Pete was puffing on a cigar when we approached and didn't seem to be too concerned about what Portia was or was not digging up.

"Hi, guys," he said. "Just thought we'd bring Portia out here for a quick dig."

"Why here?" Meg asked. "If she finds something, you'd just have to give it to the Conference Center."

"Not worried about it," said Pete, flicking a long ash into the leaves, then grinding it out with the toe of his shoe. "We're just giving her a little taste. Moosey and Bernadette have been coming by every day to see her and hounding me like crazy, but you know what? She really likes these kids. Seems to do just what they ask her. I wanted to give it a try, and Ardine's here anyway for the revival, so I don't have to take 'em home afterwards. They're going to stay for the show."

"We heard that there's a baby preaching," said Moosey.

"Yeah," said Bernadette. "The one with the tail."

"He don't have a tail anymore," said Moosey. "They snipped it off when they snipped his wiener."

Bernadette looked incredulous. "They snipped his wiener?"

"'Course they did," said Moosey, matter-of-factly, enjoying the upper hand for once. "Ma said it was a condiment."

"Covenant," I corrected.

"Right," agreed Moosey, then pulled Bernadette aside and whispered, "I'll tell you all about it later."

"Has Portia found a truffle?" asked Meg.

"I don't think so," said Pete. "But she's been digging around."

"Let me ask you this, Pete," I said. "If Portia *did* find a truffle, how would you know? Do you know what a truffle looks like?"

Pete considered the question for a moment, then said, "I know what they *smell* like."

"Fair enough," I said. "Unfortunately, the only thing you'll get to smell is our pig's sweet, sweet, truffly breath after she gobbles them down."

"You make a valid point. This evening I shall do some research on the internet and maybe print out a few pictures."

"Once you know what they look like," I added, "the trick will be to get the truffle before she eats it."

"I'm on it," Pete said, taking a long puff on his stogy.

Chapter 23

"No one's here," I said, staring up at a stained glass window depicting the patron saint of the church, Santa Hortensia Vaca Cara. A woman aptly named, I thought. Her face was as long as a country preacher's sermon on Nehemiah, which wouldn't have to be that long, but would seem like it. The patron saint's bovine visage was serene, though. Serene and udderly rapturous. Then I heard it: music that chilled me like a winter wind whipping through the ragged underpants of despair.

"They're in the parish hall," said Pedro, shivering and hiking up his underpants.

***

It wasn't long before the crowd began to move into the tent and find their seats. Unlike St. Barnabas, or any church that I knew of, the seats in the front filled up first, no doubt to get a good view of the featured speaker of the evening, Rahab Archibald Fabergé-Dupont — billed as Rev. Rahab McTavish to save confusion and because Brother Hog didn't want to have to explain why little Rahab was born out of wedlock and therefore didn't have his own last name, a minor point, to be sure. The "Reverend" title tacked to his name was legal enough. I'd shown Hog how to get the baby ordained on the internet. I also pointed out that Rahab could be a bishop for just ten dollars more, but Hog didn't want him to get the big head. "Plenty of time for that later," he said. "Besides, I don't want him to outrank me."

Brother Robert E. Lee cranked up the organ for the pre-game show. He wandered through the old favorites — *I Come to the Garden Alone, Blessed Assurance, The Old Rugged Cross, Love Lifted Me,* and a host of others. He moved from one to the next seamlessly, changing keys, changing registers, doing palm slides, glissandos, and adding the pitch bends and vibrato for which the Hammond B3 was famous. As the congregation settled into their seats, the True Branches Gospel Bluegrass Band took the stage and played a few of their signature tunes, including *I Fell In A Pile of Jesus and Got Love All Over Me,* and *Heaven Stays Open All Night.*

The crowd loved it and they received a standing ovation. Meg and I had managed a couple of seats in the fourth row and stood with the rest. Next was a testimony given by Nelson Kendrick, who'd had a recent near-death experience and had been led by this episode to share with us the hierarchy of angelic beings. He was well-informed because he'd gotten his information from the archangel Raphael himself.

"My word," exclaimed Meg. "He's got charts!"

We were enlightened as to the many spheres and their residents, including seraphim, cherubim, thrones, dominions, virtues, principalities, angels, archangels, and a "host" of others.

It wasn't a bad lecture, quite frankly, but nothing I hadn't heard before, or that couldn't be gleaned from reading St. Ambrose, Hildegarde, John of Damascus, or St. Thomas Aquinas. Nelson's model was most closely related to the Dante archetype in *The Divine Comedy*. I wondered if Dante had the same teacher as Nelson.

Before we knew it, we'd been sitting in our seats for an hour. Then, as Nelson finished up and started packing away his visual aids, Robert E. Lee began the warm-up. It was a sing-along, of course. Hymns and songs that everyone knew. *I'll Fly Away, This Little Light of Mine, Count Your Many Blessings*. The crowd sang with gusto, no big screen or song-sheets needed. The band joined in and before long the mountains were ringing with the sound of five hundred voices. *He Leadeth Me, Sweet Hour of Prayer, Power In The Blood*. Clapping now. A few of the more fervent were spinning in the aisles, eyes closed, their hands raised high. Then Brother Hog took the stage.

Hog was resplendent in his white, three-piece suit. His face fairly glowed as he stood at the pulpit and surveyed his audience. He was back in his element. Brother Hog was a preacher first, last, and foremost. Of that there was no doubt.

"Brothers and Sisters," he thundered, raising his hands into the air, as if lifting a giant, weightless, walrus aloft. "Let us praise God Almighty!"

Robert E. pounced on the keys like a chicken on a June bug. The organ leapt to life to the sound of gospel licks God loves to hear. The crowd was on its feet again jumping and shouting and hollering up a storm. Hallelujahs rang through the tent. Meg and

I got to our feet as well, more out of nervous acquiescence than a need to hop.

"Perhaps we should have chosen seats nearer the back," I said quietly, as we finally sat back down.

"No kidding," whispered Meg.

Brother Hog preached in turn on salvation by grace, accepting baptism as a sacrament, the dangers of boasting, being born again, the parable of the Great Banquet, and Abraham's promise, with a healthy dose of the Book of Daniel thrown in for good measure. Punctuated with riffs from the organist, he wrapped it all up in about forty-five minutes. By the time he was finished, sweat was running in rivers down his red face. The pocket handkerchief in his left hand that he'd been using to mop his features was wringing wet. The microphone in his right was slick, and every so often he'd had to shake drops of water off it. Now he was spent, but it wasn't over.

"I know you all have come tonight to hear the Gospel proclaimed," he said, his voice low, but amplified through the speakers so no one missed a word. "And there's someone I need you to meet."

"Rahab!" shouted a voice from the back. "Hallelujah!"

Brother Hog nodded. "Yep. My own little boy, Rahab McTavish. It wasn't long back that my wife and I discovered that this child has been touched by the Lord. He is a *preaching baby!*"

"Yes!" shouted a woman two seats down from Meg. She bounced to her feet and waved both hands over her head in exultation.

"The Holy Spirit is here tonight!" roared Brother Hog.

The organ swelled, just chords now, and people shouted and danced wherever they could find a spot to move their feet. We heard glossolalia — speaking in tongues — coming from different parts of the tent. Then he was there, on the stage: Rahab, the Baby Evangelist.

He was dressed exactly like his father in a white, three-piece suit, white shoes, and a tiny, white belt. In his left hand, Rahab held on tight to his copy of *Baby's First Old Testament, KJV,* with his pudgy fingers. Into his right hand, Brother Hog placed a black wireless microphone and pushed him gently to the front of the stage. The crowd became quiet. "Sit down, we can't see," came a voice from behind us. Slowly, from the front to the back, the congregation found their seats.

Rahab stood looking at the crowd, his chubby face split by a gigantic smile. He knew what to do, exactly what he and his father had practiced over and over in their doublewide. He put the microphone to his mouth and hollered, "Eenanah malata hasha alanaya!"

"Shwaaa!" went the organ as Robert E. Lee's fingers danced over the keys dipping into those holy chords that only the blessed know.

"Hallelujah!" erupted the crowd, back on their feet again, clapping and dancing. "Praise the Lord!"

"Sit down, we can't see!" yelled voices from the rear of the tent.

The organ backed down a little, and little Rahab began his strut. Up and down the front of the stage he paraded, stopping every few steps to proclaim another truth. "Uliamba magashami andjesta!"

"Interpreter!" came a voice from the crowd. "Brother Hog, we need an interpreter!"

"Thus saith the Lord," shouted Hog, "you will be hearing of wars and rumors of wars. See that you are not frightened, for those things must take place, but that is not yet the end."

"A prophesy!" shouted a man's voice. "A prophesy from the baby!"

"Or maybe from St. Matthew," I muttered.

"Canum acheniko ofonamachi!" hollered Rahab.

"For nation shall rise against nation, and kingdom against kingdom: and there shall be famines, and pestilences, and earthquakes."

"Hallelujah!" came the shouts.

"Miliamba andjulu!"

"But do not fear!" continued Hog. "There is salvation in the Savior."

This continued for about ten more minutes, with Brother Hog interpreting the unknown baby tongues for all he was worth.

"Wa, wa, wa, wa, wa," chanted Rahab finally, his head bobbing side to side, now entranced by the sound of his own voice over the loudspeakers. "Ba, ba, ba, ba!" Hog knew it was coming. A two-year-old has a relatively short preaching span and, although

Rahab had done better than Hog had hoped his first time out, the boy had reached his limit. Hog scooped the baby up, lifted him into his arms, and clicked off the microphone.

"Thank you, Rahab, for your gifts and the gifts of the Spirit," Hog said, his head dropping into a prayerful pose. "You have truly blessed us all tonight." He looked up. "We're going to take up an offering now," he announced, "so you can help us with this ministry, and, as we do, Sister Birtwhistle is going to sing a song for us. *Give!* Give until you can't stand to be blessed any more!"

"Hey," said Meg, "it's Goldi Fawn!"

"Sure is," I said. Keenly aware that Goldi Fawn wrote her own music, I wondered how Robert E. would do. Turns out, he did fine. Goldi Fawn provided him with a lead sheet and *I'm In The Velcro Arms of Jesus* went off without a hitch.

"Let us pray!" Brother Hog said, getting the high sign from the head usher who held up a fried chicken bucket, one of ten or so, brimming with bills. Hog passed Rahab off to Goldi Fawn and she took him off the stage. The music heightened to a crescendo, then relaxed and accompanied the people back into their chairs where they bowed their heads and finally became quiet, save for the occasional "Amen" and "Hallelujah" that punctuated Brother Hog's prayer of invitation.

We stuck around as the hundred or so folks made their way to the front of the tent for prayer and blessing. Brother Hog had three other ministers on hand to help with the task of getting the sinners right with God and dealing with the various prayer requests. It was a beautiful spring night, so Meg and I took a couple of the folding chairs and set them up under Portia's oak tree, a hundred yards or so from the blazing lights of the tent, and watched shooting stars. We'd both brought light jackets and it turned out to be a good thing. The crowd slowly dispersed, each one shaking hands with Brother Hog and Robert E. in turn, then clapping each other on the back, vowing to see them again real soon. When there were only a few dozen left, Meg and I gathered up our chairs and made our way back to the tent. Hog and Robert E. were slumped in a couple of seats on the front row. Goldi Fawn was still in a receiving line, although there were now only two people left for her to greet.

"Well, thank yeew!" we heard her say as we passed by. "Jesus just gave me that song one day while I was doing hair. I had to stop in the middle of a perm to write it down, and, let me tell you, that woman's hair was never the same." She smiled sweetly. "But it was worth it, don't cha think?"

We put the chairs back in the tent and walked over to Hog.

"Nice show!" I said. "You've still got it, that's for sure."

"Thanks for coming," said Hog. His hair was plastered against his head and his face was still red from exertion. "Noylene would've had my head. Now where's Rahab?"

I shrugged. "I don't know. Who has him?" I looked at Meg. She suddenly lost all her color.

"Goldi Fawn has him," said Brother Hog.

"No, she doesn't," I said. "She's over there shaking hands." I pointed to Goldi Fawn, now chatting up her last admirer.

It was Hog's turn to lose his color.

"Goldi Fawn!" he screamed. "*Where's Rahab?*"

Goldi wasn't used to hearing a man scream and was suitably startled. Her devotee jumped as well.

"I ... I don't know. He was here just a little bit ago ..." She screwed up her face in thought. "I was signing an autograph. No, wait ... I handed him to the guy who *wanted* the autograph. Just to hold for a second. I gave him Rahab's diaper bag, too."

"*What?*" screeched Hog. "*Who did you give him to?*"

"I can't remember!" howled Goldi Fawn, now terrified and running toward us in a panic. "Oh, my God! I can't remember!"

"Calm down now," I said, putting my hands on her shoulders. "Think for a minute."

She peered at the ground, took some deep breaths, then raised her head and looked me in the eye. "He was about medium," she said. "Not too tall, not too short. Medium brown hair. Longish. He needed a styling, that's for sure."

"A man?"

"Yes. He was wearing a sport jacket. Striped. And a tie." She nodded vigorously. "I remember now! He had a beard. A dark beard. And he was wearing a hat. One of those Panama hats, with his hair sticking out underneath. And sunglasses!" She paused. "Hey, wait a minute! It's nighttime. Why was he wearing sunglasses?"

"Oh, no!" muttered Brother Hog. His legs collapsed and he dropped to the ground in a heap.

* * *

I called Nancy and Dave and they rounded up a search party that included a couple of Helen Pigeon's bloodhounds, who got the scent from Rahab's baby blanket. The remaining worshipers, ushers, and Brother Hog's staff, numbering about thirty folks, were happy to help as well. We searched the grounds of the Valle Crucis Conference Center, high and low, for four hours.

Rahab was gone. Again.

Chapter 24

It was the end of the world all right, that was obvious. There were Baptists everywhere, all of them dancing. In the middle of the room, all the members of an older adult Sunday School class were doing the Lambada. A Yucatec mission group was jitterbugging in the corner. Clogging, waltzing, shimmying — they were going crazy. Why they were in Sarsaparilla I had no idea, but now that they were here, it was a hoochy-fest.

"I'll be danged," said Pedro. "It's the 2012 Southern Baptist Convention." He pointed into the corner past a couple of elders doing the Watusi. "There's the registration table."

"Oh, man. We should have seen this coming," I said. "SBC doesn't stand for the Society for the Betterment of Choirs. It stands for the Southern Baptist Convention."

"Hee hee!" giggled the winkle with a twinkle. "The Mayans were the first Southern Baptists and WE set them up. Thus it is written in the Blarney Codex. I'll bet you didn't know that!"

"What?" I said, unbelievably, but not unbelievably as in my incredulity was not believable, which it was under the circumstances, but what Fluffernutter said.

"And now it's the end of the world," said Pedro sadly. "I told you not to get your winkle wet."

* * *

Friday morning I picked Nancy up at the police station at 7:00 a.m. and we drove in the direction of Varmit LeMieux's house on Old Chambers Road. His Land Rover wasn't there, so we figured that our next stop was Blueridge Furs.

"Goldi Fawn says the man was wearing a striped sport jacket and a tie," I said, reiterating the information I'd gotten from Goldi Fawn Birtwhistle. I told all this to Nancy last night, but it had been late and I wanted to make sure we were both on the same page. "Medium height and weight. Panama hat, longish brown hair sticking out from underneath. Dark beard, sunglasses."

"A disguise," said Nancy.

"That's what I'm thinking," I said.

"You think it was Varmit?" asked Nancy. "I've been thinking about it all night and still can't figure out why he'd steal Rahab again. That is, if he was the one who did it in the first place."

"Can't rule it out. The last time Rahab was kidnapped, Noylene and Hog got a call within a couple of hours. They haven't heard a peep so far."

"So far as you *know*," said Nancy.

"I think Noylene would call."

I turned right on Highway 53, saw the sign for Blueridge Furs, turned again and followed a long, dirt drive to the top of a hill.

Blueridge Furs occupied the old site of the Locust Grove Dairy Farm that had bought it from Jed Pierce's grandfather who'd run a family dairy farm until the '80s. Today there wasn't a house on the property, but there were three large dairy barns; a manure storage area; an outbuilding that I recognized as the pelting shed; two new metal warehouses, long and wide with twelve-foot ceilings and large, roll-up shipping doors on the near ends; and the front office. The barns, I knew, housed the Minques that the enterprise harvested for their pelts, which were then shipped to Bulgaria to be turned into lovely accoutrements in which any fashionable woman would be happy to be adorned. Mittens, coats, stoles, vests, hats, purses, you name it. But it wasn't the Minques we were there to see.

"He's here," I said, nodding in the direction of Varmit's dark-green Land Rover.

"You want to be the good cop or the bad cop?" asked Nancy.

"Let's both be bad cops this time."

I pulled up in front of the office and parked my truck beside Varmit's. Nancy and I both got out, walked to the front door and she tried the knob. It was unlocked, so she opened the door and we walked in. Varmit, engrossed in a phone call, looked up, saw us, then said, "I'll call you back," and hung up.

"You guys are up early," he said. He was dressed in jeans and a gray sweatshirt. Work clothes. His hair was combed, but he was unshaven and looked haggard. Dark circles ringed his eyes.

"Those your casino friends on the phone?" Nancy asked.

Varmit's eyes widened, then his face collapsed and he put his head down on the desk. We stood there, silent, for about a minute, then he raised his head and said, "Yeah. You know about them?"

"We know," I said. "They were happy to confirm your indebtedness."

"They called late last night to tell me that I needed to double my payment or they'd tell the police why I'd killed somebody named Johnny Talltrees. I told them what I'm telling you. I never killed anyone named Johnny Talltrees. He's that Indian that you found behind the Beautifery, right?"

"Right," I said.

"I didn't kill him," said Varmit. "I never even met him."

"Did you meet the other two guys?" Nancy said.

"Uh-huh. I'm well acquainted with Jango Watie and George Sequoyah. They'll be coming by this morning for their money."

"Let me ask you this," I said. "If Muffy hadn't died and you hadn't come into that life insurance, how would you have paid those guys? I mean, you'd already declared bankruptcy."

Anger clouded his face. "You think I? ..." he sputtered. "You think that I could? ..."

"Of course we do," said Nancy. "Why wouldn't we? You were running the sound system when it shorted out. You cashed out on the life insurance policy the day after your wife was killed."

"Sure," I said. "You needed seventy-five thousand dollars to pay the Friendly Gaming Club and another hundred twenty-seven thousand to get you out of Chapter 11."

"But ... but ..."

Me: "You're the one who wanted Muffy to sing *Eagle's Wings* in church. You couldn't wait."

Nancy: "We just can't figure out why you bothered to take Rahab when you'd planned to kill Muffy all along."

"*What the hell are you talking about?*" yelled Varmit, jumping to his feet. "*I took Rahab?*" He was starting to hyperventilate.

"Eh," said Nancy with a shrug. "Just testing a theory." She looked at me. "FYI. Bad cop, bad cop usually doesn't work."

"Sit down," I said, putting a hand on his shoulder and pushing him back into his chair. "Put your head between your knees for a couple of seconds." He did as he was told, and a moment later looked back up.

"I would never, *never* have done anything to hurt Muffy. Sure, I got into trouble with the bank and I tried to get out of it by going to the casino. I had this Blackjack system that I bought on the internet. It couldn't fail, they said. Just keep at it, it'll pay off, they said."

"Listen Varmit. I'm inclined to believe you, as dumb as you are, messing with those thugs at the Friendly Gaming Club. We need to look around here anyway. That okay with you? We can wait for a warrant, if you want."

"No, go ahead."

"You have to come with us."

Varmit nodded sadly and got back to his feet. We walked outside, past the vehicles and toward the barns. Then Nancy said, "Hang on a sec. Is that Muffy's purse in your front seat?"

Varmit turned back. "Yeah. Mother P brought it with her to the funeral. Muffy left it in the sacristy."

"Can I look through it?" asked Nancy.

"Sure, whatever you want," said Varmit. "The door ain't locked." There was no fight in him now.

We waited for a minute while Nancy got the handbag out and dumped it onto the hood of the Land Rover. Then Varmit and I started back toward the first of the three barns.

"When does your crew come in?" I asked him.

"Eight o'clock. We're down to three guys now, plus Muffy and me. It's been a bad couple of years, but it takes that many just to take care of all the critters."

"Yeah," I agreed. "The economy. It's bad all over."

The barn was old and showed its age, one-inch-thick oaken planks over timber framing, mortise and tenon joints locked together with hand-cut oak pegs and a tin roof — probably built sometime in the 1930s, but kept in good repair by a few generations of dairymen. Varmit lifted the crossbar off the double doors.

"Hayden!" called Nancy from the car.

I turned away from the barn and saw her looking at something in her hand. She waved it at me.

"Yes, ma'am," I called back. "Find something?"

"Come on back here," she said. "You gotta see this."

"What?" said Varmit. He seemed suddenly nervous.

"Let's check it out. C'mon."

We walked back across the yard to the Land Rover where Nancy had poured out the contents of Muffy's purse.

"What did you find?" I asked.

She handed me a thin slip of paper. A store receipt. A Costco receipt. I silently read down the list of items.

Fairmont Bonded Leather Club Chair - $349.99
5 Light Pewter Chandelier - 159.99
Table lamp - 32.49
1 Set Custom Drapes - $259.99

There were fifteen or twenty other purchases on the list. Then, one from the bottom, right ahead of a Mahogany Side Table - $42.99, was a listing for Huggies Supreme Little Movers, Size 5 - $54.99. Diapers.

"Muffy?" I asked, trying to make sense of it.

"But why?" Nancy said. "Why would she do it?"

"For money, maybe. She knew about the bank note coming due."

"What?" said Varmit. "What is it?"

I looked at the cashier information on the receipt. Register 13. March 11, 11:07 a.m. Last Thursday.

"Varmit," I said. "Where's the stuff that Muffy bought at Costco last Thursday?"

"She took it to Mother P at the church," he answered, still confused. "There were some fake flowers. A ton of 'em. Some greenery, ferns, and a bunch of crap like that. A couple big loaves of bread. Some colored bottles. You know. Decorations."

"She didn't buy a Leather Club Chair?"

"Huh?"

"Didn't spend $1973.46?"

"Of course not!"

"Oh, man," I said, realization dawning. "Costco."

"What?" said Nancy.

"What?" echoed Varmit.

Just then Nancy's phone rang. She answered it. "Yeah, Dave. What?" Pause. "You're kidding! Okay, we're on the way." She snapped the phone shut and dropped it in her pocket.

"Noylene just got the call. The kidnapper wants another two thousand bucks."

Varmit looked very confused. "What kidnapper?"

"Noylene's baby was kidnapped again last night."

"And you think I did it?"

"Nope," I said. "Two reasons. First of all, you're here, so you couldn't have made the call just now."

"Oh, yeah. That's a good alibi, huh?"

"The best."

"What's the second reason?"

"I know who the kidnapper is. The murderer, too."

Chapter 25

"Should we go rescue Rahab?" asked Nancy.

"He's fine for the moment," I answered. "I know where he is. We need to go look in the warehouse."

"Which one?" asked Varmit.

"The one that Mr. Christopher was using for the set of his TV show."

"The one on the end, then," said Varmit, pointing to the building farthest from us. He's been moving stuff in all week, ever since he cancelled *Welcome to Mitford*."

"All the sets from the play. That's what he told us," I said.

"Yeah," said Varmit, as we walked across the compound. "Me and Muffy were helping him with his TV show. He was gonna film it here since we had this empty warehouse now. Then, if he hit it big, we'd charge him rent on the space, plus we'd have an interest in his show."

"Sounds like a good plan," I said.

"Costs a lot of money," Varmit said. "Not to film. That's pretty cheap what with these new cameras and all. But the buy-in for the partnership at the Home and Handgun Network wasn't chicken feed. And if you wanted any guarantees to get your show on and keep it on, you had to be a partner. That's what Mr. Christopher told us."

We'd reached the warehouse. Varmit pulled out a ring of keys, fumbled through them, then chose one and opened a side door. Once inside, he clicked the switch for the overhead lights and they flickered on, one at a time, down the length of the building. Forty feet wide by one hundred feet long, the two warehouses had been constructed to give Blueridge Furs plenty of room to grow. At the close end was a roll-up garage door, closed and locked, that looked to be ten feet tall by twelve wide. There was a small forklift parked beside the door and five wooden pallets stacked with loaded burlap sacks.

Varmit saw me looking at them. "Minque chow," he said. "High protein, high fat. Fish oil. Has some hormones mixed in as well. We have it made specially in Nebraska. It brings the Minques to full harvesting size in a year and keeps their coats lustrous."

There were no windows in the building and no air-conditioning ducts that I could see. The floor was concrete and looked hardly used. The metal framework went all the way up to the top of the twelve-foot-high gable roof, crisscrossing beams and crosspieces taking up most of the last two feet. The roof was corrugated metal. The electrical system was encased in silver conduit and fastened to the large side beams located every eight feet, then strung across the ceiling joists to power the lights. At the far end of the warehouse was Mr. Christopher's production studio, and it was in that direction that we headed.

* * *

The clouds loomed darkly and undulated ominousness as they filled the parish hall while lightning bolts crashed around us, as if Zeus was wiggling his fingers, trying out his new cubic zirconia mood rings. The dancing had reached a fevered pitch and the Praise Band in the corner was playing "Carmina Burana" for all they were worth.

"Oh, man," said Pedro, "I wish it was 2010 again."

Suddenly everything stopped. The Praise Band froze in the middle of "O Fortuna," the lightning blinked out, the clouds, although still hovering intensely and uncasually, no longer loomed.

"What did you say?" sputtered Fluffernutter O'Brannigan.

"I said, I wish it was 2010 again."

"Keeeeee!" howled the winkle. "How did you know?"

"How did I know what?"

"How did you know that I had to give you one wish?"

Pedro shrugged.

"The Big Brickle didn't know she had a wish and I wasn't obliged to tell her. When she passed me over to you, she passed the wish as well."

"Sure," said Pedro. "Everyone knows that."

"That's what you want?" the leprechaun asked. "You could have anything ... all the burritos you could eat with Santa Hortensia Vaca Cara feeding them to you for all eternity."

"No, thanks," said Pedro. "I do like burritos, though."

"The wish doesn't change events," warned the leprechaun. "Everything stays the same. The year just becomes 2010."

"Fine," said Pedro.

"And I'm free," said Fluffernutter, shaking a bargaining finger. "My servitude is over."

"Fine," said Pedro again. "I never liked you, anyway."

* * *

"This is a nice stage set," said Nancy. "I feel like I'm in Martha Stewart's living room."

"Don't let Mr. Christopher hear you say that," I said. "He and Martha do *not* get along. Not since that Home Show in New Hampshire back in '99."

"Ah, yes," said Nancy. "I remember seeing the video and thinking, 'How on earth did Martha Stewart manage to get Mr. Christopher on the floor in a headlock while wearing pearls?'"

"She's very clever," I said. "I've seen her make a shrimp cocktail out of three dead fishing minnows, a used plastic specimen cup, and a pack of McDonald's ketchup."

Mr. Christopher's set looked exactly like every other set on HGTV with the added benefit of his signature "Fourteen-pared-to-nine Layers of Style." As I remembered from our frequent one-sided conversations, the layers included paint, flooring, high-ticket upholstered items, accent fabrics, furnishings, accessories, plants, lighting, and a couple of other things. He'd laid down a bamboo laminate floor that would show up well on camera, and the flats that had, just the other day, provided the illusion of walls at the Little Theater were in place and enhanced by a lovely front door, crown molding, and a large window. The Mitford furniture had also found its way to the set. Plants, lamps, cushions, the two upholstered chairs, the end table — all had their specific space. Added to these was a leather club chair, a large desk, and a set of drapes that I hadn't seen in the theater. Hanging from a cable in the middle of the room, so it would be visible to the camera's eye, was a sparkling chandelier.

Facing the front of the set, about six feet back and ten feet off the floor, were three theater lights attached to a black bar. They were plugged up with a yellow extension cord that ran across the ceiling, down one of the side beams and dangled just below the outlet. I walked over, plugged the cord in, and the stage area lit up.

"I'll check the desk drawers," said Nancy, snapping on a pair of latex gloves that she always seemed to have stashed in one of her pockets. "Any idea what we're looking for?"

"Nope," I said, and walked back to the stage. I got down on my hands and knees, put my cheek near the floor and scanned underneath the furniture for something, anything.

"This one's locked," said Nancy, tugging on the bottom left drawer.

"Pop it," I said. I got up and walked to the door on the set, opened it, and looked backstage, such as it was. Only one thing there. A Costco tote — a big vinyl bag displaying a couple of nature photos, the Costco logo, and adorned with dark green straps. It wasn't empty. I picked it up and walked back onto the set.

"That's Muffy's," said Varmit. "At least, it looks like hers."

I opened it and looked in. There was a set of ornamental lights on a string, some speaker wire, and a ten pack of recordable CDs. There was also a slip of paper in the bottom. A receipt. I looked it over. On the paper was a list that included an American flag, artificial flowers, designer bottles in different colors, some bread, greenery, and a few other things. The information was listed as Register 13, March 11, 10:59 a.m.

"I don't think it's Muffy's," I said. "I think it's Mr. Christopher's." I pulled out the other receipt, the one we found in Muffy's purse, and compared them.

"They were both at the same Costco in Winston-Salem at the same time. Same check-out register. One right behind the other."

Nancy looked up from the desk. "They switched receipts."

"They sure did." I walked over to where Nancy was worrying the lock. "Don't worry about damaging it," I said. "Bust it open." My foot kicked something resting behind one of the legs of the oversized desk and it skittered loudly across the wooden floor.

"What was that?" asked Varmit.

"I don't know," I said, following the metal object. I reached down and picked it up just as Nancy levered the drawer open with the sound of splintering wood.

"Holy smokes!" exclaimed Nancy, reaching into the drawer.

"Holy smokes!" I said, looking at the conical, silver object in my hand.

Nancy held up a Neumann German-made taser in her latex-gloved hand.

I held up the silver tip from a cowboy boot.

* * *

"You wait here for those Indians," I told Varmit. "You don't leave here 'til you take care of it. Pay them what you owe them. No more, no less."

"But ..." started Varmit.

"Then you tell them that I already know about their extortion attempt, and if I ever see them in St. Germaine again, I will personally contact the gaming commission and see that the Friendly Gaming Club is shut down. Their bosses will not be happy with them." I gave Varmit a hard look. "You think you can do that?"

"Yeah, I can do that."

* * *

"So, what do you think happened?" asked Nancy, once we were in the truck and headed back to town.

"Three different crimes. Three motives."

"Here's what *I* think," said Nancy. "You stop me if you think I'm off."

"Go," I said.

"I think that Mr. Christopher killed Johnny Talltrees. That was first."

"Okay," I said. "We'll probably get a fingerprint or some DNA off the taser to confirm."

"So, Johnny Talltrees comes out to the farm to shake down Varmit for the cash he owes. He wanders into Mr. Christopher's studio since he's just looking around. There's Mr. Christopher setting up his living room." She looked out the window and thought for a moment. "There's an altercation and Mr. Christopher nails him with the taser. Little guy probably never saw it coming."

"That'd be fair to say."

"He dies of a heart attack," continued Nancy. "Probably not what Mr. Christopher expected, but he cleans up, puts the body in his trunk and drops it off in the alley behind the Beautifery where the garbage man finds it the next morning. How's that?"

"Almost perfect," I said.

"What do you mean, *almost?*"

"It wasn't Mr. Christopher. We found the body on Ash Wednesday. That means, according to Kent, he was killed on Tuesday between noon and four p.m."

"So?" said Nancy.

"So, Mr. Christopher was in Columbia all day Tuesday. He had a meeting with the Home and Handgun Network. Didn't get home 'til midnight."

"What? No fair! I didn't know about that!" argued Nancy.

"Police work," I said with a grin. "It never takes a lunch break."

Nancy looked irked. "Well, if he didn't do it, and Varmit didn't do it ..." She thought for a second. "Aw, crap! It was Muffy."

"I believe so. Like I said, we'll probably find a fingerprint or some DNA."

We turned off Old Chambers and onto Oak Street heading back toward town.

"Then I guess it was Muffy who kidnapped Rahab the first time," she said. "Of course! To help out with Varmit's gambling debt. Exactly seventy-five thousand dollars." She nodded to herself, making sense of it in her head. "She found out about it, and decided she could help. We always thought it was a woman."

"Nope. She didn't do it. That was Mr. Christopher."

"Aw, man!" said Nancy and slumped in her seat in disgust.

"Muffy was in the office when we got the call from the kidnapper. Remember Dave drooling all over her?"

"I remember *someone* drooling," said Nancy. "I don't recall exactly if it was Dave."

"Well ..."

"Yes, yes, I remember. So Mr. Christopher kidnapped Rahab." It wasn't a question this time.

"Yeah. No reason to buy diapers for set dressing in a play that has no babies."

"Why did Mr. Christopher kidnap Rahab?"

"He blamed someone for the failure of his last TV show."

"That was no secret," said Nancy. "He told anyone who would listen, but he never said who."

"He told us that it was a case of religious bigotry."

"So it was Brother Hog," Nancy said. "Hog turned him in to the HGTV execs."

"I don't know how the old preacher did it, but somehow he was responsible and Mr. Christopher found out. He believed that Hog should pay for his buy-in to the HHN TV network. That amount was seventy-five thousand."

"How did you know that?"

"He offered me the same deal," I said.

"Again, not fair!" Nancy griped, then said, "You don't think that Muffy and Mr. Christopher were in it together?"

"If they were, there would have been no reason for Mr. Christopher to kill her."

"Dang it!" Nancy said. "I thought maybe she was killed by accident. You know, a series of unfortunate events."

"I might have bought that except for the receipts."

"Of course!" Nancy said. "They were right next to each other in the check-out line. Muffy saw the diapers!"

"Maybe. Or Mr. Christopher *thought* she saw the diapers. But you can't get out of Costco without showing the correct receipt to the door clerk. Mr. Christopher must have helped Muffy put her purchases in her car, and at some point they got their receipts mixed up. Muffy had Mr. Christopher's in her purse and he knew she'd look at it eventually. She's the only one who knew it was his. Plus, Mr. Christopher is a topnotch electrician. I heard him giving Varmit directions on rewiring a three-way switch."

"Sheesh! Anything else?"

"Well, since you asked, Mr. Christopher was the one who staged Muffy's last performance. Varmit told me she was working with an acting coach on that song. Only one of those in town. And dipping her fingers was a last-minute change. The lid to the font had only been taken off that morning."

"So, he's the one who told Muffy to dip her hand into the water."

"Exactly."

"And why did Mr. Christopher kidnap Rahab a second time?" she asked.

"I'll bet that he still thinks Hog owes him, and, since *Welcome to Mitford* closed, the Little Theater won't be paying for the purchases he just made at Costco to finish his set. Right at two thousand bucks."

I pulled onto Main Street and a moment later we drove onto the downtown square.

"I thought we were going to Noylene's," said Nancy.

"We're going to Mr. Christopher Lloyd's house to get Rahab."

"Well, of course we are."

Chapter 26

Mr. Christopher lived in a two-story frame house on Maple Street. The clapboards were painted light gray. The shutters and trim were a darker gray. The wooden rail that surrounded the wraparound front porch was white. There was a Victorian-style turret decorated with painted shingles, and three chimneys were visible from the street. The house, like all the houses on this block, sat on about two acres, most of the property being behind the dwelling extending deep into the woods. The house was immaculate, stylish, and beautiful.

This was in contrast to the house of his neighbor, Pete Moss.

Pete also had a two-story house, but his was painted pink and trimmed in pale yellow. Why? No one knew. Cynthia didn't know. Pete didn't know. It had been painted a few years ago, and Pete had told the painter, "Just pick something." The flower-beds were unkempt (some unkind person might call them "weeds"), the grass unmown. There was a concrete birdbath filled with water that would scare algae. Pete reported that a bird landed in it once, but expired before it could struggle to the edge. Since Cynthia Johnsson had moved in, things had gotten better inside the house, but she was adamant that it was Pete's job to take care of the outside. It wasn't that Pete was lazy. He wasn't. He was just busy.

"Hire someone to take care of it," I told Pete. "You can afford it."

"Then I'd have to make decisions," he argued. "What color paint do we use? What kind of flowers do you want? What do we do with the dead kittens in the garden? I tell you, it's always something!"

We pulled up in front of Pete's house and got out of the truck. Pete and Cynthia were sitting on the front porch, both in rocking chairs, wearing bathrobes and sipping coffee. They waved at us and we walked up the ragged steps and onto the porch.

"Beautiful morning, isn't it?"

"Sure is," I said. "You seen Mr. Christopher this morning?"

"Nah. But it's only eight o'clock. He usually isn't up and about 'til ten or so."

We all heard screeching coming from behind the house. Kids.

"What's going on?" I asked.

"Moosey and Bernadette are back there playing with the pig."

"Shouldn't they be in school?" asked Nancy.

"Teacher workday," said Cynthia.

"There's a teacher workday every other week," said Nancy.

"At least," agreed Cynthia. "Not my problem. Nothing to do with the mayor's office."

"They showed up here at 7:30 and rang the doorbell," said Pete. "And this is my gol-danged day off."

"Tell 'em to go on home," said Nancy.

"Are you kidding?" said Pete. "That pig loves those kids. A happy pig is a hungry pig. We're going out later this morning."

"Who's minding the Slab?" I asked.

"Manuel and Rosa have it covered. Pauli Girl's helping with the tables."

"Why are you two here?" asked Cynthia.

"Mr. Christopher," I said. "He's got Rahab."

"He's the kidnapper?" said Pete. "You're kidding me!"

"Not only that," added Nancy, "he's a murderer."

"The little Indian?" asked Cynthia.

"No, Muffy," said Nancy.

"Oh, my God!"

"We're going over there now," I said. "If we don't make it out alive, tell Meg that I love her and was thinking about her at the end."

"What!?" said Cynthia, then lowered her voice and glanced over at Mr. Christopher's house. *"Are you kidding?"*

"Yes, yes, I'm kidding."

* * *

We walked across Pete's yard, avoiding a beaver trap, an old tire, and part of a fence, then crossed onto Mr. Christopher's lawn, the winter rye still green and lush, and climbed the front steps to his porch. I rapped hard using the brass knocker that hung in the middle of the front door. No answer. I tried the knob. Locked.

"Let's go around back," I said to Nancy.

We walked around the side of the house, taking care to stay on Mr. Christopher's property. Pete's side yard was home to blackberry bushes four feet high. Yes, we could eke our way through, carefully avoiding the thorns, but why bother?

Nancy went up the back steps and pounded on the back door that led to the porch. In the meantime, I'd been calling Mr. Christopher's home number. We could hear the phone ringing inside. No answer.

"Hey, Chief!" hollered Moosey. "If you're looking for Mr. Christopher, he left about fifteen minutes ago."

"What? Where did he go?"

Bernadette pointed back into the woods that stretched across the entire length of the block. "He went back there. Into the woods. He had a big ol' bundle with him."

* * *

I'd called Dave and he'd joined us in just a few minutes. Nancy was on the phone calling Helen Pigeon about her two bloodhounds, Buford and Flash.

"They're in Asheville," she reported. "Both dogs are down there for a dog show." Helen sent them with a handler.

"Too bad," I said. I'd gotten both the blanket and the hat — the things Mr. Christopher had dressed Rahab in the first time he took him — out of the back of the truck where I'd left them. I figured that the bloodhounds would be available. The two items were in a rolled-up, brown paper grocery bag sitting on the ground.

"How about one of those Indians?" said Dave. "They can track people in the woods, can't they?"

"Shut up, Dave," said Nancy.

Pete and Cynthia had gotten dressed quickly and now joined us in the back yard.

"Well, let's get going," I said.

"You want me to call Noylene and Hog?" asked Nancy. "Before we start out? Let them know what's going on?"

"Yeah, might as well."

"How about us?" asked Moosey, suddenly appearing. "We can help."

"Nope," I said. "Stay here."

"But we can help," insisted Bernadette.

"Oink," said Portia.

"What she's doing out?" said Pete.

"She wanted to come over and see everyone, so we put on her harness," said Bernadette. "Then she went right for that paper bag."

We all looked over just in time to see Portia the Truffle Pig rip open the paper bag, and start chewing on the hat.

"Hey!" shouted Nancy. "Stop that, you stupid pig!" She ran over and tried to pull the stocking cap out of the pig's mouth, but Portia had a good grip on it. She took a couple of more chews, then decided that it wasn't for her and let Nancy take it away. The blanket would have been next, but Cynthia scooped it up and held it out of reach. Portia sat on her back haunches, pointed her face up at Cynthia and squealed in frustration.

"What on earth?" said Cynthia. "What's wrong with that pig?"

"She's truffling," said Pete. "I don't know why."

"Because she smells truffles, of course," I said.

"What truffles?" said Dave.

"Rahab's truffles," I said. "She smells Rahab's truffle-milk. That pig's nose is ubersensitive. Even better than a dog's. Moosey, Bernadette, get that pig moving. Rahab's in the woods."

* * *

Either there were no other truffles worth finding in these woods, or the scent of Rahab's truffle-milk was so strong that Portia had no problem in following the trail. With grunts, oinks, and snorts, she led us down barely discernible paths. Every once in a while, one of us would find a broken stick or a footprint or some other sign that we were on the right track, but Portia led the way with Moosey and Bernadette in tow.

"Where is he going?" asked Cynthia. "I should have put on hiking shoes."

"I don't think he knows where he's going," Pete said. "He's just going."

"He knew we were onto him," Nancy said. "But how did he know?"

"Varmit must have called," I said. "He's the only one who had an inkling that we were headed his way."

"But why would Varmit call?" asked Cynthia.

"Probably to threaten him. Mr. Christopher did kill Muffy, after all. Once we found the receipts, it didn't take Varmit long to figure it out."

"And now Mr. Christopher's running," said Pete.

"He's got a half-hour head start on us, but he's carrying a thirty pound two-year-old. Eventually that kid's going to start wriggling and want to get down."

"For sure," said Cynthia.

"And when he does," said Dave, "he's ours!"

"Thank you, Joe Friday," said Nancy snidely.

"Joe who?" said Dave.

* * *

Forty-five minutes later, the hunt was over. We'd followed our truffle pig through about three miles of forest, up a ridge, across a couple small streams, up another higher ridge, past a waterfall, across several outcroppings with stunning views, and finally to an overlook — a huge boulder that jutted out into space decorated by a single, spindly pine tree clinging to life with roots that inched into every fissure and crevice they could find. The view was breathtaking: mountains to the left and the right, covered in blooming mountain laurel, and in front of us, just past the edge of the boulder, a gorge. We could see peak after peak in the early morning sun and the clouds were hanging like smoke. They'd dissipate in a few hours, but right now they hugged the floor of the valley.

Standing at the far edge of the rock was Mr. Christopher, his bald head glistening with sweat. He was wearing a cream-colored velour sweat suit and white Reeboks and had Rahab by the hand, the boy chewing happily on a carrot. In Rahab's other hand was his bottle. When Mr. Christopher saw us, he bent down and scooped Rahab up into his arms.

"I'm coming out to get the boy," I said. "It's over."

"No," said Mr. Christopher. "Stay where you are." Pause, then, "How did you find me?"

"Truffle-milk," I said.

If the answer confused Mr. Christopher, he didn't show it. "Truffle-milk," he said, "I should have known." Then he said, "I need a deal."

"The deal is that you send my boy back over here and I won't kill you like the pig you are," said Noylene from behind us.

"Oink," said Portia.

"Sorry, pig. Nothing personal," said Noylene. She had a .38 revolver in her right hand and it was pointed right at Mr. Christopher. She pulled back the hammer. The ominous click echoed off the sides of the rock.

"Noylene, how did you get here?" Nancy asked. She wisely had not drawn her weapon. I didn't have mine with me.

"You called me," answered Noylene. "You're not exactly the fastest group of trackers in the mountains."

"Where's Hog?" I asked.

"Coming. He's fat, you know."

I pointed at Moosey and Bernadette. "You kids go on, now. I'm not joking around. Take Portia and go back down the trail the way we came." It must have been my tone, coupled with the obvious seriousness of the situation. I got no argument from either of them and they, for once in their lives, did what they were told. Noylene watched them leave out of the corner of her eye, then focused on Mr. Christopher.

"Now send my boy over here and I won't kill you."

"Chief," said Mr. Christopher nervously, "make her put the gun down."

"Send the child over here to us," I said. "Noylene won't shoot you. Will you, Noylene?"

"Hard to say," said Noylene. "I'm getting itchy and I'm a crack shot. I could hit him right between the eyes, no problem. I just don't want him to fall off the edge hanging on to Rahab. I could shoot him in the kneecap, I guess."

"Mr. Christopher," I said again, "put Rahab down and send him on over."

He decided quickly. "Yeah, okay," he said, his eyes never leaving Noylene. "You put your gun down at the same time." Noylene nodded, and, as Mr. Christopher bent to put Rahab down on the rock, she lowered her gun. The baby's feet found the slab and he toddled happily toward his mother. She tucked the pistol into her waistband, knelt down and held out both arms to her little boy, gathered him up, turned her back on the crowd, and walked up toward the path leading back into the woods. At that moment Brother Hog came crashing out of the forest like a wildebeest.

"Mr. Christopher Lloyd," said Nancy, moving toward our suspect, "you are under arrest. You have the right to remain silent. You have the right to ..."

Ka-pow! The sound of a gunshot split the air and made us all jump. Mr. Christopher looked puzzled for a long moment, then stared down at the dark, red stain spreading across his chest. Without a sound, he took a step back and disappeared over the edge.

All of us spun around to look at the shooter. We were fairly sure that we knew what had happened and that Brother Hog, or maybe even Noylene, had taken matters into his or her own hands. We were wrong. Noylene hadn't turned around and was still walking back up the path into the woods, Rahab in her arms. Brother Hog, red in the face, was standing on the boulder, off to one side, both his hands on his knees, puffing with exertion. Neither of them had a gun. Then, on a large rock about a hundred yards up the hill, we saw Varmit, lowering his deer rifle. Without a word, he turned and disappeared into the woods.

Postlude

I sat at my desk looking out the window at a city that never slept and was therefore pretty cranky. Pedro LaFleur poured the Irish Whiskey and I lit up a couple of stogies using my new, double cigar lighter that Marilyn got me for Christmas. Marilyn was a peach. I could hear her typing in the next room, then I could hear her not typing.

"It's 2010," said Pedro. "And Carrie Oakey is still dead. You know who killed her?"

"Sure," I said. "I knew all the time."

"Yeah?" said Pedro. "Who?"

"At first I thought it was Marilyn. The window wasn't open, like I told Hammer. A pigeon had just smacked into it. So the shot had to come from inside. The doorway, actually. Marilyn's desk. But then I remembered that she'd taken the day off."

"I knew you'd figure it out," said Marilyn, appearing at the door. She sashayed across the room and porquayed onto the couch.

"So if it wasn't Marilyn," said Pedro, "who was it?"

"It was Karilyn," I said. "Marilyn's evil identical midget twin sister. From the waist up, you can't tell them apart. She was at the desk when I left, eating a radish and reading a romance novel." I shrugged. "Marilyn hates radishes and she can't read."

"Karilyn wanted to be a leprechaun," Marilyn said, "but Carrie Oakey was shutting down the franchise. Anyway, now she's fled the country. I think she's in Arkansas."

"Well, that's that, then," said Pedro, getting up. "Another case solved." He swallowed what was left of his cigar. "I've gotta go, too. I've got a date with a dame named Hortense. She owns a dairy farm over in Wisconsin."

* * *

The Indians found Varmit before we did. At least we think it was the Indians. We couldn't ever prove anything. They were pros. Varmit could have paid them off and disappeared with the rest of the insurance money, but we had put a hold on his bank account as soon as we returned to town. He could have come to us for protection, but I guess he was feeling contrary. Too bad. Blueridge Furs was seized by the bank which, in turn, called and asked the animal shelter to come and get seven hundred thirty-pound Minques. The animal shelter declined, but, rather than let the animals starve in their cages, the Fish and Wildlife Commission, upon learning that they were, in fact, sterile, took them deep into the wilderness and let them go. Actually, the word in the hills was that they took them deep into the wilderness *of Tennessee* and let them go. The reasoning was that, since they wouldn't be reproducing, they'd live for a few more years, provide food for bears, coyotes, and other predators, then die out. But really, does it ever turn out that way?

Mr. Christopher's body was recovered and sent back to Alexandria, Louisiana, his hometown.

Noylene wasn't about to let Brother Hog take Little Rahab on anymore revival trips without her, so she worked her schedule around Rahab's ever-expanding schedule. He became quite the phenomenon, eventually getting his own half-hour show on the Trinity Broadcasting Network with Dr. Hogmanay McTavish acting, of course, as his Holy interpreter. Brother Robert E. Lee went along.

Portia turned out to be quite the investment. With Moosey and Bernadette's help, the Truffle Pig Coalition cleared about twenty-six thousand dollars the first summer. We paid for the pig, put a healthy amount into both Moosey's and Bernadette's college funds, gave them a little "fun money," and still had enough left over to take a great beach vacation on Emerald Isle. Meg, Cynthia, Pete, Nancy and I rented a house for a week and ate fresh seafood every night. Dave, who had decided not to invest in our pig, was left to mind the store while we were gone. No murders were committed during that week, and Dave took full credit.

Rosemary Pepperpot-Cohosh pled guilty to one violation of The Bald and Golden Eagle Protection Act and was fined ten thousand dollars. The government didn't bother to prosecute the church. Bear Niederman tried to cut a deal and give up Mother P as the head of a bald eagle poaching ring, but, once the game wardens got a warrant to search Bear's home and taxidermy shop, there was no deal to be had. They found the tail feathers of three other eagles, plus pelts of several endangered species, including a few Carolina northern flying squirrels and a red wolf. Bear was sentenced to a year in jail and a fine of fifty thousand dollars. Mother P's fine had already been paid since the ten percent required by the court for her bond was still in the clerk's account.

Terry the Electrician never did ask Stacey the Banker out on a date, but several months later he received an invitation from a plastic surgeon in Charlotte to be the first man in North Carolina to receive a toe transplant. Terry waited until five toes were available, then drove down to Presbyterian Hospital where he underwent the six-hour procedure. Three of the toes didn't take and eventually dropped off. He put them in a jar of moonshine and kept them on his kitchen counter as a conversation piece. But two of the digits did manage to hang on and, after a few years, he was even able to wiggle them. Terry was thrilled.

The St. Germaine Little Theater decided that *Welcome to Mitford* wasn't really for them, and chose *Brigadoon* for their summer show. Goldi Fawn Birtwhistle would be directing.

Helen Pigeon's bloodhound, Flash, won Best of Breed in the Asheville Dog Show. Buford did not place.

Meg lost our Lenten bet and I held her to her promise. She cooked me hamburgers three times a week from Easter all the way to Pentecost. I had to adjust my exercise program accordingly, but it was well worth it.

We wriggled through Lent, mixing and blending the liturgy, and eventually bursting forth out the other side into a glorious Easter. Kimberly Walnut, in an effort to be culturally inclusive with our neighbors across our southern border, decided that it would be a wonderful idea to incorporate a little-known Mexican tradition on Good Friday afternoon. This tradition was "little-known" because Pete had invented it on the spot, then got Manuel Zumaya, the cook at the Slab, to back him up. Kimberly Walnut was enthralled by the very idea of being culturally diverse.

And so it was that, after our Good Friday noonday service in the church, all the young children of St. Barnabas (who were on Spring Break that week, anyway) gathered in the garden behind the church for the Blessing of the Paschal Piñata — a large papier-mâché Easter Bunny hanging by his neck from a six-foot-tall cross planted in the azaleas. Kimberly Walnut told the children the "ancient Mexican legend" about the Easter Bunny and how he swallowed all his eggs to keep them from being stolen by El Diablo, the evil fox. El Diablo captured the Easter Bunny, hung him from a tree, and beat him with a stick for forty days, but the rabbit never gave him the precious eggs. Then a rainbow appeared in the sky and El Diablo had to finally let the Easter Bunny go.

Pete and Cynthia, both in attendance, were dumbfounded. Meg was aghast. Even I was taken aback.

"El Diablo?" Cynthia said to Pete. "Forty days? A rainbow?"

"I got most of it from a *Dora the Explorer* cartoon," said Pete. "I didn't think Kimberly Walnut would go for it."

"Okay," said one skeptical kid after he'd heard the story. "But how does this have anything to do with Jesus? Isn't Easter about Jesus?"

Kimberly Walnut was taken aback. She hadn't planned for questions, preferring to start the whacking immediately after the telling of the ancient legend. "Well ..." she started, "in this story the Easter Bunny represents Jesus and the eggs represent, uh ... humankind, sort of." Then she did the expedient yet unforgivable thing and said, "What do you think, children? How is the Easter Bunny like Jesus?"

"Oh, my stars," muttered Rosemary Pepperpot-Cohosh, dropping her head into her hands. "Bev was right. She *really is* a nut."

"They both dress in white," said one little girl. "But the Easter Bunny has a bow-tie. I don't think Jesus wears a bow tie except maybe when he goes to Cracker Barrel. I think I saw him there once, but Mom said it was just a lunatic, so stay out of the bathroom."

"They're both invisible," suggested a boy. "Like that wizard in Harry Potter."

"I know!" said another boy, waving his arm frantically in the air. "I know! They both come out of a hole and make people happy."

Meg stifled a snort.

"Rabbits and Jesus both taste good with wine," said little Charlie Whitman. "That's what my Uncle Matt says."

"That's a good one," said Pete, chuckling. "A communion joke!"

"They both have long, furry ears," chirped the girl who spoke first, happy to keep contributing. "Well," she said thoughtfully, "except for Jesus."

"I get presents on Christmas *and* my birthday," said a very young girl who'd obviously forgotten the question. "I *like* to get presents!"

"That's right, honey," interrupted Mother P, intervening before things got too far out of control. "We get presents because people love us. We get them on our birthday, at Christmas, even on Easter. But the best present is from God. God gave us Jesus. On Easter, the colored eggs remind us that God loves us more than anything. Does everyone understand?"

All the heads nodded.

Mother P quickly blessed the piñata and the children took their sticks and thumped the Easter Bunny vigorously until he broke apart and all the plastic Easter eggs spilled out. It took a while, but the kids were happy to oblige. "Take *that*, Easter Bunny!" yelled the little girl who liked getting presents. "Take *that!*"

Each of the eggs contained a scripture promise and a chocolate kiss. Most of the kids ate the chocolate, threw the scripture lessons on the ground, and went home. It was at that point that Rosemary decided to forego the blended service for the foreseeable future and vowed to have several stern meetings with Kimberly Walnut.

St. Barnabas turned its sights toward the coming year. Easter Season would be followed by Pentecost, then eventually Advent, and another Christmas. Our adventures would continue. It is Meg's opinion that in St. Germaine, North Carolina, anything is possible. Anything? No. *Everything* is possible.

* * *

"Hmm," said Marilyn, after Pedro had gone. "It's 2010. Ain't that something?"

"Yep," I said. "Pedro bought us a couple of years. Enough time to get our lives in order, do some serious repenting, go to church, tell our loved ones how we feel about them ..."

"Or," cooed Marilyn, giving me a come-hither wink and languoring longly on the sofa, "a couple of years to do just about anything we want." She patted the sofa cushion beside her and smiled like Mona Lisa right after she ate that canary. "After all, the end of the world is right around the corner."

It's good to be a detective.

About the Author

Mark Schweizer lives in Tryon, North Carolina. He used to be a church choir director. He used to be a college music professor. He used to be an opera singer. He used to be a lot of things including "employed." Now he writes books. Be afraid, be very afraid...

Just A Note

If you've enjoyed this book—or any of the other mysteries in this series — please drop me a line. My e-mail address is mark@sjmp.com.

Also, don't forget to visit the website (www.sjmpbooks.com) for lots of fun stuff! You'll find the Hayden Konig blog, discounts on books, recordings, and "downloadable" music for many of the now-famous works mentioned in the Liturgical Mysteries including *The Pirate Eucharist, The Weasel Cantata, The Mouldy Cheese Madrigal, Elisha and the Two Bears, The Banjo Kyrie, Missa di Poli Woli Doodle,* and a lot more.